A Hero and a Rogue

by

JoMarie DeGioia

PUBLISHED BY:

Bailey Park Publishing

ISBN: 978-1-944181-24-6

A Hero and a Rogue

Book Two of the
Gentlemen Undercover Series

by

JoMarie DeGioia

Chapter 1

Sussex, England 1824

Matthew, the bloody fool.

Diana Ashley huddled beneath her thick wool cloak, her fingers and toes, her ears and the tip of her nose, tingling from cold as she stood on the bluff above the River Arun. March had never seemed so bitter. On a night like this she almost regretted the promise she made four years ago.

She shifted her feet in an attempt to warm them and turned her back on the river. Thank God their mother couldn't see what her younger brother Matthew had become. Addlepate.

She glanced up the bluff, her gaze drawn to the gothic beauty of Shelby Manor. A light shone in one arched window, winking at her as if it knew all of her secrets. Did Mr. Shelby know what went on right beneath his handsome nose? Did he care?

"And you'll know nothing of this, Mr. Shelby," she vowed as she turned away.

She watched the smugglers make a successful landing, as more illegal goods from the sea were dragged along the bottom of the River Arun from Littlehampton. Matthew and the others would soon complete the run upriver. She could breathe easier now.

With one last glance up at the manor, she began the long, lonely walk home.

***

Bitter wind buffeted the mullioned windows of Shelby Manor, causing their leaded panes to rattle. The weather, and the late and desolate hour, suited Robert Shelby's mood. The great house was quiet, the servants long abed.

He limped across the room to the sideboard, the ache in his right leg dull and persistent. After two months spent in Hell, and more than a year passed since, his injuries were healed save for his blasted leg. On cold nights such as this it pained him like the very devil.

Damn his cousin's blighted soul. Nearly killing Robert then holding him captive just to keep his own vile secrets safe. He grabbed one of the bottles of brandy left by his attentive staff and poured a generous amount into a glass.

Setting the bottle down once again, Robert slumped into the chair beside the hearth. A dismal fire sputtered behind the grate, but he wouldn't call a servant to remedy that. No, he was content to wallow in self-pity with nothing to warm him but the liquor. He drained the glass.

A flicker of light flashed from the river, drawing his tired eyes for a moment. The free traders plied their craft tonight, dragging goods upriver from the coast.

"The devil take them," he grumbled in dismissal.

He closed his eyes, waiting for sleep to take him.

The next morning Robert awoke in his big bed to a familiar collection of discomforts. The brandy sat sour in his belly and his head rapped a discordant tune. He shifted to a sitting position, the fine linens rustling loudly in his ears. He shook his aching head—a mistake to be sure. The room spun for a moment and he rubbed his burning eyes.

He groaned and stood. His wounded leg held, thank God, and a squint-eyed glance toward one sunny window showed him that the clear weather was the reason. A splash of cool water from the washstand in his dressing room helped his wits settle.

He would ride into Arundel today. A visit to Constable Ashley might yield some information, and perhaps even a case. The man was surely up to his ears dealing with the smugglers, though. Perhaps he, too, had seen the signal light, the beacon that caught Robert's eye last evening.

Robert wiped his face and dressed himself as befit his station, tan breeches accompanied by a white shirt and yellow waistcoat. He could have called for his valet, but he'd had enough coddling during his overlong convalescence. He pulled on brown boots the man had shone to a high polish, his right leg held at an awkward angle.

He stood and shrugged into his brown jacket, finally turning to regard himself in the cheval glass set in one corner of the room. Aside from red-rimmed eyes, his face bore no evidence of his overindulgence. Small blessing, that.

He left his chamber for the well-set sideboard awaiting him in the breakfast room belowstairs.

***

Diana hurriedly served herself breakfast, loath to encounter her brother over eggs and ham this morning. Last night's mind-numbing worry and toe-numbing cold still stung.

"Good morning, Sister," Matthew called as he entered the room.

Diana rounded on him, biting her tongue to keep from admonishing him for last night's efforts. The boy bore no evidence of his dark errand. His glossy black hair was neat, his merry blue eyes bright. He was the very picture of a carefree country gentleman of eighteen years.

She forced a smile on her face. "Good morning, Matthew."

Matthew hummed as he filled his plate at the sideboard, oblivious to her pique. And Diana could say nothing, for the promise to their mother. Her mother had known of his wild propensities and had kept it from both her husband and her daughter until she'd known her time was near. Her father still continued in ignorance, which was as it should be at present.

What would Matthew say if Diana told him she knew of his actions? Run far away from Arundel, no doubt. The hope that he would give up his shady work one day soon was her only comfort as she watched him on those moonlit nights. And if she were to lose him forever, what then? Biting back a sigh, Diana joined him at the cherry wood table.

The clink of fine china and the scent of cinnamon told her tea would soon be served. It was a costly drink in their home, as her father didn't purchase his stock from the fruits of Matthew's labors. Ironic, that.

Diana nodded to the maid who set the tray beside her

and took up the pot, filling two cups. "What are you about this day, Matthew?"

Her brother settled his lanky frame across from her and grinned. "Clive promised to meet me for lunch at the inn."

Once more, Diana bit her tongue. Boorish and rude, Clive Stilton insisted on pressing his suit on her. Her brother's blind hero worship only added to her dislike of the lout.

Matthew consumed his breakfast at a rate that never ceased to amaze her and stood. "Good day, Diana," he offered with a bow. "I trust you will spend the day in your usual fashion?"

Yes, she answered inwardly. As a flighty young lady with nothing to occupy her mind save for shopping and gossiping in the pretty shops on High Street? Not likely. "I shall endeavor to occupy myself."

The smile he gave her filled her with warmth. It was so much like Mother's. In a flash he was gone, leaving in his wake a jumble of feelings. No longer hungry, Diana pushed her plate aside.

The sound of voices from the direction of the

entryway soon drew her notice. One belonged to her father. The other gentleman's was deep and familiar as well. That voice caused a flutter in her belly, as it had since the first time she'd seen the man attached to it.

Diana rose and took small steps toward the entry. The carpet beneath her feet muffled her footfalls, and she rounded the corner just in time to see her father's visitor disappear into the constable's office. A glimpse of golden hair, taken with that wide breadth of shoulders clad in a fine jacket, told her the visitor was indeed none other than Mr. Robert Shelby.

As she had done on previous occasions too numerous to count, Diana stepped closer to her father's office. Her duties toward keeping the secret of Matthew's late-night activities carried into the morning hours now and again. On this day she had to know what Mr. Shelby knew of the smugglers and what, if any, information he might share with her father. She leaned toward the closed door as she strained to hear something of their exchange.

"How does this morning find you, Shelby?" she heard her father ask.

"Well, Constable," Mr. Shelby answered in that wonderfully deep timbre. "How did you fare with the free traders last evening."

Diana held her breath as she awaited her father's answer.

"I leave them to the Landguard," the constable said.

Mr. Shelby made no comment she could hear. Their conversation lowered in volume and Diana leaned closer to the wood panel. She heard nothing for the space of a few minutes, then a click of the door latch set her heart pounding. She slid away from the door and feigned interest in the calling cards set in the salver on the table just outside the office. She saw that the door opened a crack out of the corner of her eye.

"Do stop by when you return to Arundel, Shelby," her father said amid a shuffle of papers.

Diana knew then that he would remain in his office for hours, as usual.

"I shall," Mr. Shelby said. "My work in Middlesex should not occupy me long, more's the pity."

Diana frowned. Did he truly despise Arundel that much? He spent plenty of time at his mysterious public house in Middlesex. What "work" drew him there?

She leaned a bit closer to the door again. With a whoosh it was pulled open. Cursing to herself, she kept her eyes to Mr. Shelby's shining boots. He filled her senses, though. The masculine scent of him, the lean length of him.

"Was there something you needed, Miss Ashley?"

Diana slowly raised her eyes, unable to resist taking in the splendid picture he made in his tan breeches and fine waistcoat. She'd found him imposing from behind, to be sure. She scanned the breadth of his chest and shoulders. Oh, he was handsome from the front.

When her eyes met his at last, she bristled at the ire swirling in his blue-gray gaze even as her cheeks began to burn. "I…" She swallowed past the lump in her throat. "N-nothing, I assure you."

One golden brow arched and she longed to trace it with her finger. She placed her hands behind her to deny them the pleasure.

His eyes flicked over her before settling on her face. "Then perhaps you should not listen at doors to matters that do not concern you."

Her mouth dropped open in shock. When he stepped closer Diana could only stare up at him, her knees shaking as her skin heated. Finally, with a curl of obvious disdain on his beautiful mouth, he turned away from her.

Diana drank in the incredible picture of a fit man striding purposefully down a hallway. What did it matter if he hurried to be out of her company?

He favored his right leg as he turned the corner, reminding her of his injury. It certainly didn't take away from his appeal. She leaned against the little table and let out a ragged breath as she waited for her heart to slow.

"Silly girl," she chided herself.

"Diana?" her father called.

Closing her eyes, she took a moment to collect herself. At last she dismissed Mr. Shelby's fine figure from her mind and entered her father's office.

"Good morning, Father."

Constable Ashley smiled. "How are you this day, my dear? It has been damp and chilly of late."

Diana started. Did he know of her late-night errand? "I am well." She settled herself on the chair opposite his large desk, smoothing the skirt of her rose-sprigged day gown.

He studied her for a moment, his eyes sharp. "You seem flushed."

She shifted in the chair. She couldn't let the conversation continue in this direction. "Matthew has already taken his leave."

A look of exasperation came across his face. "I do not know what the devil occupies that boy. He used to vex your poor mother to no end." He waved a hand. "Ah, well. No harm has come to him yet, nor have I heard any tales of his breaking the laws I uphold."

Diana's hands fisted and she hid them in her skirts. The Ashleys had more respect than money, and her father would surely die if they lost their standing in the community.

"What did Mr. Shelby want?" she asked, hoping to turn her father's thoughts.

"He is leaving for that public house of his in Middlesex. He wished to advise me to send for him if I find myself in need of his particular talents in his absence."

Diana leaned forward. "His talents, Father?"

A brief raise of the constable's thick brows assured her that he wouldn't satisfy her curiosity.

She came to her feet. "I have to speak with Mrs. Small about tonight's menu. The Stiltons are coming to dinner."

"Yes, yes."

A touch of regret colored his words. Her inherited sense of intuition came to full alert and she spun to face him.

"Father, please don't tell me Clive is coming as well?"

"Yes, my dear. Clive will attend with the squire and his aunt."

Clive, that miserable groping clod!

She managed to leave her father's office before giving voice to the string of muttered curses that trailed behind her all the way to the kitchen.

Chapter 2

Diana sat at her father's elbow, facing the leering Clive Stilton across an expanse of linen and china. Did the brute see nothing but the bodice of her gown? His muddy brown eyes seemed incapable of rising from her bosom.

His clothing was expensive, yet the cut of his gray jacket did little to flatter his frame. The man was wide and the cravat tied elaborately about his thick neck only accentuated that feature. His big hands dwarfed the fine silver, and his thick lips smacked as he anticipated consuming quite a bit of her father's fine fare. The hunger with which he eyed the large serving platters was too much like that he shot in her direction.

She knew her sapphire blue dress was well suited to a girl of nineteen years, and very fine. Yet dressing for this evening hadn't given her the tiniest flink of joy. *Flink.* An odd smuggler's term for a signal light. How fitting. She faced this evening's dinner with as much enthusiasm as she did her nighttime watches.

Fine lamb was served this evening, accompanied by winter root vegetables. The wine was poured and the food sent up its aroma. A merry fire burned behind the firescreen.

At least she wasn't down by the river this evening. Diana sipped her wine. No, tonight Matthew was safely at the other end of the table.

"How does this evening find you, Miss Ashley?" Squire Stilton asked from his place beside her.

Diana set down her glass and faced him. A successful man and Clive's uncle, he couldn't be more different from his nephew. Though he was as large as the oaf, he carried himself like a wealthy country gentleman. His hair, brown streaked with gray, was neatly dressed and his clothing fit him well.

"I am quite well, Squire Stilton."

A benevolent smile spread across his round face. "No gentlemen pressing their suits to the point of annoyance?"

She refrained from turning a meaningful glance in Clive's direction and managed a smile. "I am not plagued by such, Squire."

"Humph." This from Mrs. Stilton, the disdain in her voice clear from across the table. "I find that hard to believe. A tolerably pretty girl like you." She paused to dab a napkin at the corner of her wide mouth. "Though your years might soon become a hindrance, I wager."

Diana refused to rise to the bait. She had heard the

story of the Stilton's marriage when she was a little girl, from the gossips in Arundel. Mrs. Stilton had been Miss Stilton before marrying her cousin at an advanced age. A matter of inheritance had drawn her husband to her, money that might have gone to the gentleman through entail instead of to the lady had such arrangements been in place.

Mrs. Stilton wore her role as wealthy matron excessively. Her dress, a light green, was ill-suited to her florid face. Large pearls encircled an equally-large neck, and looking at her clearly showed Clive's lineage.

"Miss Ashley is of a perfect age in my opinion, Aunt," Clive declared around a mouthful of lamb. He swiped a piece of bread over his plate, spilling gravy over the edge to darken the linen beneath. His beady brown eyes didn't appear to notice, fastened as they were on her breasts. "She wears her years quite well."

Diana turned from his attention, her face flush with anger. The squire turned a speculative look in her direction, causing her cheeks to burn hotter still.

"Miss Ashley obviously cares for her father." The squire nodded. "He is most fortunate to have such an attentive child living with him."

Matthew began to cough, his laughing eyes meeting Diana's. She shook her head at him, praying he would keep his opinions to himself.

"My sister cares for our father, that is true." Matthew glanced at his hero. "But I would wager she won't be on the shelf much longer."

Well, isn't this a pleasant topic of conversation? Diana flicked her gaze around the table. Clive beamed at her, puffing out his chest until his buttons strained. Her father seemed befuddled, since he obviously viewed her as the child she had been when her mother died. Squire Stilton smiled into his glass of wine while his wife glared viciously in her direction.

Mrs. Stilton did not care for Clive's pursuit? Capital! Laughter bubbled up, which Diana kept quiet behind her napkin lest they think her daft or, worse, happy to have a connection to the wealthy Stiltons of Arundel.

She came to her feet. "I will see to the sherry and sweets, Father."

Clive lumbered to his full height, bowing his head in a show of deference. She knew it was a bloody charade; whenever he found her shopping in the village he treated her like a common maid not worthy of such regard. Diana left the dining room for the temporary solace of the kitchen.

Why couldn't she have her own hideaway like Mr. Robert Shelby? Then she could escape her responsibilities and obligations, with no suitors to bother her. Well, perhaps one particular suitor would serve. An image popped into her mind, one of a man well-formed and handsome, tall and imposing. A curl of disdain on his gorgeous mouth. Mmm.

Shaking her head, she pasted a pleasant smile on her face and rejoined their guests.

***

Robert sat in the crowded dining room of The Hideaway, absently noting the changes to the place since before his captivity. Fine linens dressed tables sporting silver and china and candles of beeswax. Even the clientele was different from before. The public house didn't look much like one now, in his opinion. And thankfully, it bore no resemblance to the stinking waterfront pub that had been Robert's prison for those long months.

Robert's sister, Taylor, had come to The Hideaway following his disappearance, seeking his partner and best friend Blake's help. She'd managed to capture Blake's heart and Robert had yet to meet a happier man. He smiled into his mug of ale. Taylor had changed more than the pub's decorations and the like.

He had spent the ride here reviewing the folders of pending cases. His current clients were nothing out of the ordinary. One gentleman who swore his finest and fanciest watch fob had gone missing. Another man who feared his mistress entertained others in his absence. How he came to that suspicion Robert wouldn't guess, but the notion of following a woman looking for wealthier benefactors didn't interest him. Perhaps another case would present itself this evening.

He glanced around the dining room and a red-headed maid caught his eye. Annie, who in the past had served Robert both belowstairs and above, grinned back at him. He set aside his empty plate and lifted the mug of ale to his lips again. It wasn't brandy, but it would dull all but his basest senses.

Annie set down the platter she held and wiped her hands on an apron that did little to conceal her generous figure. She took up a pitcher and sauntered over to his table.

"Evenin' Mr. Shelby." Annie filled his mug to the

brim and perched one hand on her hip. "Ya' been gone too long, I daresay."

Robert eyed the plump flesh displayed above the tight bodice of her work gown and felt a twinge of want. "I believe you've the right of it." He took a long sip of ale and set the mug aside once more. "Any visitors in my absence?"

"One gentleman." Annie glanced about the room and leaned closer. "Ain't been here in a fortnight, but came back last night lookin' for ya.'"

His gaze moved from her cleavage to her face. "Who?"

She shrugged. "He didn't give his name, but it be the same one what come 'round last time."

Robert could guess: the suspicious gentleman with the wayward mistress. "Damn."

"Looked desperate."

Bloody wonderful. "Thank you, Annie," he said. "I am certain that he will revisit The Hideaway once he knows I've returned."

Annie nodded, her red curls bobbing. She turned to go, then stilled as she glanced over her shoulder at him. Robert recognized the invitation on her face and let that knowledge show in his gaze.

"Later, Shelby?"

A practiced shrug was all the answer the girl needed. A bright smile on her face, she went about her duties. Perhaps he should consider their coupling. His mind would be vacant for that brief moment of release, and he could ignore his bothersome cases. And any thoughts about the pretty little snoop he'd left back in Sussex.

Nothing important had been discussed in the Constable's office this morning, yet when he'd found Miss Ashley eavesdropping in the hallway he'd snapped at her. She had simply stood there, so close to him he could smell her sweet scent. Her breath had come fast, and when she'd put her hands behind her back, her breasts had pressed against the confines of that pretty flowered gown and brushed against his waistcoat.

He drank more of his ale. "Troublesome chit."

When had she grown so lovely? He had scarcely paid her notice when she visited his sister as her bosom friend. Thick lashes as black as her hair framed large eyes of deep blue. Her face was a perfect oval, and her skin was clear but touched with a blush of pink. He smiled. That blush was undoubtedly brought on by her embarrassment at being caught in the act of snooping.

When her lush pink lips had parted, he couldn't help but stare… and step closer still. Both pique and desire nettled him. No matter. She was merely the nosy daughter of the constable and he wouldn't think any more about her.

After the last patron was gone and the final table cleaned, Robert still sat at the table. More ale than he'd allowed for swam in his belly. He stood and sucked in a breath. Sitting at the blasted table for hours, after sitting so long in the blasted carriage, had his leg shouting in protest.

"Yer leg painin' ya'?" Annie asked.

Robert gave a shrug.

"Let me help ya', Shelby."

Robert allowed the girl to wrap an arm around his waist. Why the hell not?

He let her lead him abovestairs, to the fine chamber set aside for his use. Nearly as large as the one used by Taylor and Blake when they were in residence, the room was far from what one might expect in a public house. More evidence of Taylor's magic. Ah, but he would soon lose himself in the fine linens if not in the willing serving girl.

For tonight that was enough.

***

Diana collapsed on her bed, her eyes wide open despite the lateness of the hour and the fatigue filling her body. Tonight she felt the effects of her task to her very bones.

The riverbank had teemed with young ones tonight, children forced in one manner or another to serve the smugglers. Matthew had escaped her line of vision a few times, causing her heart to give a lurch. She'd reminded herself he was eighteen years old, but more danger surely lurked for boys on the crest of manhood. Opportunities for work more dangerous, and more attractive to her carefree brother, lurked around the corner. Danger was the primary draw for Matthew.

"Oh, Mother. Why must this continue?"

She knew the answer her mother would give. As much as she had loved Diana, Matthew had been the one utmost in her mother's concern. Squeaky carriage wheel and all of that. And Diana's love for both brother and father kept her to her vigils. Surely it would kill her father to learn of Matthew's involvement in such illegal dealings. And what if Matthew were to be taken from them? The Lord only knew how it could affect her father's health and well-being.

At least no unwanted guests had plagued her this evening at dinner. Her father had seemed pleased to have her to himself, which he would no doubt prefer as the years passed. But she would wed someday, although not to whom the Arundel matchmakers might expect. She couldn't bear the thought of being in Clive Stilton's company for the space of a meal let alone the rest of her life.

At last she began to succumb to the fatigue dragging her into the linens. And as she closed her eyes an image swam before her. Tall and golden-haired, a mocking smirk on a beautifully masculine face. Mr. Robert Shelby, that mysterious gentleman who secluded himself in his manor.

Was she actually contemplating wedding herself to a man who had nothing for her but disdain? A tired laugh bubbled out of her and she rolled onto her side.

"Not bloody likely," she murmured.

Sleep found her and, despite her conviction, Robert Shelby filled her dreams.

Chapter 3

Robert cursed as he crouched behind the cottage, his leg protesting the position. He'd trailed the unfaithful mistress, if one could indeed call a rich man's ladybird unfaithful, to this cottage so like the others set in this part of London. His client was right. This particular bird knew how to ply her trade: get cozy with one man while feathering a little love nest of her own just in case.

Murmured voices reached him, high-pitched feminine cries coupled with the deep groans of a man in the throes of pleasure. Robert cursed again and shifted to peer through the lace curtains dressing the window. He needed the man's identity in exchange for the high fee he would charge, so he had to set eyes on him.

The couple shifted, allowing Robert an eyeful. The girl was generously endowed and enthusiastic as she rode her bedmate. Robert ignored the discomfort in his leg and crept higher.

"Markham!" the girl cried out.

"Markham?" Robert muttered.

It struck him then. Markham, his client's bosom chum and second in line for an earldom. Robert wasn't surprised. It had been his experience that the *ton* exhibited as little consideration for a friend as for any enemy. But bearing the news would no doubt prove complicated. Markham was also his client's brother-in-law.

"Bloody wonderful," he grumbled.

The sounds of passion issuing from the cottage covered his exclamation. Robert pushed himself away from the window and took a few steps to ease the limp caused by the cramped position. He shook out the folds of his greatcoat and continued past a few houses to the plain hack he made use of when investigating.

The Hideaway beckoned, and he looked forward to another night spent drinking tart ale. He had ultimately turned down Annie's offer of companionship, and would more than likely do so again tonight. He should crave losing himself in a willing woman, but the disquiet that had plagued him in Arundel dogged him still. Arundel. Just a fleeting thought of the village brought Diana Ashley to mind.

What would the pretty little snoop be like in her release? Would her deep blue eyes grow deeper still as he moved within her? Would the musical lilt of her voice, her breathy sighs, ring in his ears as he drove them both to satisfaction?

For a long moment he allowed himself the luxury of imagining Diana Ashley pressed against him, her slender curves etched in his memory from that all-too-brief contact outside her father's office. He let out a groan and held one hand over his closed eyes.

Miss Diana Ashley had no place in his mind, let alone in his bed. She was a lady, if not in title. Like his sister she was meant for hearth and home, and he was most assuredly not.

He would keep himself to The Hideaway. He could work his cases from there. That would serve to keep him out of Sussex in the foreseeable future. And away from temptation.

The ride from London to The Hideaway in the northern part of Middlesex did not take long. Robert alighted the carriage when it stopped in front of the public house, allowing the pull of the place to draw him inside. He rubbed absently at his leg as he looked into the dining room. The room still boasted several gentleman well in their cups. In little mood for company, Robert made his way toward the office he shared with Blake.

He sat down at the wide mahogany desk and withdrew a folder from the stack set on the glossy surface. He added a few notes describing the circumstances surrounding Robert's discovery of the mistress's paramour, keeping his words blessedly succinct, and that piece of business was closed in his mind.

A rap came at the door.

"Come," he called.

The door opened and Annie walked into the office, a tray held before her. The remains of Mrs. Mott's fine fare served this night. The beef was cold now, but lean and thinly sliced. Some of the cook's fine bread accompanied the meat, and a generous slab of cheese. A mug of ale finished the meal.

"Thought ya' could use a bit o' somethin'." Annie set the tray on the desk and straightened.

Robert placed the folder aside and grabbed up the crusty bread to take a healthy bite.

"Ya' be wantin' anythin' else, Shelby?"

He stopped chewing and regarded her. Ever open, she asked for nothing save for an hour of pleasure and the bit of extra coin in her pay packet. The lure of mindless pleasure with no attachments pulled at him. And yet…

"Not tonight, Annie."

Without a look of either disappointment or pique, Annie nodded and bade him good night. Robert swallowed as the door clicked shut. He was never one to deny himself what was given so openly without any threat of attachment. Why, then, had he declined Annie's offer?

He took a bite of juicy beef and washed it down with the ale. Tasty, though not remarkable. The reality struck him then. His mind's odd little sojourn in the hack had given him an appetite for something he couldn't find at The Hideaway tonight. Miss Diana Ashley.

The mere thought of innocence wrapped in a tempting package had spoiled him for the touch of Annie's experienced hands.

***

Diana walked down High Street, the heels of her slippers making pleasant note of her progress. The morning was bright, with the promise of spring at last in the air. Her cloak was suitable cover over her muslin gown, and her straw bonnet shielded her face. With one hand she held a basket at the ready should anything strike her fancy. For once she was on no errands save for her own.

She planned to visit the milliner's. Certainly she was due a new bonnet. She longed to peruse the dressmaker's book of designs. Perhaps at the next country dance she could wear something a bit more daring. Wasn't she old enough to exchange her girlish pastel gowns for something more elegant?

Several of the shopkeepers nodded and called out their greetings and Diane returned the gestures. The wide street bustled with activity. The butcher shop and market boasted many customers and she took care to keep clear of the horses and carriages making their way over the cobblestones. The smells of baking sweets and blacksmith's iron mingled with the scent of horses and the nearby riverbank to strike a chord within her.

This was Arundel. Home.

Diana savored a deep breath as she turned her face toward the sun. Warmth peeped beneath the wide brim of her bonnet and she closed her eyes. A shadow fell across her face then, dousing both light and warmth. Her eyes snapped open and she gazed up at the mountain of man before her.

"Miss Ashley," Clive Stilton offered with a jerky bow.

Diana instinctively took a step back, tightening her fingers on the basket handle until the reeds pricked her through her glove.

"Good morning, Mr. Stilton." She forced herself to be calm. What was it about Clive that affected her so?

As his brown eyes slowly ran over her she recalled precisely the reason. She stepped around him but he fell into step beside her.

"Out for a bit of shopping?" he asked.

"Yes."

They continued on. She looked about the shops, eager for any excuse to leave the brute's company. More than one young woman on the street gazed longingly at Clive. His appeal was completely missed by Diana. The butcher's daughter beamed from the doorway of the butcher shop until her father grabbed her arm and tugged her back inside. A group of young ladies sighed as they walked past, barely acknowledging Diana as they bumped into Clive.

"Good morning, Clive," one plump blond chirped, soon echoed by her two companions.

Clive nodded but kept his attention to Diana. His long legs ate up the ground but she didn't try to keep pace with him.

He circled around her and came to her other side. “Had me a pleasant time at your father’s home, Diana.”

She tripped as he used her given name. Spinning on him, she glared. “Do not address me as such, Mr. Stilton.”

“But you’re meant for me.” A grin split his face. “Diana.”

For a moment she could say nothing. He took advantage of her shock. He grabbed her by the arm and urged her to the side of one of the shops, shielding them from prying eyes and wagging tongues. And the safety of High Street in the height of the day.

Alarm trilled through her. She clenched her hand into a fist and sought to free her arm. “Release me.”

Clive did, but immediately leaned his big body closer to her. His chest nearly crushed her and she shrank against the rough wooden shingles at her back.

“I want you, Diana.” He shrugged. “Even though my aunt isn’t for the match.”

“Wise woman.”

He scowled down at her. Shaking his dark head, he flashed what he no doubt believed a winning smile. “My uncle's fond of you." He pressed himself against her belly, his body hard and unyielding. "The squire would like to see us wed. And I'll have my uncle's money and your respectability. You can't deny it would be a good match."

Her mind worked furiously. Wed this man? Never. She took in their position then, and knew that should anyone see them she would be ruined. She had to put some space between them.

"*I* do not favor the match, Mr. Stilton," she stated, wriggling to get away from him.

He let out a groan and his eyes glittered as he pressed tighter against her. "You're a hot wench, ain't you?"

With a strength borne of disgust she pushed at him and at last earned a bit of freedom. She took quick advantage of it and skirted around him and back out onto the street. In a flash he reached out and grabbed her wrist with a crushing grip. He began to twist her arm and she let out a yelp of pain.

He pulled her closer. "You think you can just walk away from me?"

"Help!" a child called.

Diana's wrist throbbed when Clive released it, but she refrained from drawing attention by rubbing the injury. She turned her gaze to the child, quickly guessing him at about eight years of age. The boy was one of the Potter children who ran about Arundel. But she had never seen such a look of alarm on any of their identical round faces.

Dismissing Clive from her notice, she crouched before the shaking boy. “What is it, Ben?”

“Oh, Miss Ashley!” he cried. “Get the constable. There be a body by the river!”

She brought her hand to her mouth and ran toward the bridge. The sight below on the riverbank confirmed it. The boy was right, but he’d failed to mention the age of the deceased. Why, it was a child no older than Ben himself! The face shone ghostly pale in the sunlight and her stomach lurched.

Clive lumbered to her side. “One of them river rats.”

Others soon gathered on the bridge as the butcher and several of the men of the village made their way down to the bank. Clive then puffed out his chest and assumed the air of a man in charge. His transformation didn’t surprise or impress her.

“I will fetch my father,” Diana said to no one in particular.

She ran from the bridge, gaining her home in record time. She dropped her basket in the entry, she hadn't even realize she still carried it, and ran to her father's office.

She threw open the door. "Father!"

The constable looked up in surprise, his mouth agape. "Diana, my dear! What is the matter?"

"There is a body near the river, Father." She took a breath to rein in her alarm. "A little boy's body."

Her father moved like a man half his age as he donned his jacket and left the house. Diana could only stand there, her heart still racing. Who was that boy? And how did he come to be in the river? Was he one of the smugglers' boys as Clive suggested?

Nausea churned in her belly and she sank into the chair facing her father's desk. Another innocent, far younger than Matthew but on the same path. Why hadn't she seen anything of it last night, when Matthew's welfare kept her attention from all else? Her vigils had become perfunctory, little more than keeping a watch on her foolish brother. And now a child was dead.

She closed her eyes and prayed for forgiveness.

***

"Came for ya' on the mornin' post."

Robert eyed the note Annie held. He took it from her and settled behind his desk as the maid took her leave. He welcomed the distraction. His client had ranted and wailed and pounded his chest in outrage but no meeting at dawn would settled the two gentlemen. How could the man call out his wife's brother for bedding *his* mistress?

Robert flipped the missive over and read the address penned on the other side.

"Hell," he muttered.

He opened the constable's letter and quickly scanned the content. With his heart pounding, he sat straight in his chair. The body of a child? Left by the river like so much garbage. The constable's writing bore evidence of a trembling hand. And if the constable was upset how, pray, would Robert find the man's daughter?

He left the office and called for his carriage, climbing the steps to see his belongings readied for his return to Arundel. To home.

Chapter 4

Home. The prospect jarred him. Robert had ceased to think of Arundel as home soon after his rescue. Odd that, since during the whole of his captivity in that stinking chamber on the waterfront he could think of nothing other than returning to Shelby Manor and the loving company of his father and sister.

He'd insisted on investigating the case of stolen goods in London over two years ago, against Blake's warning. But he' had never dreamed that his own cousin was the ringleader of the operation. And a sound beating from Trevor's henchmen followed by a dousing in the Thames had been his last recollections until Blake and Taylor had come to his astonishing rescue two long months later.

But those months were well and gone. Now his father was gone as well. His sister Taylor was absent for long stretches of time, caring for her own family. Her daughter was nearly one year old, and Robert had yet to spend much time in his niece's company. Little wonder at that, since he turned down each of Taylor and Blake's invitations.

Guilt whispered in the back of his mind, guilt over the fact that he'd brought all of it down on their heads. He knew full well why Taylor made no appearances in Arundel, and why she kept her precious little angel far from the people in the village.

"Bloody gossips," he grumbled.

And the lovely Miss Ashley was no doubt counted among the tale carriers. She had snooped outside her father's office. What else, pray, drew that lady's notice?

Ah, who was he to judge a woman's mind? He knew his sister loved Blake, for Taylor was an open book. But other fine-bred ladies, and less than fine, as his client's mistress proved last evening, could be duplicitous.

Sterns met Robert in the entry of Shelby Manor, surprise rounding his eyes for a brief moment before his usual composure settled into place. "We did not expect you so soon, sir."

"Nasty business calls me back, Sterns."

The butler nodded his gray head. "The child."

Robert blinked. Servants' gossip wouldn't serve his investigation at present, however. He must stop at the constable's and then head for the riverbank to search for clues.

"Yes. Pray, tell the staff that I may not return for

dinner this evening."

Sterns nodded sagely and turned to instruct the placement of his master's effects. Without another thought of such trivialities, Robert left for Ashley House.

The town seemed much as it had been when last he'd ridden over the cobblestones, though the streets were not crowded due to the lateness of the hour. As he passed the brightly lit windows of the Inn at Arundel he saw that it did a brisk business as usual. Laughter and conversation spilled out as one patron opened the door but, though his mount shied at the sounds, he easily resisted the lure to join them.

The constable's house was soon before him and he dismounted. Finally he hesitated. Was it merely the constable's summons that drew him here? Or did the lovely Miss Ashley and her possible upset urge him on? He set aside any lingering disquiet regarding his pull toward the man's daughter. Now was not the time.

He secured his horse, climbed the steps, and rapped on the glossy blue door. A maid opened it, a plump older woman who bobbed her mop-capped head in deference and directed him to the constable's office. She paused in the doorway and he realized then that the constable wasn't alone.

"But what of the child, Father?" came Miss Ashley's plea.

The emotion in her lilting voice caused a beat of something Robert dared not identify in his chest.

"How is it that we don't know his identity?" she went on. "Has no one cared to report him missing?"

"Now, now my dear," the constable said. "Not all is like it is here in Arundel, where everyone seems most adept at following each other's business."

Was that a snort the girl uttered? The thought brought a reluctant smile to Robert's face.

"Mr. Robert Shelby, Constable," the maid announced.

Both Ashleys turned toward him. The gentleman wore his relief on his face and his daughter stared in open surprise. He couldn't resist returning the favor, looking deep into those gorgeous dark blue eyes.

Diana blinked impossibly long lashes and turned to her father. "You sent for Mr. Shelby?"

"Yes," her father said.

"Oh, good," she sighed.

Robert stared at her again. Diana blushed prettily and stood, the skirt of her lovely purple dress swirling about her shapely ankles.

"I'll leave you to your business." She paused in the doorway, one graceful hand resting on the handle. "Will you take your dinner with us, Mr. Shelby?"

"Yes, thank you."

He surprised himself with the answer, but the wistfulness in Diana's voice pulled at him in a way that even her upset had not. She closed the door and left them in peace, which he found favorable at the moment as he could scarcely think in her presence.

He sat himself opposite the constable. "What have you learned thus far?"

"Precious little, I fear." The older man let out a breath and ran his hand over his graying hair. "At first we had thought the boy drowned but the physician believes he died from a blow to the head."

Robert had given the situation much thought on his ride from The Hideaway and believed he knew the reason the boy's body was found on the bank of the River Arun. Now the news of the nature of the child's injury brought a darker thought to mind.

"Perhaps one of the batmen got over zealous with his

weapon."

"Smugglers' infantry," the Constance muttered. "True, they like their clubs. But why would they turn on their own? And could a child truly be involved in smuggling?"

"In my line of work, Constable, I have seen many children used abominably to the ends of someone who should have kept a more careful watch over their well-being."

The other man nodded sagely. "Pederasts and pickpockets."

It was Robert's turn to nod his agreement. "And free traders."

"But here in Arundel? Surely the Landguard keeps that rabble to the coast."

"We are not far from the coast. A short trip upriver from Littlehampton." Robert let his words penetrate for a long moment. "And with the canal leading to the Thames, Arundel is a most attractive route."

Constable Ashley rubbed his face and let out a sigh. "I have been lax."

"No," Robert was quick to counter. "Your business is the people of Arundel and its environs. You are not the only one to leave the smugglers to the Landguard, overtaxed as they most certainly are."

Ashley looked at him in question.

Robert took a breath. "I admit I have seen the signal lights below my own home."

The older man shook his head in dismissal and folded his hands on the desk. "Something struck me as odd about the boy's appearance, Shelby. It may mean nothing."

Robert's senses sharpened. "What?"

"Well, he was dressed as an urchin. That is true. But he appeared… soft. Almost fresh-faced."

Robert thought for a moment. "Perhaps he was new to the work." This seemed reasonable, though the significance of the boy's condition would bear more contemplation at a later time. "That could explain his boss's vexation."

"Well, smugglers or no, we must learn what happened to the child."

Robert agreed. "Anyone who can harm a child is a danger to all in Arundel."

***

Diana couldn't help but watch Mr. Robert Shelby across the width of the cherry table. This dinner was far more pleasant than when the Stiltons had dined with them. Clive

Stilton's lack of manners and close scrutiny had been unpleasant indeed.

Mr. Shelby moved with such grace, even when cutting a bite-sized piece of rare roast beef or simply lifting his glass of wine to his beautiful mouth. He conversed with her father, seated to his left, and paid her little attention. That suited her well, since in that case she had some hope of hiding her conflicting feelings where the gentleman was concerned.

Relief had filled her when he'd entered her father's office. He just seemed so capable. The gossips of Arundel spread tales of his cases despite his continued silence regarding his work. In fact, secrecy seemed to increase his value here. More was the pity, in Diana's estimation. She knew how intrusive the villagers could be and the harm such gossip could do. She had seen families shamed and ladies ruined by the tales spread along High Street.

If she were being completely honest with herself, she would admit that she felt more than relief at his appearance as he'd stood in the doorway of her father's office. He looked incredible even now in the dining room. Fine clothes befitting a man of his station dressed his large frame to perfection. His golden hair caught the light from the candles set on the table as he nodded at something her father said. A flash of white teeth caught her eye as he smiled his agreement and her heart tripped in response.

The bits and pieces of the conversation she'd overheard in her father's office struck her now. She supposed he was correct in his assumptions, to her shame. The smugglers were no doubt to blame for the boy's death. But the conviction in Mr. Shelby's voice filled her with hope that all would soon be set to rights. Not that it would absolve her in her share of the guilt. Diana shook her head and turned her attention to her fine meal.

"I apologize for monopolizing your father's attention, Miss Ashley."

She eyed their dinner guest closely, searching for any of the disdain she had seen so clearly when he'd addressed her outside her father's office in the recent past. He appeared in even temper at present, so she took his words at their given value.

"Arundel is in danger, Mr. Shelby. You are the only—" One golden brow arched as before and she rushed to correct her blunder. "That is, you and my father are the only gentlemen who can resolve this heinous matter."

He lifted his glass to her in mock-salute. "I thank you for your vote of confidence."

Was that a smile teasing the corner of his mouth? The possibility caused her heart to flip again. She reached for her own glass to occupy herself.

"What the devil…?" Mr. Shelby asked. "Forgive me. What happened to your arm?"

Diana froze, her gaze falling to her wrist. Clive's bruises stood out against the white skin peeping out from beneath the hem of her sleeve. She dropped her hands to her lap, hiding her wrist from view.

"Are you injured, Diana?" her father asked, half out of his seat as he leaned toward her.

Silence blanketed the table as her mind worked. She raised her head to face her father. "I dropped a tray on my arm yesterday morning, Father," she lied. "It is nothing, I assure you."

Her father seemed placated as he sat back down, but a tentative glance toward their guest showed he hadn't lost his scowl of displeasure. She reached for her wine glass with her left hand and drank down a healthy gulp. At last he turned those blue-gray eyes away from her and let her finish her meal in relative peace.

After sherry and dessert were served her father and Mr. Shelby once again adjourned to his office, leaving Diana alone in the parlor. The pretty rose-tinged room held enough occupations: cards in one of the carved side tables, needlework set close to the settee on which she rested beside the hearth, sherry on the silver tray set near the tall windows. Even so, she did little but fear Mr. Shelby's reappearance. He rejoined her just as she rose to retire. She peered around him in search of her father but found the doorway empty behind him.

"Your father is otherwise engaged, Miss Ashley."

"Oh, I…" She cleared her throat and bobbed a quick curtsey. "Well, then I must bid you good night."

"Good night," he said.

But he simply stood there, filling the parlor, and apparently wouldn't turn his eyes from her. She lowered her head and began to walk past him.

In a flash his hand shot out, encircling her right wrist. With his other hand he pushed her sleeve up and out of the way. "You will tell me what happened to your arm."

Diana bristled but held her ground. "I explained at

dinner, Mr. Shelby. And it is really none of your concern."

He turned her hand palm up, now tracing one finger of his other hand over the angry purple bruises Clive had left on her flesh. She sucked in a breath as he stroked and soothed her.

"These marks are not from dropping a tray," he said.

She wouldn't involve him in the sordid business of Clive and his unwelcome advances. It would serve nothing and the embarrassment would surely cause her cheeks to flame further. "Again, sir, this is not any of your—"

"Someone put their hands on you," he cut in, his voice rumbling from deep within his broad chest. "Someone hurt you." His eyes met hers. "Tell me what happened."

Giving a shake of her head, she tried to extricate her wrist from his grasp. He pulled her closer, lifting her wrist closer to his face. As she watched he brushed his lips over her flesh. Shivering slightly, she couldn't look away from him. Thick lashes brushed his finely-chiseled cheeks as he dropped another tender kiss on her wrist.

"Mr. Shelby," she whispered. What, pray, caused her voice to tremble so? "Mr. Shelby, please."

He lifted his head and she was caught by his beautiful

eyes. Before she could guess his intentions, he brought his lips to hers. Firm yet soft, his mouth teased her. Diana knew nothing of kissing, save for Clive's horrid attempts at seduction over the last few months. But this kiss? This kiss was unlike anything she'd ever imagined. She leaned toward him, letting her eyes drift closed.

She let out a soft sound, almost a purr, and he growled in response. Surprise caused her to open her lips, and he touched his tongue to hers. Oh! She pulled away and he released her.

He blinked rapidly. "Miss Ashley, I…"

She whirled away from him, rubbing her hand over her wrist as if she could remove every trace of his touch. But she didn't touch her fingers to her lips. No. That caress she wished to savor just a few minutes more.

She risked a glance at him, astonished to see something far different from his usual disdain. He looked almost hungry.

He stepped closer to her. "Miss Ashley."

She stared up at him, trying to rein in her racing pulse, her rapid breathing. "Good night, Mr. Shelby."

After a long moment he gave her a curt bow and left

the parlor. She sank back down on the settee and closed her eyes. She could still taste him, a flavor hot and heady with a hint of spice. When he'd touched his tongue to hers! Oh, and that compelling expression she'd seen etched on his features. Let him chastise her in the future or treat her with irritated disregard.

She would keep the memory of that hunger she'd glimpsed in her heart.

***

Robert left the constable's house as if the Landguard was after him and he carried a cask of smuggled brandy. What had he been thinking? He cursed himself as he urged his mount to a brisk trot down High Street. What was it about Diana Ashley that caused him to take leave of his senses? Last week, when her very presence inflamed him with ire and wanting. And tonight…

She had tasted hot and sweet, and he'd nearly lost himself. When he'd pulled her closer, bringing that delectable body in full contact with his, he couldn't help but deepen the kiss.

When she'd faced him at last, her cheeks a charming pink, he could only stare at her. But her eyes, huge and deep,

deep blue, but by God, he could get lost in those eyes.

The bruises marring the delicate skin of her arm were not put there by a simple household mishap. Robert knew that as well as he knew his own name. Someone had put their hands on her, someone with hands large enough to leave that particular pattern of bruises on flesh. He had seen enough cases of battered women in his line of work to recognize the marks of a bully.

Conviction filled him in the next moment. He would learn the identity of the coward. And he would make him very sorry that he had ever dared to touch Diana.

Chapter 5

"Pity about the young one."

Diana turned from the dressmaker's collection of ribbons to give the speaker her attention. A stout woman draped in too much lace was in loud conversation with another similar female resident of Arundel. Apparently the crowded shop was as desirable a venue as any for their declarations. They didn't speak to Diana directly though, as usual, little was done on either side to keep their words private.

"That's what comes from letting your children run about," the other matron answered with a nod, sending her chins bobbing.

Diana knew they spoke of the Potters, whose only apparent misstep was having too many children and earning too little money. The two cackling hens nodded and clucked as they reinforced their belief that poverty leads to poor innocents found dead by the river. That unfortunate child was no Potter, but that was apparently immaterial to their conversation.

"You cannot know what you are saying," Diana blurted out.

Both women stopped their chatter, turning their round faces in her direction.

"Miss Ashley." The first woman sniffed and shook her head, the long feathers on her bonnet swaying. "A child found dead is a serious matter."

"Yes, indeed," her companion chirped, more feathers bobbing.

"I am well aware of that," Diana began. "But—"

"The boy wasn't from Arundel," the first woman said. "No doubt his parents have little care of his whereabouts."

"Are you saying that the child was not wanted?" Diana fisted her hands at her side. "That he hasn't been missed?"

A cluck of dismissal came from the first matron. "What's one urchin among a pack of them. Am I right Nan?"

"Run like rats along the river, they do, Fran," the second matron said.

Diana was fairly shaking as she held her mouth closed by shear will. She deliberately coiled the wide rose ribbon she held and brought it to the counter. Mentally counting to herself as the women resumed their two-person tirade on the other side of the shop, Diana managed to smile at the dressmaker.

"Is this all for you today, Miss Ashley?" the woman asked her.

"Yes, thank you."

Placing the small parcel in her basket, Diana turned and made her way for the door. She valiantly fought the urge to once more stick her nose in the distasteful business as the chattering went on around her.

"There be Mr. Shelby," one of the matrons said, either Nan or Fran.

Now that stilled Diana. She had thought of little but that wonderful kiss last night in the parlor, a caress that still caused her to shiver with pleasure. And there he was indeed, fit and fine in the afternoon sun. He wore no hat, and his golden waves ruffled in the breeze. He rode a fine brown horse past the dressmaker's shop, his destination unknown to Diana.

"Pity about him, it is," one of the gossips said.

"What?" Diana couldn't keep from asking.

"So alone up there at the Manor," the other woman added.

"And at his age?" the first put in. "We should find him

a bride we should, Nan."

"There was that nasty business with Mr. Trevor, though, Fran."

"We shouldn't let that color Mr. Robert's prospects, Nan."

Diana ground her teeth together and took another step toward the door.

"Now, the scandal about his sister must be addressed," Nan said.

Diana stilled again and began to count to herself once more. *One, two, three, four, five…*

"Miss Taylor was always a flighty child, Fran. We weren't surprised when we heard of her shame."

…six, seven, eight, nine, ten…

"But she's caught herself a baron," Fran said. "Maybe loose morals thrown in the right direction—"

"That is enough!" Diana shouted. Both biddies stopped, their fat mouths gaping open as Diana warmed to her topic. "Miss Taylor Shelby was and is a lady. Lady Thompson, to be exact. A baroness. She has always comported herself as such, and you two have no right to speak ill of her character!"

They both blinked their beady bird eyes at her and still stayed dumb. A glance toward the nodding dressmaker told Diana that she agreed with her.

“Mr. Trevor Shelby was a vile passer of lies, ladies,” Diana said with a firm nod. “His crimes against both brother and sister are well known, and still you continue to give credence to his hateful tales? I am ashamed to share the same space with you.”

With that Diana left the shop, one misstep on the threshold the only flaw in her otherwise dramatic exit. She stood outside, still shaking, and let out a soft string of curses as she squeezed her eyes shut.

“You shouldn’t speak so, Diana,” a man said to her side.

She peeped open one eye to find Clive standing close to her. Bloody, bloody Hell! “I’ve no time for you today, Mr. Stilton.”

She held her head high and turned toward her father’s home. Clive’s beefy hand came down on her shoulder and she jerked away from his grasp.

“You will not put your hands on me again,” she hissed.

He apparently had the good sense to take a step back. "You made me angry." He shrugged. "You should refrain from doing so in the future."

She gaped at him with what was no doubt the very expression Fran and Nan had turned in her direction not five minutes ago. "Now see here, you pompous fool."

"Easy, Diana." The warning was there in his voice, and it was her turn to take a step back. The bully followed her and she felt a shiver of alarm as he narrowed his eyes at her. "I'm not gonna to hurt you. But know this. You belong to me."

Diana squared her shoulders and prepared to tell Clive just what she thought of his attentions when the lout turned from her and sauntered down the street.

***

Robert had hoped to see something the villagers had missed, but the riverbank yielded nothing to his eyes this day, not so much as a sign of a struggle. Odd, that. Had the villain merely left the child here after the vile deed? If so, why? He mounted his horse and turned toward town.

As he neared the shops on High Street he spied Diana Ashley. Her hair was upswept with several curly tendrils catching the breeze and as her cloak rippled in the wind he glimpsed a pretty dress of dotted cream muslin beneath. Then the young man had joined her, one he recognized as Stilton's nephew. Clive Stilton placed his hand on her shoulder and the girl's reaction told Robert all in an instant. She had jerked away from him and squared her shoulders. Robert knew then that Clive was the brute who had left the marks on her arm.

Robert made his way toward the pair, but checked his movement in the next instant. She seemed to have a lot to say to Clive despite his physical intrusions. She was decidedly tongue-tied when she was with Robert, however. Did she welcome the clod's attentions as well as his words?

He put the girl and her predicament out of his mind as he turned toward Shelby Manor. It appeared that she was able to fend off the dolt's attentions this day. He wouldn't pry into Miss Diana Ashley's affairs, unless he saw some proof of another injury.

He would focus on the case of the dead boy today. He needed information, and the people of Arundel would no doubt bend his ear should he approach them on the subject. But gossip wasn't precisely what he needed at present. He needed evidence. Something to give a clue to the boy's identity.

He hadn't forgotten the words the constable had used to describe the child: soft and clean, fresh-faced. Perhaps a trip to Bow Street in London would yield some answers.

He muttered to himself as he gained his home, the picture of Diana and her suitor clear in his mind. She let that man put his hands on her. Did she allow him access to that succulent mouth, that delicious little body? Bloody Hell.

"Then I will leave her be," he grumbled as he opened the door.

"Are we acquainted with the young lady, sir?" Sterns asked.

Robert came to a halt in the entry, turning to glare at Sterns. The old man had the sense to keep further comment to himself, but Robert glimpsed the shadow of a smile on his thin lips as he took himself to the back of the house.

"Presumptuous old…" Robert ceased his mutterings and took himself to his office. Was that a rusty chuckle he heard Sterns utter before he closed the door?

Chapter 6

Robert sat in the dining room of the Inn at Arundel, brooding over his adequate meal of beef stew and root vegetables. It didn't compare to anything that issued from Mrs. Mott's kitchen at The Hideaway. Nor from his own cook at Shelby Manor, for that matter. But tonight he'd had little desire to endure Sterns's censure.

Robert knew from growing up beneath the butler's watchful eye that the man missed nothing. Many was the time he and Blake had pulled a prank and believed themselves out of danger of discovery only to have Sterns barring the door to Shelby Manor, some incriminating piece of evidence dangling from his bony hand. A reluctant smile curved Robert's lips as he recalled the vicar's pilfered shoe or a matron's lorgnette held up as proof of his trick. My God, he missed those days. Sterns had kept every one of Robert's secrets. That was certain. But that gave him no cause to pry into his business with Diana Ashley.

The inn was quite busy as usual, and Robert used the time spent eating to study the patrons. Most of them he recognized from years of familiarity, for many raised in Arundel never left. Thankfully, Robert had The Hideaway and regular escape from country life. That sense of homecoming he'd felt yesterday was absent tonight. Surely that wasn't due to his seeing Diana and her suitor.

Chatter went on around him, though nothing of much import that he could fathom. Older men, portly and skinny, gray and balding, traded stories as they drank deeply of ale. Young bucks out for an evening of tamed debauchery pinched the bottoms of giggling serving girls. Robert glimpsed the moon through one of the windows, and knew the smugglers wouldn't be active on this particular clear night. Which of these upstanding citizens of Arundel stood to lose money due to tonight's clear skies?

No one in the place looked excessively vexed to his eyes, but he knew full well how deceiving looks could be. His cousin Trevor's foppish appearance had hidden a violently criminal soul. No, he wouldn't give another thought to the bastard who'd kept him from his family, and from his father in the man's last days. Trevor was beaten to death in Newgate and his sister Taylor was safe. That was all that mattered once that horrid chapter was closed. He longed to get on with his life.

The puzzle of Diana Ashley inexplicably popped into

his mind. Even as the memory of their kiss warmed him he grew angry to think of the Stilton pup's audacity. She hadn't seemed overly receptive to the boy's suit, but she might be practicing that act of beguiling refusal that coyly led a man to believe he did indeed have a sliver of a chance to do more than touch her.

She was a snoop. Of that, he had first-hand knowledge. More than once he'd found her watching closely as he spoke with her father, thinking herself out of his sight as she stood close to her father's office door. He'd caught a whiff of her sweet scent more than once, too. And she undoubtedly shared gossip with the people of the village, for what else was there to occupy a young woman without a husband to direct?

He pushed aside his empty plate and raised his tankard to signal the serving maid. Generous of figure, the girl swayed as she came over to him. She kept her face downcast, which struck him as odd since the girls at the inn were usually quite forthcoming in their manner.

"More ale, Mr. Shelby?" she asked into the pitcher she held.

Robert nodded in answer. At his silence, she raised

her head a notch. A smudge darkened one cheekbone, faint in the candlelight but clear to him. The flesh beneath her other eye wasn't marred, so he didn't think she suffered from any particular malady. Save for a violent lover, he mentally added. The marks on Diana's wrist came to mind.

"Yes, thank you," he said at last.

The girl refilled his tankard and slid away from the table. He lifted the mug to his lips, stilling as Clive Stilton entered the dining room.

"Place is full," the squire's nephew said in a booming voice.

"I'll find us a table, Clive," the man's companion said as he rushed to the innkeeper's side.

Robert watched Clive as he worked the room, a smile on his wide face as he postured in his fine yet ill-fitting clothes. Pompous ass.

"Found us a table, Clive," the young man said with a bright smile.

Robert knew immediately the identity of the younger man. That thick black hair, those deep blue eyes, could only indicate his relationship to Diana Ashley. This was obviously Matthew, a pup of little note in Robert's memory. And if

Matthew Ashley counted Clive Stilton as a chum, the boy had not grown any wiser over the years since Robert had known him as an idle troublemaker.

The two young men settled themselves, and then Matthew made certain that the serving maid saw to their needs directly despite the crowd.

"Ale, miss," he said. "And two platters."

Robert watched as Clive studied the maid, his stomach churning. He'd seen many a lascivious glare in his day, had given them himself to pleasing effect, but the cast on Clive's face spoke of more than carnal intentions. The girl with the bruised cheek must have recognized it as well, for she brought their meals and didn't linger at the table. Interesting. And telling, he would wager.

"And how is your sister, Ashley?" Robert heard Clive ask rather loudly.

"Well," young Ashley answered. "No doubt making certain our father doesn't work himself too hard."

Clive snorted. "The constable takes his direction from a chit?"

Matthew blinked in apparent surprise as Clive's derisive tone, earning a dash of respect from Robert as his dark brows drew together.

"My sister cares for the family, Clive." The boy smiled then, ease once more in his countenance. "Admirable trait in a wife, wouldn't you say?"

Clive barked out a laugh before taking a drink of ale and wiping his mouth on his sleeve. "She has many admirable traits."

That was it, in Robert's estimation. The time had come to make himself acquainted with the reigning dandy of Arundel.

He stood and sidled over to their table. "Good evening, gentlemen."

Clive looked him up and down and plastered on as false a smile as the young man's uncle ever demonstrated.

"Shelby," he said with a nod of his large head.

"Hello, Mr. Shelby," Matthew put in, an open expression on his face. "Pray, join us?"

Clive scowled in Matthew's direction, but only for a moment. "Yes, Shelby," he said with a decided lack of enthusiasm. "Do join us."

Robert hid his smile and settled himself at their table. He took a deep drink of his ale before setting it down. "I take it you two gentlemen are free of any engagements this evening?"

A flicker of something, shame or disappointment, flickered in young Ashley's eyes.

"We ain't needed anywhere," Clive stated.

Robert regarded him for a moment, just long enough to cause the big man to squirm a bit in his chair. Well-versed in the art of interrogation, Robert found it best to simply remain quiet at times. Often his subject would find it necessary to fill the empty spaces in the conversation.

"We dined at the Ashley's the other night," Clive offered. "Pleasant time."

Robert nodded and folded his hands on the table. "I find the company at the Ashley's most agreeable."

Clive's eyes narrowed as he sought to wrap his dull wits around Robert's meaning.

"Yes," Clive said at last.

"My sister inherited her gift for entertaining from our mother," Matthew offered with a slight smile. "My father will no doubt miss her when she weds."

To Robert's amazement, Clive's chest expanded. He wouldn't have been surprised had the ape pounded it with his beefy fists. The clod thinks to wed Diana Ashley? Not bloody likely.

"Is she engaged then?" Robert asked. He fixed a smooth grin on his face. "I am surprised to hear of it, if so. Why, last evening when we spoke she made no mention of any sort of arrangement."

"You spoke to her?" Clive cut in, his face going red. "When, pray?"

Robert brushed a speck of lint from his sleeve before answering Clive's pointed question. "Why, last evening. I dined at the Ashley's, Stilton." He turned to Matthew. "I did not see you there, however."

The young man blushed to the roots of his hair, a telling trait he shared with his sister. Though on her Robert found the blush appealing. On her brother it could only portend guilt.

"I…," the boy uttered. "I, um, was otherwise engaged."

Clive looked ready to blow. Whether his anger was directed toward his companion or him, Robert didn't care.

"I daresay your sister is a wonderful hostess," Robert said at last. "Most accommodating."

Clive fisted his hands in obvious effort to restrain himself. Ah, Robert had not brawled since before his captivity. And smashing his fist into Clive's leering face would give him immense satisfaction. Instead, he raised his tankard to signal the girl once more. She came over with obvious reluctance. Robert engaged her in conversation, watching the reactions of the two younger men at the table. Matthew eyed the girl, smiling until he saw evidence of someone's violence on her pale face. His brows rose and he lost his friendly grin. As for his loutish companion, Clive glared at her until she slunk away again. Robert drank from his mug, his ears attune to Clive and Matthew.

"Her face, Clive," Matthew said in a soft voice.

Robert watched from the corner of his eye.

Clive gave a shrug. He drank his ale and wiped his mouth. "Sometimes a wench needs to know who's master."

Robert's respect for Diana's brother grew as a flicker of unease filled his eyes. Perhaps the boy wouldn't be so eager for his sister to tie herself to the bully. As for himself, it was all he could not to take Clive's thick neck in his hands and throttle him.

"Well gentlemen, I shall leave you to your meal."

Robert came to his feet and turned to Matthew Ashley. "Do give your sister my regards."

He glanced at Clive, pleased to see the rage choking him until his face flushed purple. After a quick bob of his head, Robert crossed to his table. He dropped a bit of money on the table and turned, eager to keep his own counsel at Shelby Manor.

***

Diana rested on the settee in the parlor, her needlework held in her lap. Embroidering tiny flowers and ribbons on squares of linen served to occupy her time and her mind. Her father had retired early, fatigue etched on his face as he bade her good night. Her brother was out and about, but she knew the smugglers didn't work on this bright, clear night.

She could glean no new information regarding the dead boy despite her foray into the village. After her horrid exchange with Clive she'd taken herself to the milliner's but that shop had yielded nothing as well. Oh, people discussed the boy. In words nearly as dismissive as the lauded Fran and Nan. Her heart nearly broke to think of a child in such danger, at the mercy of men stronger than he. She began to feel a bit of what her mother must have when Matthew took his first step off the path of good-natured pranks to outright lawlessness.

She trimmed one completed flower, done in a lovely shade of violet, and threaded her needle. Her wrist caught her eye, the vibrant bruises at last beginning to fade from her skin. The marks brought Clive's violence to her mind, of course. But due to a certain gentleman's tender application two nights ago, the sight of the marks caused a pleasant warmth to fill her.

The memory of Robert Shelby's beautiful mouth pressed to her flesh, her pulse beating as his lips caressed her, sent any lingering thoughts of Clive from her mind. She glanced toward the spot of cream carpet on which she'd stood, rooted to the floor as he'd pressed closer to her for that too-brief kiss. She licked her lips and she could almost taste his mouth again, and the sherry he'd had after dinner. She nearly felt that tender exploration as his tongue touched hers. Diana closed her eyes and shivered at her mind's musings.

"Oh, my," she sighed.

"What ails you, Sister?"

Diana stiffened, her eyes snapping open as she turned

her head toward the door. Matthew stood there, a look of confusion fixed on his face.

"Oh, Matthew," she rushed out. She held up the piece of linen. "I couldn't sleep, so I thought to work the needle a bit. I believe it has done its work. I am quite fatigued at last."

He seemed placated by her answer. He walked to the round table holding spirits and poured himself a glass of sherry. "My evening was exceedingly dull as well," he offered as he glanced out the tall window.

She followed his glance at the bright moonlit sky. She forced a look of mild interest on her face and nodded. "What did you do this evening?"

Matthew turned toward her. Taking his drink, he settled his long frame on the matching settee opposite her. He gazed at the fire behind the grate. The flames were low but still issued sufficient warmth.

"I dined with Clive at the inn," he stated. "The meal was pleasant."

Something in his tone struck her as odd. Normally, after an evening spent in the company of his idol, Matthew extolled the man's imagined virtues. He will be rich one day Diana, she'd heard him predict. A lady would be most fortunate to align herself to the Stiltons, he would often elaborate. But tonight, inane comments regarding Clive and his family were not forthcoming.

"Oh."

Matthew took another drink and studied her for a moment. "Diana," he began, his blue eyes intent on her face. "Has Clive ever…?" He cleared his throat, his gaze going to the fire again. "Have you ever noticed a proclivity in him toward… forcefulness?"

She tugged her sleeve down over her bruises and chose her words most carefully. As much satisfaction as she would take in diminishing Clive in her brother's eyes, she had little desire to raise Clive's anger. When confronted, she didn't doubt that Clive would turn that anger toward Matthew in a flink.

"Clive is indeed forceful," she said. Matthew looked at her, alarm on his face. "Do not fret, Brother. I have no true fear of him."

The worry visibly eased from her brother's face, but his dark brows remained fixed in a slight frown. "You would tell me should anyone approach you in a manner not befitting your station, Diana?" He leaned toward her. "You would trust me to see you safe?"

Hardly, she answered inwardly. But this show of gallantry and an interest in someone other than himself was so unusual and wonderful to see, she dared not discourage him. "Certainly, Matthew," she answered with a bright smile. "You are my brother. We should look out for each other, is that not so?"

Confusion touched his features. No doubt he wondered what purpose her attentions would serve him. She folded the square of linen and carefully placed the needle in the fabric.

"Robert Shelby was at the inn," Matthew said.

She started. It was fortunate that the needle's point was nowhere near her fingers, for surely she would have done herself an injury. "He was?"

"Yes." Matthew reclined on the settee and drank more of his sherry. "A most pleasant man. So unlike his cousin."

"Trevor Shelby was a monster," Diana said.

He nodded at her words. "Mr. Shelby informed us that he dined here the other night."

Diana stood and brushed her hands over her skirt. "He is helping Father on the matter of the murdered child."

Matthew's gaze skittered away, his mouth turned down in a slight frown. "Horrid, that," he said, his voice soft.

Diana studied her brother in the light of the fire, seeing an inkling of the fine man he could become one day. His heart was tender, and his sense of true right and wrong still appeared very much alive. Perhaps if he separated himself from Clive's ill influence…

"Robert Shelby does not care for Clive, I daresay," he said.

Diana hid her smile. She was certain Robert Shelby was a good man. And if his opinion of vile Clive Stilton was any indication, her instincts were not misled on that point. "Oh?"

Matthew flashed that smile so like their mother's and nodded. "I believe he was goading Clive. He said he much enjoyed his dinner with you and Clive nearly choked on his ale."

Diana laughed at that, a sense of lightness filling her as it had not in so very long. Matthew's deep chuckle joined hers and for a moment the siblings just looked at each other, at ease.

"Mr. Robert Shelby is most clever, Matthew," she told

him. "His words do not always mean what one might believe at first."

"Are you saying that he did not enjoy himself here?" Matthew teased.

Diana bit the inside of her cheek to keep another laugh from bubbling forth. "He did," she nodded. "He did. But I believe he said as much to gain a reaction from Clive. His investigative prowess is well-known."

"Yes," Matthew mused aloud. "I wonder at his profession, his and Lord Blake Thompson's. Most interesting, that."

Oh bother, she sighed inwardly. Now he found the prospect of making inquiries most interesting? At least he was giving thought to activities on the proper side of the law.

"I bid you good night, Brother." She dropped a kiss on his cheek. "Pray, do not stay up too late."

Matthew clicked his tongue at her, a smile lifting one corner of his mouth. "I am no longer a child, Diana."

She nodded and left the room.

If only his sensibilities would catch up with his body.

Chapter 7

A few days later Robert made his way up High Street on foot, intent on gleaning what information he could from the gossipy villagers. Sitting up on his mount wouldn't serve him today. He would be on their level and they would be more likely to tell him what they'd heard.

"Good day, Mr. Shelby," the butcher called from the doorway of his shop.

Robert returned the greeting and approached him. "How does this day find you, Hollis?" He smiled at the girl peeking from behind her father. "Miss Hollis?"

Robert wasn't certain of the young woman's precise age but she acted younger than her appearance might suggest. She giggled, a shy blush staining her plain features.

"We be well 'nough Shelby, Gertie n' me." The butcher, a big man, snorted and wiped his hands on the apron straining to cover his belly. "Though if it weren't for yer man and Miss Ashley, it wouldn't be so."

"Miss Ashley?" Robert asked. "What has she to do with Sterns?"

"They be the only ones want pricier cuts of meat, save for Mrs. Stilton." He held up one hand. "Not that I'd put them in that woman's class. They be pleasant, not like the squire's wife."

Robert smiled a bit. No, Diana Ashley was nothing like any of the Stiltons. "Surely you can endure the woman's manner for her business, Hollis?"

"Aye," the butcher laughed. "I like her money, well 'nough."

Robert nodded as he chose his next words carefully. "What have you heard of the child?"

The mirth left the man's ruddy face and he shook his head. He looked over at his daughter. "Go see to the sweepin', Gertie." When she left them, her father continued. "Haven't heard nothin', I'm afraid. Ain't no one gives a care for the mite nor where he came from."

"Yes, I believe you have the right of it." Robert inclined his head. "Pray, tell me if you hear any gossip worth repeating, Hollis?"

"Aye, Mr. Shelby." Hollis's thick brows drew together. "If anybody was to put a hand on me simple Gertie… Ain't right, hurtin' a child."

Robert agreed. He bade the man farewell and made his way farther up the street. He soon spied Clive Stilton, walking about High Street as if it were he and not his uncle who was squire. He thought back to that evening a week ago at the Inn at Arundel, to Clive reigning over the dullards as they hung on each monosyllabic word the lout uttered.

Apparently the females of the village thought Clive cock of the walk as well. Three girls dogged Clive's heels, their round faces wreathed in smiles as they gazed adoringly up at young Stilton. Matthew Ashley rounded out the party, looking much as he was, a carefree young gentleman out for a day's pleasures.

Robert decided to arrange an encounter with the clod Clive, if only to goad him on the matter of Diana Ashley. Whistling, he crossed the street and planted himself directly in the party's path. One of the village girls, he couldn't remember one from the other and each was equally silly in his opinion, bumped into him. She managed to rub her ample breasts against his chest as he turned in mock-surprise.

"Oh, forgive me, miss," he said with a sweeping bow.

The girl stared up at him with a hunger he found misplaced on so young a face.

"'Twas nothin', Mr. Shelby," she gushed.

The other two girls took note of Robert then and

regarded him with a level of interest to rival the first girl.

He nodded to each in their turn. “Good day, ladies.”

“Good day, Mr. Shelby,” they said in unison.

He heard Clive Stilton grumble something under his breath. Robert then faced the two gentlemen. “Mr. Stilton,” he said with another bow. “Mr. Ashley.”

“Hello, Mr. Shelby,” Matthew Ashley said with a genuine smile.

Young Stilton had much playacting to do to approach his companion’s affability. Clive took a breath, which caused his neck to thicken beneath his cravat, and sneered more than smiled. “Shelby.”

No friendly greeting, then? Robert arched a brow, the import of which the dolt missed. He faced Matthew. “I take it that your sister is well, Ashley?”

“Quite.”

“Capital.” Robert nodded. “She is such a lovely girl. So accomplished.”

“Accomplished?” Clive snarled.

“Why, yes,” he returned. “The girl runs her father’s house quite well and has a gifted hand at entertaining. I had a most pleasant time the other afternoon.”

Stilton's dull brown eyes seemed likely to bug out of his florid face. "You… you visited the Constable's again?"

Robert shrugged in his most dismissive manner. Surely his sister Taylor would be most diverted to see Robert assume such an air. "Of course. The constable and I have business." He took a breath and turned a wolfish smile on Clive. "And passing a bit of time in Miss Diana Ashley's company is not without its own rewards."

Matthew Ashley seemed to accept Robert's words, if he was also a bit startled by them. The gaping girls now eyed Robert as the man not-quite-within reach, and they sidled closer to him.

"Miss Ashley's passin' pretty, Mr. Shelby," one remarked. "Though dreadfully dull."

"Aye, dull," another nodded, her bosom brushing Robert's forearm.

"Aye," the last added. "She's so… proper."

"Shut yer mouths," Clive spat. "You won't speak of her."

Clive's defense of Diana didn't endear him to Robert for he knew full well the motivation behind it. The bully wanted her as a wife. Well, Robert would no sooner condemn

Diana to the man's violent hands than he would have his own sister.

He disengaged himself from the clinging young women and offered them another bow. "Ladies, I will leave you to your walk." He faced Matthew and Clive. "Gentlemen."

"Good day," Matthew offered with a smile.

Clive Stilton said nothing, but Robert reasons he could nearly feel the man's eyes burning through the back of his coat as he continued up High Street. Robert caught a glimpse of a slight figure outside the dressmaker's, and knew it could only be Diana. Her grace was evident even from here, as she strolled with her maid. He was grateful for the servant's company, as Clive would no doubt abandon his hangers-on in an instant should the opportunity present itself to get her alone. In his mind Robert could still see those horrid bruises on her delicate wrist.

Robert used his skills to keep to the occasional shadows, and watched her make her way toward her home. He would make certain she got home safely. Years of plying his trade had taught him much about concealing one's position, and Diana didn't noticed his attention as she fairly float over the cobblestones. She wore a smile as she greeted those she had probably known all of her life. Just watching her move so caused his body to heat. She was lovely.

He glanced up the street and noticed that Clive and his party continued away from her. He saw that Diana took note of that as well, and knew it was relief that caused her shoulders to relax. So she didn't welcome Clive's attentions. He told himself that was fortunate only due to the man's violent nature. Surely Robert didn't want her affections secured elsewhere.

He turned away from both Clive's party and Miss Diana Ashley and made his way toward the milliner's shop.

"Mr. Shelby!" The booming voice belonged to Squire Stilton, who was waving one hand from across High Street. The man made his way toward Robert, a look of concern fixed on his round face.

"Good day, Squire," Robert offered.

"Good day. I take it you're investigating the child's death?"

"Yes." Robert paused a beat. "The constable has asked for my assistance."

The squire nodded vigorously, though his lips pursed

for a moment. "Capital, capital," he rushed out. "And, pray, have you learned anything of the child's identity?"

That was an odd question. Robert watched the man, whose thick brows were furrowed over his sharp eyes. "I've yet to glean any information on the *murderer's* identity, Squire."

Stilton blinked. "Murderer? Oh yes. Of course, of course. That is of the most importance, I agree with you."

"I will continue my investigation in London."

At this the man straightened. Was that relief on his florid face? "Excellent notion, Shelby," Squire Stilton nodded. "Capital."

"I am glad you approve," Robert returned dryly.

The squire took his words at face value and offered a magnanimous smile. "I care deeply for the good people of Arundel. And if your investigations can help put this nasty mess behind us all, then I hold your efforts in great esteem."

With that, the squire bobbed his head and hurried up High Street. Robert watched him go. The squire held his efforts in great esteem, did he? As if the man's benevolence had any bearing on his work. Bloody odd comments regarding the dead child. That was certain. Though Robert had no evidence to that end, he doubted the squire's only concerns were the worries of the people of Arundel.

He set the puzzle of the benevolent squire form his mind and made his way to Shelby Manor instead of the milliner's. Perhaps London would yield answers after all.

Robert gazed out the window of his office at Shelby Manor late that evening, his back to the useless bits of information he'd gleaned regarding the boy found murdered on the riverbank. The trip to Bow Street had yielded nothing, though he shouldn't have been surprised. Hadn't Blake told him time and again that the Runners gave no care to the poor children of London? It seemed that Robert alone would have to see justice for the nameless boy buried in the yard beside the church.

A flash of light caught his eye, bobbing from beneath the bridge. The signal was passed, and flashed further up on the bank. A successful run at the coast had no doubt yielded much contraband this evening. Robert suspected the smugglers brought more wares up from Littlehampton.

He had never given much notice to the smuggling trade, seeing little he could do to halt the progress of an activity that served so many in Arundel. More than a bit of the tea and brandy in the Manor could indeed have come from the smugglers' crops.

But now that a boy had been murdered, left like so much refuse at the side of the river? That put the case squarely into his realm, in his considered opinion. True, no one offered payment for his work on this case. But that didn't matter. He would see justice, if only for the poor little soul if not the boy's unknown family.

A shadowy figure suddenly caught his eye, moving across the bluff below the manor. He was shrouded in darkness and a voluminous garment, most likely a greatcoat. And slight in stature, Robert guessed from his viewpoint. Well away from the scurrying below, the figure obviously spied on the bank itself. Could this person be the lander, the connection to see the goods distributed? Surely the man would know something of the boy's death. He might not be forthcoming with his information, however.

Robert smiled, the effect almost ghastly in the reflection of the glass. He would take great delight in gaining the man's cooperation.

***

Diana crouched lower against the stunted tree, the

bark pinching her even through her thick cloak. Dark as night and much too large for her, the garment effectively hid her from any notice. The smugglers' boys worked with efficiency as she watched. And her brother was in the thick of it. He called out instructions often, his voice hushed and nearly unfamiliar in the fog-laced air. The smaller figures moved in a kind of dance to her eyes. The shallow boats dragged the goods seemingly in unison, and soon they would land at last and begin their ride by cart and wagon. The canal to London awaited. At least her brother had to her knowledge never accompanied the goods into the Thames. That trip would present more danger than she cared to ponder.

She wrapped the cloak around herself and settled back against the familiar, uncomfortable stump. A sound rustled behind her and she turned her head to ascertain its source. Nothing met her gaze. No surprise there. Darkness and fog held the night, and she could see little save for bobbing lights and shadowed outlines. She shivered and took a breath.

"Calm yourself, Diana," she whispered.

A week had passed since Matthew asked her about Clive's forcefulness, and he hadn't mentioned Clive again in her company. She had managed to eluded the "forceful" Clive

Stilton in the past week, as well. She'd seen Clive and her brother strolling at one end of High Street on more than one afternoon, though they thankfully gave all of their attention to the brazen village girls who accompanied them. Her maid Jane had joined her, and that wouldn't change in the foreseeable future. On one particular afternoon Diana had the distinct impression that someone was watching as she'd made her way home. Oh, nothing had seemed truly out of place. And yet she could nearly feel someone's gaze on her.

Suddenly, that odd sensation came again. She stood and whirled about, narrowing her eyes to catch a glimpse of the intruder. As before, she saw nothing. She turned back to the riverbank and squared her shoulders, intent on resuming her lonely vigil, when a pair of hands roughly grabbed her arms.

"I have you," her captor growled.

The voice was deep and intense and frightened her to the core. She struggled, kicking back with her booted foot and connecting with her attacker's shin. A string of inventive curses met her ears but she didn't let that deter her. She resumed her struggle, wrenching away from him at last.

Diana ran up the bluff, her heart pounding in her ears

as her half boots sought purchase in the damp sand. She could hear him behind her, biting out a curse as he lumbered closely behind her. He caught her blasted cloak and pulled, yanking her away from the purchase she'd begun to claim in the muck. With a muffled scream she fell, tumbling toward the hulking figure. The man caught her in his arms and stood, his arms tightening as she began to struggle again. Her voluminous hood covered her eyes and she fought against the unseen attacker with renewed vigor.

"Stay still, you bloody rotter," he cursed.

Something familiar in that voice struck her, and she froze. Oh, no. Bloody Hell. She kept her head down and attempted to shrink inside the hood of the damnably large cloak.

"You are no more than a child," Robert Shelby said, disgust lacing his cultured voice. He held her in one strong arm and reached up to throw back her hood. "What the devil…?"

Diana lifted her face to look him squarely in his rounded eyes. "Good evening, Mr. Shelby."

He blinked at her in obvious confusion for a moment, at last turning a scowl of immense displeasure on her that she could sense more than see. "You little fool." He gave her a shake. "Do you not know the danger, Diana? Out here alone, with no means of defending yourself?"

Diana blinked back tears and managed to keep her trembling chin high. "It is none of your concern."

"Much like the bruises that clod put on your arm, I take it?"

That surprised her, though perhaps it shouldn't have. His anger at her injury had been most evident the night he'd dined with her and her father. She realized then that he still held her, and sensed the intensity of his gaze on her face. "Mr. Shelby, if you would kindly—"

He crushed his mouth to hers, silencing her and causing her body to shiver with something other than the cold. His tongue brushed over her lips and she opened her mouth willingly. This time he took her mouth, the kiss almost bruising as he made the most provocative sounds in the back of his throat. She found herself pressed to his body, chest to thigh, and swallowed a gasp of shock. His big hands ran over her back, finally settling on her bottom as he pulled her even closer.

He broke off the kiss, cradling her to his chest as he

rested his chin on the top of her head. “My God,” he rasped. “Do you not know what could have happened?”

Diana gave a shake of her head, earning another pleasant squeeze from his arms. He placed his fingers beneath her chin then, lifting her to face him.

“Mr. Shelby—”

“Why are you out here?” he asked.

She couldn’t tell him, not without giving her brother’s actions away. “I merely thought to take a stroll.”

“Try another tack, Miss Ashley.” She turned and he caught her hands in his. “My God. You are chilled through.”

She glanced down at the large hand cradling hers and bit her lip. He was so strong, yet she doubted very much that he would ever use that strength to harm her. She thought back to the mighty struggle he had given her. Perhaps it was true that he wouldn’t use that strength now that he knew full well who she was, anyway.

Easing her hand away from his, she focused her attention on her cloak. Wrapped up once more, she sought to put as much distance between them as possible.

“You are coming up to the manor,” he said, grabbing her arm once more.

She dug her heels into the sand, gaining little purchase. “I cannot leave yet.”

She covered her mouth with her hand. The fog shifted and the moon shone as he turned those blue-gray eyes on her, the intensity showing her in an instant the persuasive effect he had on subjects of his investigations. “Why must you stay?”

She gulped and attempted to maintain her composure. She couldn’t tell him. He pulled her along, cursing with every uneven step he took. She threw one last glance toward the riverbank and then focused on the lighted windows of Shelby Manor.

Here was another mess she could lay at Matthew’s feet.

Chapter 8

Robert's leg protested both the uneven terrain and the forced activity tonight. Diana had kicked him, surprisingly hard and directly on his wounded leg. If her presence there on the bluff had surprised him, his own reaction had stunned him. Stark fear and intense longing had warred for a time, both only appeased as he'd pressed her to him. He longed to do that as soon as they gained his home, too. To kiss her senseless in front of a roaring fire.

But he would have answers from the stubborn package first.

She was still as a stone, the moon showing her averted pale face as she moved with grace over the sand and rocks. The overlarge cloak wrapped her figure, but Robert had felt the lush curves it concealed. With mind-shattering clarity. He was still hard from the contact despite the cold, wet air. And he would see more of that delectable body once he got her out of the cloak and before the fire. His body reacted in anticipation. "Bloody Hell," he grumbled.

"Pardon?" She faced him, her eyes wide and her mouth agape.

Turning from the alluring picture she made, he

continued up the bluff until they strolled through the still-dormant gardens. *She* strolled. He limped.

A few more steps and they were through the double doors and safe in his parlor. He released her and closed the doors behind him. Tight.

He saw that the fire still burned, brighter than before. Sterns's handiwork, he knew without question. No doubt the man knew of Robert's brief absence and anticipated the need for warmth after the damp chill. He removed his greatcoat and draped it over a chair near the hearth.

Diana took small steps over the carpet, the ugly cloak dragging the floor, and looked about the room. "This is lovely."

Robert glanced about, taking in the green and ivory furnishings, the cherry wood and marble tables. The carpet was done in a floral design of green and rose and cream, and she suddenly stood still as if afraid to drop more sand from her dainty booted feet. He swallowed a curse as he rubbed at his leg. Dainty indeed.

"Is your leg paining you?" she asked.

Robert waved her question away and stepped closer. "I care not about my leg at present." He removed her damp cloak. "Although the chill air and a race through the sand is most certainly not conducive to its condition."

"I am sorry I kicked you," she murmured.

He snorted. "Yes, well. I suppose I'm glad to discover that you are not completely without defenses."

She nodded and rubbed her hands over her arms.

"Are you still cold?" he asked. "Pray, come closer to the fire."

Diana nodded, her loose curls bobbing from the action, and floated over to the crackling fire. She held her hands out to the warmth, and Robert took a moment to admire the way the light shone through her muslin gown. Little wonder she'd donned the overlarge cloak for her excursion.

"Why were you on the bluff?" he asked.

She sighed and her shoulders slumped a bit. "I must keep watch."

That stunned him anew. "You work with the smugglers?" he asked, incredulous.

A laugh without much evident humor issued from her lips. "Hardly. But I must keep watch just the same."

Robert's gifted mind worked. Her father didn't police the banks of the River Arun. And she could no longer work with the free traders as he himself could. The child, then. That made sense.

"You must keep watch for the young ones," he stated.

She turned, her graceful brows arched above her lovely eyes. A stiff nod came then. "Yes."

He knew in his gut there was something more here. He also knew that Miss Diana Ashley would share none of it with him this evening.

He limped to a table set beneath one of the windows at the back of the room and poured two generous glasses of brandy. He offered her one, which she took with another nod. Slender fingers wrapped the glass, and she lifted the drink to her lips. As Robert drank his own he watched her, unable to keep from following the descent of the liquor. Her throat worked a bit as she swallowed and she gave a delicious little shiver as the brandy found its mark.

She turned a tiny smile in his direction. "Thank you."

He swallowed his own drink and eyed her closely. She'd given him a run for his efforts there on the beach, as fast as the weight of her cloak and the unsteadiness of the ground had permitted. And when he'd caught her?

The brandy began to soothe his leg if not his body's

other discomforts. He placed his empty glass on the table deliberately and stepped closer to her.

He should send her home. He took the glass from her and set it down on the nearest side table. She didn't belong in his home without chaperone. But he had tasted her desire along with his own out there on the bluff. And he couldn't bear to go another moment without tasting it again.

She gazed up at him, still and beautiful. He cupped her face in his hands and brought his mouth to hers and she opened to him immediately. *Amazing.* Their tongues met, and he tasted brandy and desire and Diana. He took from her and then kissed her throat, delighting in the purr she gave as she tilted her head back. Robert felt the pulse at the side of her neck as she murmured sweetly.

"Oh!"

"Mmm, Diana…"

She could have come to great harm there on the bluff. He worked the buttons of her bodice free, caressing her through her chemise. She was so sweet. So delicate. He lifted his head and gazed down at her full round breasts. She wore no stays tonight. No wonder she'd been able to struggle so freely.

"Beautiful," he rasped, his hands covering her.

She trembled at his touch. Robert brushed his thumbs over her nipples, thrilling at her response. The pink buds puckered, and he couldn't resist dropping a kiss on one of them through the thin fabric.

"P-please." Her voice wavered

Robert froze. With a jerk he lifted his head to find her on the verge of tears. She didn't beg for more attention. She was an innocent. Damn it to Hell. He closed her dress over those lovely breasts and straightened.

"Forgive me, Diana," he mumbled. "Miss Ashley."

As before in her father's study, she turned away from him. His hands itched to grab her, while his heart longed to take her innocence and bind her to him forever. *That* thought doused any lingering passion clouding his mind.

"I will see you home."

"No!" she cried. She rounded on him, and dashed an errant tear from her cheek. "My father must not know of this."

Robert sobered. "I would never disclose this, Miss Ashley. Despite my actions of this evening, I am a gentleman."

She conceded that point with a nod. Astonishing, even as the image of her there in his parlor, her hair mussed and her lips rosy from his kisses, moved him as none had ever before.

"I suppose I could take one of your horses," she said.

"And how, pray, would you explain that on the morrow? No, allow me to call the carriage." He tilted a crooked grin at her. "As adept as you are at eluding your father's prying eyes, I am most certain that you can find a way to alight the vehicle at a location different than your own doorstep?"

She laughed lightly at that, a musical sound that warmed him more than the brandy or even her kisses had.

He saw her bundled once more in the ugly cloak and deposited her in his carriage for the short ride to her father's house. Closing the door as the horses began their progress, he took a breath. He had nearly taken her. Indeed he'd taken more liberties than a lady of her station should expect. And though his attentions had caused distress, he saw no abhorrence or censure on her lovely visage. She had responded to him.

"My God."

"Had a bit of an adventure this evening, sir?" Sterns asked.

Robert shook his head at the butler now standing in the entry. "Thank you for the fire and the brandy, Sterns."

The man hesitated and Robert arched a brow at him in question.

"I take it the lady is safe?" Sterns asked.

Robert muttered beneath his breath. "Yes, Sterns," he said on a breath. "And she will remain safe, if I have anything to say about the matter."

Sterns lost his worried look and nodded. "I bid you good night, sir."

"Good night," Robert grumbled.

He crossed to the table and poured another generous glass of brandy and sank down onto the settee to study the fire and think of Diana.

***

Diana cuddled into her sheets, the warmth of the brandy still in her belly. The ride from Shelby Manor had been blessedly short, and it appeared that no one took note of either her progress or her arrival. The house was quiet, her father asleep and her brother about his dark duties. But she wouldn't think about her continued deception of one excellent man nor her continued surveillance of a careless one. Only one man, different entirely from either father or brother, filled her thoughts at this late hour: Mr. Robert Shelby and the wonderful sensations he had effortlessly elicited within her in his lovely parlor.

His lips on hers, his breath moist on her flesh, caused a shiver of delight to course through her even now.

"Astounding," she sighed aloud.

But she knew that he wouldn't put off his investigations much longer. He would come to her for answers.

And she had no bloody notion what, precisely, she would tell him.

"No one has a word to say of the boy," Diana heard Mr. Shelby say late the next morning.

Diana stilled in the hallway, her head cocked to one side to glean more information from Robert. She hadn't been aware of his arrival, closeted with the cook as she'd been for the past hour or so. Her father wasn't a difficult man to please but Diana was determined that more than mutton and bread be served at every evening's meal. She also wished to make certain that fine fare be available should Robert Shelby dine with them again.

She turned toward her father's office, to her familiar spot near the salver. Her father's responses were muffled by the door, though Mr. Shelby's diction was quite clear to her. After last evening, she suspected she would recognize his voice in as dense a fog as ever enveloped Arundel.

The poor little boy with no name had been put to rest, but she doubted his soul had found any peace. Such a violent death after so short a life. Diana sniffed and shook her head.

"The Runners had no information to impart," Robert said. "Nor any interest to investigate,"

She let out a gasp of outrage and both men stopped talking. Taking quiet steps away from the door, she nonetheless stilled as it opened.

"Miss Ashley," Robert said.

She turned and offered him a smile. Mr. Shelby returned the expression, the remarkable effect lending him the air of the man he'd been before his disappearance. He hadn't looked so last evening. But the intensity etched on his face then had thrilled her as much as this smile did at present. Knowledge swam in the blue-gray depths of his eyes, knowledge of what he'd done to her and how she'd responded. She felt her cheeks flame.

"Mr. Shelby," she said with a quick curtsey.

He bowed his head and sobered his expression. "Do join us."

"No, I couldn't."

"Diana, my dear," her father called.

She let out a breath and with resignation entered the office, passing close to Robert's large frame as she did so. Ignoring the pull of the body she knew to be most fit in spite of his leg, she held herself away from him and faced her father. "Yes, Father?"

"Shelby tells me that you may have some information to impart regarding the boy, Diana." The constable peered at her. "Pray, do share?"

"I… I've heard nothing of import in the village."

"Did you not speak with the gossips?" Robert put in from behind her.

Diana gave an unladylike snort, covering her mouth with her hand in the next moment. She glanced at Robert and dropped her hand. "The people of Arundel have little to say for the child, save that it was most obvious that no one missed the boy."

"I feared as much," Robert said as he folded his arms across his chest and lounged in the doorway.

Diana let her gaze flit over him—how could she not, he was posed there so masculine and beautiful?—before turning to her father once more. "Father, I believe there is a connection between the boy and the smugglers."

She held her breath as her father weighed her words. Out of the corner of her eye she watched Robert as he studied her. Would he give her secret away? For some reason she didn't believe he would. And though he believed that she kept vigil solely for the benefit of the poor children who were used and discarded, she had little desire for her father to know that for years now she had sneaked out of his house and gone out into the night alone.

"I concur with Miss Ashley," Robert said. "On the face of the matter, in any event. The child was not from Arundel, and at present there can be no other explanation for his being found here."

She shot him a look of gratitude and relaxed a bit. She couldn't bear to be in such close quarters with the man for much longer, however. "Well, I have household matters to attend," she rushed out as she made her way toward the door.

"Miss Ashley."

Oh, so close. Swallowing a sigh, she faced Robert. "Yes?"

"Pray, may I have a word with you?" She gaped at him and he turned to her father. "I wish to question her further about gossip."

"Ah," her father nodded.

Did her father also believe that she had so little to occupy her time and energy outside of village gossip? That was a sad prospect indeed.

"Well…," she began. The intent on Robert's face told her that he would settle for nothing less than agreement. Hadn't she known as she lay in her bed last evening that he would question her again? "Yes, of course."

"I daresay we are finished here, Shelby," her father said. "Diana, pray show Mr. Shelby to the parlor."

As she eased past Robert through the little bit of space left by his body, she felt the heat of him. He was so close, their bodies nearly touching. She wouldn't look at him. She would steel herself against his pull. She was in her father's home! Not in Shelby Manor, where she had allowed far too many liberties with the vexing man.

"After you, Miss Ashley," he said, that grin making a reappearance on his handsome face.

Her eyes on her slippers, she walked briskly down the hallway to the parlor.

Chapter 9

Robert watched Diana as she walked before him with her slight shoulders squared as she attempted an air of disassociation. He had seen the blush infuse her exquisite features however, and suspected more than embarrassment put the color there. He had to know more of her sojourns to the bluff to watch the smugglers. And as his present course of investigation in Arundel and London was proving tiresome and less than fruitful, he would take a pleasant tack this morning and pass a bit of time in the presence of a beautiful young woman with a few secrets of her own.

"Here we are, Mr. Shelby." She shrugged as she crossed to an ivory settee near one long window and perched herself daintily upon it. "I do not know what you wish me to tell you."

The sun slanted through the panes, catching the dark curls that had escaped the braids coiled at the back of her head to frame her face. Dressed in a demure day gown of pale pink, she was nonetheless an appealing picture. Giving his head a shake, he closed the double doors which led from the corridor. She let out a gasp, her eyes round, and he arched a brow at her.

"You do not wish your father to hear of the events of last evening, do you, Diana?" he asked.

At his use of her given name, he saw recognition fill those deep blue eyes even as she gave a quick shake of her head. He felt a flush of that desire that had filled him last evening and tamped it down.

"Miss Ashley," he went on, turning his attention to the waking garden visible through the window behind her. "Last evening you indicated that you frequently keep watch on the bluff."

She waved her hand, a graceful motion that caused an odd stirring in his chest as it caught his notice. "Not frequently. Not precisely."

He snorted at that and it was her turn to arch a brow in question.

"You watch the smugglers. You admitted as much to me," he pointed out. "Why?"

She nibbled her lower lip and Robert let his gaze settle on that ripe pink flesh. Her lashes lowered and she gave a tiny shake of her head. "I cannot tell you," she whispered.

"Then tell your father. He is the constable. It doesn't serve that his daughter is out alone."

"I cannot tell anyone."

Irritation filled him and he stalked over to her. "You repeatedly put yourself in danger and you will not divulge the reason?"

She shook her head again. "Do not press me on the matter."

"You little fool." He grabbed her by the arms and pulled her to her feet. "A child is dead, Diana. More than likely in his duties for the smugglers. They are a dangerous lot, and if they were to learn that you watch them—"

"They won't!"

Robert threw a meaningful glance toward the doors. Clearly she sensed his meaning, for she eased a bit in his grasp.

"Tell me what drives you?" he asked, his voice low. "I cannot bear to think of you out there alone. In danger."

She raised her eyes to his and he saw the defiance there, defiance mixed with vulnerability. His blood heated in pique and desire.

"I am not one of your cases, Mr. Shelby," she asserted. There was the hint of a tremble in her voice. "You will cease this and leave me in peace."

"Not bloody likely." He pulled her to him and pressed his mouth to hers. Releasing his hold on her arms, he let his hands trail over her slender back. To his delight she wrapped her arms around his neck and gave herself up to the kiss. She tasted sweet and pure and he took what she gave.

His tongue stroked hers and she returned the motion, setting him on fire. Her body was in full contact with his and he felt her curves brand him. Never before had a simple kiss moved him so swiftly to the point of acute wanting.

He broke off the kiss and brought his lips to the base of her throat, lightly tonguing the little hollow there. She let out the tiniest moan of pleasure and he echoed it with a louder one of his own. "My God, Diana…"

She tangled her fingers through his hair and clutched him to her as his mouth slipped lower. "Robert…"

Robert stilled and lifted his head. The sound of his name on her lips caused unnamed emotions to snake through him. He kissed her again.

Footsteps of a passing servant came from beyond the double doors and he released her. She swayed a bit on her feet, gazing up at him. Her lips were rosy, her eyes a bit out of focus. She was wholly adorable. Unable to resist, he dropped another kiss on those rosy lips.

She seemed to collect herself and stiffened slightly. "Mr. Shelby."

"Robert," he corrected.

She shook her head and turned away from him. "That is not proper."

Her dismissal raised his ire. "Propriety seemed to escape you the moment your tongue entered my mouth."

She yelped in outrage and faced him, her eyes glinting. She was a sight to behold.

"You, sir, will leave me."

Robert threw up his hands. "Pray, spare me from your maidenly protestations. I am no despoiler of virgins." He stalked to the doors and pulled them open wide. "But know this, Diana. I'll not yield on the other subject."

She raised her chin and dared him to press her further. He growled and left her there, bound for the fresh spring air and the freedom from the obstinate girl.

He fumed as he mounted his horse. Once again Diana had managed to wring a tangle of feelings from him. The ache between his legs would make for an uncomfortable ride home. She appeared unaware of her power over him, however.

"Thank God for small concessions," he muttered as he shifted in the saddle.

The mystery of the boy wouldn't be solved here in Arundel. And London would bear no further information. There was truly nothing to keep him here in Sussex. He would leave for The Hideaway to make use of the fine rooms, the delicious fare and the friendly serving maids. Miss Diana Ashley couldn't enter his mind if he filled it with other matters.

He nodded absently at the shopkeepers who waved greetings as he passed, resolved to separate himself from Sussex and all that resided here.

***

Diana buried her face in her hands and sank down onto the settee once more. *Shameful.* Once more the beguiling man had wound his magic around her, leaving her breathless. And senseless. There they had stood, in her father's home, and she'd allowed him to kiss her.

"More than allowed," she softly admitted.

She lowered her hands and stared at the flowered carpet. If she were being completely honest, she would acknowledge that she had welcomed his caresses. The opportunity to get lost in his strong arms, to feel his lips, his tongue, on her flesh was all she had longed for in those reckless minutes. He had certainly seemed more than willing to oblige her. Oh, she was surely in a muddle.

She leaned back in the settee and held her hand to her bosom. Taking in a deep breath, she sought to at last collect herself. She would stroll High Street today and speak to the gossips. She had to make certain that no one learned of her aborted trips to the bluffs nor last night's visit to Shelby Manor. She wouldn't shame her father in that manner.

"Nearly too late for that," she mocked herself.

She left the parlor at last, in search of her maid's company to assure that her separation from Clive Stilton continued.

"Diana," she heard her father call.

She found him in his office, a thoughtful expression on his face. He didn't seem to make note of her arrival for a long moment, at last turning an absent smile in her direction.

"I trust you and Mr. Shelby had a pleasant discourse?"

Her mouth dropped open, which she quickly covered with a bright smile. "Mr. Shelby wished to know what information, if any, I had to impart, Father."

"Yes, yes. The man said as much." That thoughtful cast came into his gaze again. "And did you?"

"Not beyond what he has already learned, I am afraid."

"More's the pity," the constable offered. He coughed into his hand before continuing. "He believes the smugglers had a hand in the boy's death."

She chose her words carefully. "And is that your conclusion as well?"

Her father shrugged and rubbed his hand over his face. "I've always found his deductive reasoning quite sound," he admitted. "Even before his disappearance, he was always one to hold on to a subject until he was satisfied."

Diana nodded, refusing to see the double-meaning in her father's innocently-spoken words. But the image of Mr. Shelby, that intensity in his beautiful eyes, made her wonder for a moment what satisfaction he would seek with her. Her cheeks flamed and she was grateful that her father once more studied the top of his desk.

"Um, yes," she murmured.

He nodded and faced her. "Are you going out into the

village, my dear?"

"Yes, Father."

"Pray, be careful. The miscreant who harmed that child could live right here in Arundel."

"I will be careful," she said, leaving him to his work.

She closed her father's office door and walked toward the back of the house. She didn't wish to believe he was correct about the child's killer. Maybe a smuggler from London was responsible. She doubted that was the case, however. It was more likely that someone here in Arundel had killed a boy and left him, cold and alone, by the river.

And she feared that someone Matthew worked with would turn out to be the villain.

She kept vigil again that night, wrapped once more in the overlarge cloak to ward off the chill. The operation went smoothly, as far as she could see. Huddled against the tree stump, she focused on Matthew and the young ones as they dragged the goods upriver.

She wouldn't think of last evening, of the terror that she'd felt when she'd been grabbed from behind, or that unnamed sensation as her captor made his identity blatantly clear. She gave a delicate shiver and wrapped her arms around her middle. It must be the cold.

She'd heard much of Robert's reputation as a bit of a rake, both before his captivity and since, and didn't doubt that. One look from those stormy eyes, a lift of one corner of that beautiful mouth, and even she was compelled to give him anything were he to ask. Or to simply take, as he had with his lovely kisses.

He despoiled no gently-bred ladies in Arundel, at least to her knowledge. His angry words in her father's parlor rang true. But surely he took his pleasures with the maids at the inn as most men in town did. Those silly girls in the village spoke of the serving wenches with a kind of envy. Little wonder that, as they were no doubt as generous with their favors as those paid for their services. Didn't they fawn over that fool Clive?

Would they readily give themselves to Robert should he turn an ounce of his charm in their direction? The thought of him holding any one of those vapid young ladies, kissing them as he had her, caused a pain to niggle at her belly.

"What concern is it of mine?" she asked in a whisper.

Voices reached her then, in obvious high spirits. She let out a breath and closed her eyes for a moment. Another night's work concluded, and her brother had survived yet again. She rose and stretched, brushing the sand from her bottom. A glance up at the manor showed no light in the room she guessed was the pretty parlor. Robert was no doubt at The Hideaway, mired in his own work and Middlesex amusements. No matter. Neither his work nor his diversions were of any concern of hers.

Decidedly dejected, she stomped the sand from her half boots as she made her way up the bluff toward High Street. Avoiding the lights of the Inn at Arundel, dimmed to better suit the seasoned clientele at so late an hour, she safely made her way home and into her room.

After lighting a lone candle, she removed the hateful cloak and set it aside for Jane's attentions. Her room was a pretty chamber, done in colors of rose and gray. Her mother had taken great pains in giving the room a feminine air, and the light wood of the furniture and the airy window coverings gave the room the dainty freshness of a nosegay of spring blooms. Her mother was very much present in the room. They'd passed much time there. She would tell Diana stories of adventure and handsome princes and, later, of the task that drew her from the house when all others were abed. The promise came then, and soon followed Diana's vow to continue to watch out for Matthew when she was gone. Diana shook her head to dispel all but the most pleasant recollections.

She donned a nightgown of lawn and sat at her vanity, seeing to her own needs as she was wont to do after her late night excursions. She always made a point of leaving off her stays on these nights. Even Jane wouldn't know of her mistress's late night activities. Not solely from the condition of the damp ugly cloak.

Releasing her hair from her braids, Diana took the time to carefully brush it. The moisture in the night air had caused curls to twist the dark strands, and she bit back a curse as one particular tangle caught her brush.

When her hair was smooth at last, she rose from the vanity. As tired as she was, she had little desire to seek sleep in the satin-and-lace covered bed. Her eyes burned with tears she wouldn't shed. She was so weary of it all. The time has come for her to confront her brother at last. She would screw her courage to the sticking place and see it done.

Oh, Robert would undoubtedly continue his investigation of her actions each and every night the smugglers ply their trade, but he could only speculate at her part in it. Nevertheless, she wouldn't give up another evening to her thankless vigil. Her brother would know of her own reluctant involvement with his smuggling tomorrow.

And Matthew would stop this before something so horrible happened that neither her father nor Robert Shelby could save him.

***

"At long last you grace us with your presence, Brother."

Robert walked through the door of The Hideaway and smiled at the sight before him. Taylor, with as bright a smile as he'd ever seen on her lovely face, stood in the entry. Her arms crossed, she regarded him with one golden brow arched.

"Did you miss me, Sister?" he teased.

Her blue-gray eyes clouded a bit. "Always, Robert."

He sensed the hurt in her voice and felt a stab of guilt. He grabbed her to him and lifted her off her feet. Too much time had passed since he'd held her. Before Trevor's machinations they had been as close as a brother and sister could be. And as it was she and Blake who had bravely rescued Robert from that dank chamber, he held his sister in great esteem as well as affection.

"About time you showed your pretty face here, Robert." This from Blake Thompson, Robert's best friend turned brother-in-law, standing beside the stairs. Blake lounged against the railing and regarded Robert closely. Robert planted a kiss on Taylor's cheek and lowered her to her feet, extending his hand as he stepped toward Blake. Blake grasped his hand and shook it, followed by a sound pounding on Robert's shoulders.

Robert returned the gesture with equal warmth. "How did you know I was coming?"

Taylor placed her hands on her hips and tilted her golden head to one side. "The staff informed us of your last visit over a fortnight ago. We deduced that you wouldn't remain in Sussex much longer before visiting again."

"I had business in Arundel. Or I would not have left The Hideaway at all," Robert grumbled.

"The child," Blake said.

Robert arched a brow. "Is there nothing you don't know, Blake? Pray tell me, then, who killed the boy and why?"

Blake barked out a harsh laugh and shook his dark

head. "Our case files show me nothing more than what you wrote before your return to Sussex."

"Yes," Robert admitted. "And Arundel yielded little information to add to that particular file."

"The gossips had nothing to impart?" Taylor asked. "I find that surprising."

More than mirth colored Taylor's words. The meddling folks of Arundel spread tales true or false with equal zeal.

"They dismiss the boy," Robert said. "As he obviously came from elsewhere, he is not their concern."

Taylor clicked her tongue as she shook her head sadly. "Pity. A child is the same no matter his home or family connections."

Robert nodded. "And what of my niece?" he asked, thinking to turn the subject down a more pleasant road. "Is she here?"

"Hardly," Blake put in. "Lily is safe at Thompson Hall, her doting grandfather seeing to her every comfort."

Robert smiled at that. "How did you leave the earl?"

"Quite well."

"And most pleased to have me out from underfoot, no

doubt," Taylor laughed. "I admit the place has proven quite the challenge for my decorating talents."

"Yes, and The Hideaway has come as far as it will, I daresay," Blake quipped.

Taylor swatted him on the arm and Blake caught her hand and pressed a kiss on her palm. Robert smiled at their exchange, well pleased for the two most important people in his life.

"Come, Robert," Blake said, setting his wife free. "I wish to hear all of the case, despite your avowal that little information exists."

Robert nodded his agreement. "At the very least it will serve to divert my mind from—" He caught himself. "Never mind, pray."

He glimpsed the spark of interest in Taylor's eyes and braced himself for an inquisition.

"Why do I believe more than this case vexes you in Arundel, Brother?"

"Let it go."

"What is this?" Blake put in, the grin returning to his face. "Only a female can cause that level of discomfort in a man, believe me. Do not tell me a woman has caught your notice in Arundel."

Robert wouldn't speak of Diana Ashley. These two could have no true notion of his actions in Sussex, let alone his involvement with the constable's daughter. "The case, Blake."

Blake and Taylor exchanged a look, whose import he didn't wish to decipher. Robert stalked down the corridor to the office he would now share with Blake.

Blake joined him and closed the door, thankfully saying nothing more of women.

Or of Arundel, save for the case of the nameless child buried in an unmarked grave.

Chapter 10

Robert paced in his comfortable room at The Hideaway, working the puzzle of Diana Ashley in his thoughts as he worked out the tensed muscles in his leg. Their antics the other night on the bluff still bore fruit, though the discomfort to his mind concerned him more than that of his troublesome limb.

She watched the smugglers each time they made use of the River Arun, that much he knew. She wouldn't admit to the reason for her involvement, though he suspected the death of the child drew her. But the resignation he'd glimpsed in her stance as he sneaked up behind her that night told of a frequent occupation rather than an impulsive action brought about by the recent heinous development.

In the week since leaving Arundel, he'd sought to lose himself in the paltry cases brought to Blake and him for solution. Blake gave himself up to the cases, encouraging Robert to aid him in finding stolen jewels or misplaced lovers. Taylor occupied herself in the public house, seeing that the food and ambience reflected her tastes and desires for the place. But both would soon depart for Blake's holdings, he knew.

Their daughter Lily drew them, as well as the lure of domestic bliss. Envy bit into Robert. How wonderful would it be to return to Shelby Manor in a like pursuit? To find his life mate waiting for him, a smile on her beautiful face, her deep blue eyes sparkling, her glossy black curls arranged in an artful mass that simply begged for his fingers to disarray?

"What the devil…?" he bit out.

Here he was at The Hideaway, with any number of amusements before him, and he could only think of Diana Ashley? True, she was the most beautiful girl he had seen in recent memory. And more intriguing than any he'd ever met. She was clever at keeping her secrets. That was certain.

But she wouldn't evade his investigation for long. He would unravel her mysteries. The memory of their embrace at Shelby Manor—of those searing kisses in her father's parlor!—heated his blood. A smile curved his mouth. Ah, but what a bloody marvelous time he would have inciting her to divulge much more than her connections to the smuggling in Arundel.

Once more he'd declined the offer of female companionship from Annie, raising Blake's brows a notch. Taylor seemed almost satisfied to him, no doubt pleased that her brother wouldn't debase the fine young women who served the patrons at The Hideaway. As if Blake hadn't availed himself on any number of them before his nuptials.

Robert's anger dissipated even before it could be roused, for in the past few weeks he often found himself yearning for more than sexual adventures with no true connection. Innocent kisses, and not so innocent caresses, from a certain dark-haired girl had left the prospect of any other encounters pale despite their vigor. With nothing to truly draw him for the rest of the evening, he readied for bed.

The next morning, his suspicions regarding Blake and Taylor proved correct. The couple took their leave, but not before threatening to pay a visit at Shelby Manor in the near future.

"I will know the identity of the girl who keeps you from Arundel, Brother," Taylor promised.

One knowing look from Blake told him that she wouldn't abandon her quest in the foreseeable future.

"Now see here, Taylor."

"You have been alone for far too long, Robert," she softly insisted, effectively silencing him as surely as if she'd shouted. "Pray, allow me to indulge my curiosity?"

Robert rolled his eyes heavenward. "Your 'curiosity' is not what troubles me, Sister," he told her. "Your insistence that you know what is best for me? That is what vexes me greatly."

"Enough," Blake put in. He clasped Robert's hand and gave a shake. "We will see you soon?"

Robert nodded and turned to his sister. Taylor hugged him and Robert closed his eyes against the sting of emotion. He smiled winningly at her and she returned the expression after a moment's hesitation.

"Kiss Lily for me?"

"Certainly. But it will not be long before she begins to insist on her uncle's fond presence as well as his absent kisses, Robert."

Robert said nothing to that, his throat curiously tight. He saw them off in Blake's fine carriage, emotion warming him even as it served to put him on his guard. A final glimpse of Taylor, one dainty hand waving farewell, caused his own to reach out for them. He glanced at his hand, outstretched in an obvious bid for attachment, and fisted it at his side.

Work beckoned, a case that would serve to divert his attentions from familial obligations, emotions, and the longing for a connection. Several clients would see him today, and he more than welcomed the distraction.

Perhaps then Miss Diana Ashley would not intrude on his thoughts.

A scant week later, he hid himself in his office, the room now empty of both his friend and the camaraderie he'd enjoyed for his too-brief visit. The sense of emptiness due to Taylor and Blake's departure persisted. Liquor aided his cause. The brandy dulled his mind and his spirits.

He stubbornly refused to let thoughts of Diana Ashley enter his consciousness, as even as the tiniest flash of her image brought about an arousal that urged satisfaction he wouldn't find at The Hideaway. His colorless existence was broken only by his work, to which he gave himself with vigor to rival his manner before his captivity.

Sitting himself down, he eyed the folders at his elbow with a befuddling mixture of irritation and relief. He withdrew one particularly vexing file and opened it, smiling once more to see the latest addition.

The letter had arrived last evening, a relief to him. Immediately he'd penned a note advising Blake of the information within, guessing well his friend's pleased response. He read the few words the solicitor had written again, that welcome sense of resolution filling him.

"She is safe," he said aloud.

"Where the devil is the bastard?" he heard from outside the door. "Shelby, show yourself!"

Robert's smile widened. Ah. Grimes, at last. He returned the note to the folder and set both aside, standing as Annie opened the door.

"A Mr. Grimes for ya', Mr. Shelby."

Grimes, a decidedly ugly bull of a man, glowered from the doorway. Annie bobbed a curtsey and closed the door behind her.

"Grimes." Robert grinned. "What brings you to The Hideaway this fine morning?"

"Cease that prattle, Shelby," the man growled. He ran his short fingers through his springy brown curls and spat out a curse. "She ain't been home all night, damn her unfaithful hide."

"I take it you speak of your wife?"

Grimes's thick brow lowered over his small black eyes. "Ya' know my meanin'!"

Robert clasped his hands behind him and took

measured steps around the desk. "Your wife is gone, I take it?"

Grimes pounded on the desk. "Where is she?"

Robert took a moment to savor his disclosure as he stood before the bully. "Where you will never touch her."

"Son-of-a—"

"Easy, Grimes," Robert said, his voice a low threat. "Should you dispel my sunny disposition this morning, you will not be pleased with the result."

"She's my wife, damn your hide!"

"And you chose to reward her foolish notion of marriage to you with the generous application of your fists."

"What of it?"

The man seemed genuinely puzzled, causing Robert's stomach to churn with distaste.

"She is gone, Grimes. You would do well to rethink your attitude toward women in general and wives in particular." He turned a chilling smile on his client's husband. "You may find your next spouse far less submissive."

Fear flickered in the dolt's dull eyes. *Good.*

"Well, she ain't proved herself worth nothin'," Grimes muttered. "I s'pose it ain't right to keep meself to her when she be so disrespectful."

Robert bit back a sharp retort. "Yes," he said flatly.

Grimes took his leave and Robert let out a breath. The man's wife was in protection well to the north, due to the safe house provided by Robert and Blake's solicitor. He and Blake had seen too many battered women to safety in the past few years, and those cases were the ones in which he agreed with Blake's notion that any amount of payment was adequate to see that particular brand of justice.

Men who would use their size and strength against someone weaker didn't deserve the breath in their bodies. Robert knew this in his soul. The battered body of that little boy bore evidence that children were victims as often as women. Any bruises inflicted on a woman turned Robert's stomach, the thought once more bringing the injuries to Diana's tender skin to his mind.

Let Clive Stilton so much as think to hurt her again. Robert would do more than merely see Diana safe.

***

"I must see to my work, my dear."

Diana nodded absently as her father took his leave from the breakfast table. She sipped her tea, wishing she could gain strength from the brew. At any moment her brother would saunter into the room, a carefree smile on his face. She would take no delight in revealing her knowledge of his actions these long years. But she would be lying to herself if she didn't admit that she longed for the release from duty the admission would afford her.

All morning she had worked on the approach in her mind, the predawn hours filling her with conflictions. Her mother's words, her heartfelt entreaties repeated numerous times while she'd lived, still echoed in Diana's mind. Her mother's visage floated before her now, at last a look of resignation fixed on her ageless features.

Diana's reputation was indeed at stake should the people of Arundel learn she spent her evenings traipsing about unchaperoned. She'd been in Robert's house. In his arms. But Matthew's very life depended on her convictions today. Admitting to her nightly sojourns was a small price to pay.

"It is time, Mother," she whispered. "Pray, give me strength."

Movement at the open door of the breakfast room caught her eye. Matthew entered, a bit unsteady on his feet.

She took in his appearance, so altered from his usual gracefully-attired self. His clothes were rumpled as if he'd slept in them. His hair was more tangled than artfully tousled. His eyes seemed sunken in his pale face. A niggle of worry chased down her spine.

"Good morning, Matthew."

He gazed at her as if unseeing, finally blinking his red-rimmed eyes. "'Morning."

Diana watched as he chose his morning meal with little care, his hands a bit shaky. "Are you quite all right?"

He turned from the sideboard and stared at her. At last he offered her a smile, but it was merely a shadow of his usual expression. "I am fine, Sister."

Diana drained her tea cup and folded her hands, prepared to wait for the moment to divulge her wishes to him. No such moment seemed ready to present itself, and she eyed the meager amount of food he absently consumed from his plate.

She took a breath and forged ahead. "Matthew, I need to speak with you."

He looked up, his dark brows knit with worry. Her apprehension swiftly turned to alarm.

"What ails you?" she asked.

His mouth opened, but nothing audible readily came forth. "I cannot speak of it," he rushed out at last. He stood and dropped his napkin to the table. He took a few halting steps toward the door and spun back to her. "Is Mr. Shelby back from Middlesex?"

"I… I do not know. What business could you have with Mr. Shelby?"

His hand worked on his limp cravat. "I merely… Never mind, pray."

With those confounding words he ended their discourse and quit the room. And any hope she'd had of begging him to abandon his activities followed on his scuffed and dusty heels.

"What in the world?" she murmured.

No matter. She would confront her brother soon and make him see reason. His actions and demeanor this morning puzzled her greatly, and she suspected Clive Stilton was involved. Matthew's moods often matched his involvement with the lauded young Mr. Stilton, though until this day he'd always seemed most pleased to mention the lout's very name. She hadn't asked after Clive. But had she done so, would the worry have fled his features? Or would his alarm have increased?

Anger caused her to fairly shake. For so long she'd despised the invisible hold Clive had on her brother. If that reprobate had done so much as think to harm him? Her defense shouldn't have surprised her, but the vehemence of it did.

And what, pray, could Matthew have to do with Robert Shelby? Such could portend no good. That man's work wasn't illegal, if the tales told in town could be believed. But it wasn't without its own danger. Hadn't it led to Trevor Shelby's keeping Robert captive for those long months?

She had no notion if Robert was home nor of when he would return to Arundel. If the past did indeed repeat itself, he would stalk back into her life sometime over the next fortnight. But would Matthew's difficulties wait until then?

Letting out a breath, she stood. She would go into the village and find out what could be learned from the gossips. Perhaps something would indicate the nature of her brother's dilemma.

She could only pray it was nothing so dangerous that

she could not save him from it.

Raised voices reached her not much later, as she returned from her fruitless trip into Arundel.

"Took her virtue, he did!" a man's voice declared. "Beat her bloody and left her for dead!"

Diana froze, her hand at her throat. She stood on the step, peering through the open door at Mr. Hollis as he yelled for her father. The butcher was beside himself, rage and fear and upset warring expressions on his ruddy features. Her stomach churned as her heart began to pound.

"Hollis, please," her father soothed. "Do calm yourself and tell me what has happened."

Diana stepped into the house, one hand outstretched to Hollis. "Mr. Hollis, do listen to Father."

Hollis looked at her, his eyes wild, and shook his head. "W-what I got to say ain't fit fer yer ears, Miss Ashley." He rounded on her father once more. "I'll have justice fer me daughter. Just see if I don't!"

"I do not know what you're talking about, Hollis. If you would—"

"He took her! He… He hurt her."

Her father's face paled, raising the tiny hairs on the

back of Diana's neck.

"Who, Mr. Hollis?" she asked.

"Me daughter. Me Gertie!" Hollis shook his fist in her father's face. "He took her against her will, he did. And I want his hide for me wall! I'll hang him in me window, I will. As bloody and beaten as me sweet girl."

Hollis fell to broken sobs that pulled at Diana's heart.

Her father placed a hand on Hollis's shoulder. "We will find the man who hurt her, Hollis," he stated. "Believe me on this. We will learn his identity."

The man sucked in a mighty breath and fixed his glassy eyes on her and her father both. Trepidation flashed through her as if she knew what he would say before the words left his mouth.

"No need to learn who the bastard be, Ashley," Mr. Hollis said. "He be yer son!"

Diana gasped a breath as the man's meaning struck her. Matthew's odd behavior and appearance this morning would lend him guilt had anyone else seen him. But she knew better. Her brother wasn't violent and would never raise his hand to a woman. Mr. Hollis's daughter was slow, as sweet as a child and just as guileless. Surely the man was mistaken!

"No," she gasped.

Both men gave her no notice as she turned and rushed out of the house. Her father's hushed and fervent tones fell behind her, no doubt seeking to both soothe Mr. Hollis and convince him of Matthew's innocence. But she'd seen her father's eyes when the accusation came. The doubt there had cut her deeply, for her brother's sake as well as her own.

She raced down High Street, a route she'd taken countless times before on her nocturnal vigils. Why, pray, did today's task make those others seem like mere amusement?

As she made her way she paid no mind to those littering High Street, folks bent on gossip of the most awful kind who stared at her.

"Where's your brother, Miss Ashley?" the blacksmith shouted, his big soiled hands clenched into fists. "Where's he hidin'?"

She shook her head and continued, keeping her swift strides even so that no one would feel compelled to follow her to what they would most certainly deem Matthew's hiding place. He didn't do this. He couldn't!

"Mr. Matthew Ashley is nowhere to be found, Miss Ashley!"

This from Fran or Nan, a smile peeping through the expression of matronly outrage at such a development. Again, she persevered and made her way past the shops and crowds and turned toward the bluff.

Her knock on the glossy ivory door of Shelby Manor brought its swift opening. An elderly butler stood there, shock clear on his dignified features.

"M-miss Ashley!"

"Hello…"

"Sterns, miss."

"Sterns." She offered him a quick smile as she glanced about the large marble-tiled entry. "Is Mr. Shelby at home?"

"Why no, miss. He is in Middlesex at present."

"Oh, oh no—" She recovered. "Do you know when he will return, Sterns?"

"I am sorry, miss, but no. I daresay the household is never advised of Mr. Shelby's comings and goings."

Oh beautiful, she silently cursed.

"I told Mr. Ashley so, when he came—"

"My… my father?" she asked in confusion. "The constable was here?"

Sterns blinked at her and shook his gray head. "No, miss. Mr. Matthew Ashley was here earlier."

She sharply drew in a breath. "Matthew was here? When, pray?"

The butler considered her question for a moment. "Above three hours ago, miss. He seemed most intent on finding my master." Sterns shrewd gaze met hers unflinchingly. "Much as you are now."

Diana felt her cheeks heat a bit but wouldn't indulge in a bout of missish coyness. "Did Matthew say anything? Anything that would indicate his next destination?"

"Destination, miss? He did seem most put out when I told him Mr. Shelby was out indefinitely. He turned on his heel and left."

Diana nodded, her mind working. She had to find Matthew. But where the devil could he have gone?

"Thank you, Sterns," she said to the butler. "Pray, advise Mr. Shelby of my visit?"

"Certainly, miss," the man bowed. He took a step closer. "And if I can be of any assistance, Miss Ashley, pray don't hesitate to call upon me?"

She blinked in surprise. The sincerity on the elderly

servant's face set aside any silly notions of propriety. Offering him a shaky nod, she left Shelby Manor to plan her next course of action.

Chapter 11

Robert walked the narrow street bisecting the tiny village of Homerton where The Hideaway was located, his mind on the upcoming evening of mindless amusement. Two days had passed since the abusive Mr. Grimes' visit and no additional cases of such import have called to him. Stolen pocket watches and necklaces, unfaithful wives and duplicitous mistresses. Those possible cases did little to draw his interest.

The walk about in the chill and damp night air caused his leg to stiffen, and with each swing of his right leg he swallowed a curse. Sore muscles were little to endure, though. He couldn't delay his return to Arundel much longer. He would be forced to face the unsolved mystery of the dead boy. And the beguiling mystery of the smugglers' watch girl.

He had gotten no answers from Diana when last he questioned her in her father's home, and the Lord knew he'd gained nothing save frustration when he'd posed those same questions the night he'd found her keeping watch. What was it about Diana Ashley that drove him mad?

True, she was beautiful. Achingly beautiful, were he to be completely honest, with slender curves and rosy lips that promised pleasures. She was quick-witted, if her slippery evasion of his interrogation tactics were any indication. And she was compassionate, for didn't she keep watch over the smugglers so another child wouldn't be harmed? At least that was what she wanted him to believe.

"Bloody damnable chit," he grumbled.

He looked up to find himself on the doorstep of The Hideaway, not fully cognizant of the walk that brought him back. He vaguely recalled stepping out on his ill-advised quest for fresh air, after indulging in too much of Blake's ale and not enough of Mrs. Mott's food. No doubt his leg would hurt like the devil when the ale wore off.

Pushing through the door, he found the public house empty. A few candles sputtered in the dining room, enough to show him that the room had been set to rights. He removed his greatcoat, draped it over the nearest chair and made his way toward the taps.

"Ale, Shelby?"

Robert squinted, at last spying Annie holding aloft a tankard. "Annie."

The serving girl smiled and stepped closer. "Thought you'd be needin' this when ya' stumbled back here."

He offered her a grin that felt false but had its predictable reaction. The girl giggled and handed him the ale, which he drained immediately.

He set it down on the table. "Good night, my girl."

He turned and she caught him as he tripped over his own feet. Pain shot up his right leg and he cursed loud and long.

"Leg painin' ya'? Small wonder."

Robert shook his head, ale and thoughts of Diana clouding his mind. "I am a bloody fool."

"Never that, Shelby." Annie clicked her tongue and steered him toward the staircase. "Come on. Let's get ya' abed."

A harsh laugh came from him, sounding odd to his ears. "Abed. That's my girl."

Annie chuckled her assent and led him up the stairs.

***

Diana shivered as she stepped down from the hired hack. The hour was late, later than she'd ever spent on her vigils by the riverbank. The ride from Sussex had been blessedly uneventful, though guilt stabbed at her as she had once more made a secret escape from her father's home.

No sign of Matthew could be found, and the dejection on her father's beloved face told her that Matthew's disappearance might very well indict him in more eyes than those of the villagers in Arundel. But for once in her life she decided to use the gossips of the village to her own advantage.

Ready information met her ears as she discreetly inquired after the location of Robert's Hideaway. It hadn't even taken a moment's hesitation before she found herself compelled to go to the one man who could set matters to rights.

Her brother was innocent. But the foul storytellers in Arundel wouldn't rest until they found what they believed was justice for the poor sweet daughter of Mr. Hollis. Her father couldn't hold off justice for long, even though it was misplaced and aimed at his own son.

She shifted her hastily-packed satchel to her left hand and raised her fist to rap on the rough wooden door. The sound carried little beyond. She peered through the mullioned windows to see but faint flickering light within. Dejection threatened and she leaned her forehead against the door. The thick panel gave slightly, its latch giving up its scant hold on the doorjamb with a click.

"A blessing?" she asked on a soft laugh of relief.

Taking this as the boon it was, she entered the public house and closed the door behind her. She set her satchel at her feet and took a breath. "Hello?" she called out softly.

No sound came to her in answer. The faint smell of charred wood and the stronger one of ale assailed her nostrils. The doused fire behind the grate in what must be the dining room explained the first; the barrels set against the far wall of the place, the second. Several tables filled the space, all with chairs neatly set beneath. Save for one chair that supported a great coat draped over its back. She recognized that great coat even in the dim light.

"Thank God," she whispered.

She removed her cloak and draped it over the chair beside Robert's greatcoat. Setting her bag down, she turned toward the staircase. Surely he was abovestairs, then. She climbed the stairs, the carpet deadening her footfalls, and stood for a moment on the landing at the top as she peered down the hallway. A soft sound met her ears, unintelligible but no doubt human. And vaguely masculine.

Light shone from around one door set near the end of

the corridor, the wooden panel slightly ajar. He must still be awake at this late hour. As her heart hurried its beat, she continued on toward the room.

She raised her fist as she had belowstairs, stilling as another sound came from within. This was most assuredly masculine, and most intriguing. Her curiosity piqued, she peeped through the crack of light coming from the room. As the door swung open on silent hinges she froze, stunned at the image before her.

Robert reclined in an upholstered chair, his head resting on the wide back. He wore only tan breeches, his smoothly-muscled torso and arms bronzed by the fire burning merrily behind the grate set in the hearth beside him. He gripped the arms of the chair, his throat working as another beguiling sound issued from his well-formed lips.

That was precisely when she took note of the scantily-clad girl kneeling before him.

***

Robert squeezed his eyes shut as a mixture of pleasure and pain gripped him. The pain in his leg was almost bearable as the throbbing seemed to move toward his cock. Annie's hands worked over his chest and he gave a shiver. Her lips followed her hands, pressing kisses on his flesh as her fingers kneaded his thighs. She dropped a kiss on his stomach and he sucked in a shuddering breath. He knew what was coming next, even though he had denied himself for weeks now.

Annie trailed her fingers over the bulge in his breeches before working first one button free, then another. As Annie lowered her head to his lap he heard a gasp. Robert turned toward the doorway and opened his eyes. Recognition slammed through his muddled brain. *Diana?* "What the devil…?"

Diana opened her mouth, but no sound came forth that he could hear. Annie came to her feet and gathered her discarded dress from the floor. To Robert's amazement she bobbed a curtsey to Diana before fleeing the chamber.

"Dia— Miss Ashley?" Robert stammered.

Diana nodded, her eyes tracing over his chest and stomach toward the loosened front of his breeches. He followed her gaze and spat out a curse as he buttoned his breeches, coming shakily to his feet. "Why are you here?"

She swallowed and closed her eyes for a moment. "This is about Matthew," he heard her murmur. She met his gaze at last. "I need your help."

He stared at Diana for several beats. What the devil was she doing here? In his chamber at The Hideaway? The recollection of his and Annie's actions just moments ago struck him and he bit back a curse that would surely blister Diana's ears. Her eyes raked over him, once more settling somewhere south of his chin. He rolled his eyes heavenward and said a silent prayer of thanks. Had she not made her presence known when she had, she would have seen far more than his bare chest.

"Forgive me," he muttered, shrugging into the shirt he'd abandoned some time ago. "Why are you here, again?"

He faced her and she at last dragged her gaze from his form, settling instead on her kid slippers.

"I need your help," she said again. "My brother…" A sob caused her voice to crack. "My brother is in trouble."

Without thinking, he wrapped his arms around her as she broke into soft sobs. He had never before seen this vulnerability in her and it moved him more than he wished to admit. She melted against him and he couldn't help but revel in the sweetness of her surrender.

Too soon she recovered herself and placed her hands on his chest. She held herself away from him and he let her go. Sniffling, she turned from him and fixed her gaze on the fire behind the grate.

"Tell me what happened," he urged.

She nodded, squaring her shoulders. He took in her appearance as she gathered her composure. Modest muslin dressed her figure and no bonnet covered her dark curls. Where was her cloak? Belowstairs, no doubt. Precisely how long had she stood there in the doorway as he'd nearly indulged in activities beyond her maidenly comprehension?

Tucking his shirttails into his breeches, he chose another tack. "Matthew Ashley always struck me as a feckless youth, Diana. But I have little faith that he could have gotten himself in such dire straits as to drive you to come here in the middle of the night."

She turned, shaking her head. "Matthew has been a fool, that's true. But this… No. I cannot lend it credence."

Robert shook his head, sorely wishing that he hadn't indulged in any number of vices this evening. The ale still clouded his mind, but at least the echo of Annie's promised pleasure had at last fled his body.

He took a step closer to her. "Tell me."

She took in a breath and released it in a rush.

"Matthew has been working with the smugglers. For years now."

Her late-night vigils now made perfect sense, even to his murky thoughts. None other than familial obligation would induce her to keep watch for so long.

"That explains your keeping watch."

"Yes."

"But why come to me, Diana?"

Tears swam in those clear blue eyes. "He's been accused of… of…"

She trembled before him, and he couldn't keep himself from gently grasping her arms.

"Of what, pray? What has your brother been accused of?"

Her eyes fluttered closed. "Of forcing himself upon a defenseless woman," she whispered.

He stood there, how long he didn't know. But when she fell to sobbing anew, he cradled her to him.

"He did not do it," she vowed softly. "He could not."

He believed her. There was little in Matthew Ashley's character to indicate such a monster lurked beneath his carefree exterior. True, in his profession Robert encountered many a gentleman who hid his perverse proclivities beneath a gentile façade. Matthew's demeanor had never given him any cause to believe he was anything other than what he seemed however, and Robert prided himself on his judgment if little else.

"Where is your brother now?"

"I do not know. He… he fled."

"What? Why?"

She rubbed her cheek against his chest, her tears seeping through his linen shirt. Her sigh brushed across his flesh and he fought to ignore the sensation.

"He could not face his accusers, I believe," she said. "They are so ready to think the worst." She sighed again. "As always."

Bitterness colored her words and he led her over to the chair. She sat, her hands folded in her lap as her shoulders slumped. He knelt before her, his intent far different than Annie's when she'd held this position not fifteen minutes earlier.

"Tell me all of it," he said.

"You know full well the damage the tale-tellers happily inflict, Mr. Shelby."

"Robert."

She blinked and gave him a reluctant nod. "Robert. And the poor girl…" Shudders racked her form as she bit her lip.

Robert covered her hands with his. "Who was it?"

"The butcher's daughter."

An image of the slightly-dimwitted but sweet girl filled his mind. Anger pooled in his belly, twisting sickeningly. "But she is like a child."

Diana nodded. "And her attacker…" She fisted her hands in obvious outrage. "He beat her."

Robert straightened, the truth striking him. "Clive."

"W-what? No. He couldn't… Oh, he could!"

His stomach clenched at the fear stamped on her face. He had to know the extent of the bastard's abuse, no matter the pain the recollection would cause her at first.

"Diana, has Clive ever forced you? Has he done more than hurt your arm?"

"You knew?" She gaped at him. "How?"

"I recognize a bully when I see one. And Clive Stilton surely fits the order."

"Yes."

A world of import filled that single word.

"Has he ever touched you?"

She stared at him, guileless. Those beautiful eyes widened and she gave a shaky of her dark head. "No, thank the good Lord."

He let out a breath he hadn't realized he was holding. "Indeed."

She gifted him with a tiny smile which broke through the darkness of the moment. He realized his position at long last. She was here, unchaperoned and in his chamber.

"You cannot stay here," he said.

Alarm filled her eyes as she sprang to her feet. "Oh, you cannot send me away! You must help me. You help people, Robert. Tell me the tongue-wagging people of Arundel have not misled me in this!"

"Be easy, Diana," he soothed. "I merely meant that you must quit my chamber." Her shoulders sagged in obvious relief now. "Where are your effects?"

"I left my cloak and satchel belowstairs when I arrived." Her cheeks redden and she eyed the chair she'd just vacated with dawning horror. "Oh, forgive me! I cannot believe what I saw. That is, I did not know that you were indisposed."

"Easy, love."

She eyed him with dismay at the endearment, so easily-spoken. As he watched, she gathered that remarkable spirit about herself and affected a prim stance despite their muddled circumstances. Desperation showed in her pale features nonetheless. "You will help me, then?"

Bloody Hell. There was nothing else for it. He raked his fingers through his hair and let out a breath. "Yes."

To his astonishment, she closed her eyes as if in prayer and swooned into his arms.

Chapter 12

Diana awoke the next morning in an unfamiliar chamber. Comfortably furnished, the low-ceilinged room wasn't quite what she'd been expecting when she'd fled from Arundel yesterday. Oh, so much had happened since her flight.

She stretched and glanced toward the small window to her right. The sunlight streaming through the sparkling panes, piercing the lovely lace curtains dressing the window, told her that it was most assuredly late morning.

One glance at her body showed that she wore only her chemise. However had that happened?

"Oh, no," she groaned.

Some of the events of last evening came rushing back, the most distressing was her falling into a maidenly swoon! Robert had no doubt seen to her care after that embarrassing encounter. Too fatigued to give much struggle, she'd apparently allowed him to see her to bed. However would she face him this morning?

She rose from the bed and eyed the chair opposite. It was smaller than the plump one in Robert's fine chamber. An image flashed, one of the girl kneeling at the feet of the most splendid man Diana had ever seen. She groaned again.

She saw to her morning toilette behind a pretty privacy screen set in one corner of the room and washed her face from the fine china washbasin. The dress she'd worn the previous day awaited her behind the screen as well, draped with care over a wooden straight-backed chair. Leaving off her stays, she donned the dress and fastened the tiny pearl buttons marching up the bodice. Had Robert's fingers worked these buttons? A flush infused her. Would the embarrassment of this morning never end?

A smallish vanity sat just beside the small, lace-dressed window and Diana sat herself at it, peering into the oval mirror atop. Her hair was a fright. That was certain. She looked about and found her satchel sitting in wait at the foot of the narrow iron bed. Withdrawing the few items she'd brought, she hung a handful of dresses and underclothes on the pegs set behind the privacy screen and took out her more personal effects.

Her brush in hand, she worked the tangles out of her hair. No benefit of bonnet would hide her curls today. She swiftly braided her hair and coiled it in a simple style.

A knock came at the door. She turned toward it with

curiosity. "Come."

The door opened and a serving maid entered. A red-haired serving maid. Oh, Lord.

"Good morning, miss." The girl dropped a curtsey. "Mr. Shelby wishes ya' to join him in the dinin' room."

Diana nodded, unable to speak. True, the girl wore clothes befitting her occupation this morning, with a crisp white apron over serviceable brown work dress. Her face showed neither shame nor anger over Diana's intrusion last night. In fact, she wore a friendly smile Diana couldn't help but return in some measure.

"Thank you…"

"Annie, miss."

"Annie."

Another curtsey and the girl left Diana in solitude. Befuddled, Diana eyed the open doorway. Shaking her head, she came to her feet and left the chamber, bound for the staircase.

She descended the stairs to find herself nearly in the dining room, and she found it a pleasant space now that she viewed it in the daylight. Linens dressed the round tables topped with silver candlesticks and small vases filled with flowers. The wide-planked floor shone from polishing. The welcoming scents of fresh bread and sausage and eggs reached her and she suddenly realized she was famished. She'd left before dining last evening and now she could think of nothing more wonderful than indulging in some of the fine food covering the sideboard.

The tall figure leaning against it gave her pause, however. "Good morning, Miss Ashley," Robert said.

He appeared his usual handsome self, but the smile on his face wasn't one she'd glimpsed before. It was most welcoming, aided by a dimple set in one cheek. Fine clothes dressed his figure, but it didn't take much imagination on her part to envision the magnificent arms and chest hidden beneath the white linen and brown jacket. She would never forget what he'd looked like last night.

She swallowed. "Good morning."

She crossed to the sideboard, her nose tingling pleasantly. The serving girl, Annie, set a tray of sweet rolls beside the other platters on the sideboard. The rolls gave up the wonderful scent that had first drawn Diana's notice.

"Oh, these look scrumptious," she said.

Robert nodded to Annie, who went about her duties,

and smiled at Diana as he began to fill his plate.

"Mrs. Mott is famous for these sweet rolls," he said.

She followed his lead and lifted a china plate. As she served herself from the fine fare offered, she sought to ignore the masculine form so close to her. "Everything looks wonderful."

He gave a chuckle. "Are you a bit hungry this morning, Diana?"

She nodded. "Yes, I admit. I left last evening before dinner."

He fell silent and she glanced at him to find a worried frown marring his brow.

"You must tell your father you are here. He is surely frantic with worry."

Diana thought a moment. "Perhaps you can write him? No, no. You've done enough, though I daresay I shall trespass on your generosity a bit more before all is resolved."

Robert indicated the nearest table and waited for her to sit. She set down her breakfast and did so, awaiting his response as he gracefully sat himself across from her.

"I would be happy to pen a note to the constable."

She thanked him. "Please do not tell him of the

circumstances surrounding my arrival?"

A golden brow arched in question. "Circumstances, Diana?"

She felt her cheeks heat, in sharp response to anger as well as embarrassment. "Do not tease me, Robert. I am ill-accustomed to such a manner of living as yours."

He blinked and soon appeared contrite. His brows knit and he leaned toward her. "I meant nothing by my words. Allow me to apologize? I am ill-accustomed to the company of young ladies of breeding, save for my sister's."

She read his sincerity and relaxed a bit. At her nod of acceptance, he flashed a smile and fell upon his breakfast and she followed his example.

Her meal proved as tasty as it appeared, the eggs fluffy and the sausage savory. But the sweet rolls!

"Oh, your Mrs. Mott deserves any praise she receives for these."

"Yes. Of which she assures Lord Thompson and myself at every available opportunity."

Diana smiled, now eager to meet the woman who held her own counsel in the presence of such commanding gentlemen as Lord Thompson and Robert Shelby.

Red-haired Annie served them tea and Diana managed to meet the girl's eyes briefly. The maid left them and Diana's gaze settled on her tablemate. Robert chewed mechanically and kept his eyes downcast. And was that embarrassment coloring his finely-carved cheekbones?

He at last met Diana's gaze. "I cannot begin to tell you how sorry I am about the events of last evening," he rushed out. "I had no notion… Ah, hell."

She thought to turn his thoughts, and hers, from what had transpired in his chamber to what happened after he agreed to help Matthew.

"Last evening. After I," she began. "I must apologize for imposing upon your chivalry."

"Chivalry?" he smiled, that dimple winking once more into view. "Ah, the swooning. Pray, do not trouble yourself."

"I swooned." She shrugged and sipped from her tea. "I admit I was overset. The circumstances… Well, you are aware."

"Yes." He drank from his cup and set it down deliberately. "I must know everything, Diana. You will tell me all you know of it."

She fixed a guileless look upon him. “Of course.”

***

Robert led her to his office and indicated the chair facing his desk. She settled herself, running her hands over her skirt and looking everywhere but at him as he sat behind the desk.

He’d read the trust in her open gaze in the dining room and was still taken aback. What, precisely, did the girl know of him, save for what the gossips of Arundel have told her? No doubt they’d all but led her here to The Hideaway, with their flapping mouths. But her confidence that he would see matters set to rights?

He found her faith as astonishing as her arrival on his doorstep. Not precisely his doorstep, his mind insisted. The image of her frozen in the doorway of his chamber, still and lovely as shock rounded her eyes and dropped her jaw, came to him and he chastised himself again.

She looked a pretty picture this morning, in her slightly-wrinkled day dress. Her hair, that glossy mass of curls, was simply dressed yet very pretty. Last evening, after she’d fallen into his arms, he’d been seized with a wave of protectiveness unlike he’d ever experienced. She’d roused soon enough, to his great relief, and he'd then led a very sleepy young woman to the chamber not far from his.

Thankfully the room had been ready for any occupant, as was the norm at the public house. He'd soon saw her settled into the narrow bed, her face nearly as pale as the fine linens on which she rested. He wouldn't think about her delectable body, clad in only her chemise. No, to do so would surely lead him to madness.

That worry was once more on her face, a face he was relieved to note now bore no evidence of either her flight from Arundel or the impropriety she'd encountered here.

"I am eager to see this matter settled," she offered in a tight voice. "I cannot bear to think of Matthew out there, frightened and alone."

"I am in full agreement with you." She opened her eyes wide in surprise and he thought to elaborate. "If he did not commit this heinous crime—"

"He did not."

"Pray, let me finish. If he did not hurt Hollis's daughter, the real culprit will be eager to see him blamed. And punished."

"Do you truly believe Clive is the villain?"

He saw the burgeoning hope in her gaze and was loath to dash it. "I'll not condemn the rotter without evidence."

Disappointment clouded her eyes, but she gave him a reluctant nod. "I see." She brightened. "But your investigative skills are well-known! You will prove Matthew's innocence. I know it."

Ah, if only he were worthy of her faith. He stepped out from behind his desk as she watched him, trust clear on her features as she gazed up at him. "I shall prove nothing if I cannot find your brother."

She came to her feet in the next instant, pacing about the office in agitation. He didn't attempt to stop her but watched as she worked the matter out in her mind.

"Matthew, the fool!" she muttered. "He has always kept his own counsel, save for that scoundrel Clive. I have no notion of where my brother would go."

She stopped and held her hand over her mouth. As she had last evening, she fell into soft sobs. And to his chagrin, his response was also as anticipated.

"Hush, love," he soothed, wrapping his arms around her. "I know you are upset, and that is more than understandable. But you cannot take all of this upon yourself."

"But I must," she whispered through her tears. "I promised."

He took her chin and lifted her face to his. "Whom did you promise?"

She gave a hiccup and shook her head.

"Whom did you promise, Diana?"

"My mother."

He could say nothing to that. His own mother was a dim memory, dead since he was a boy.

She dashed the tears from her cheeks in a show of bravado and pushed at his chest. His admiration for her grew.

"There is no need for this," he said. "You are overset."

Staring at him, she sniffled again and bit her lower lip. With her limp in his arms and her face so soft and open, he couldn't resist. He framed her face with his hands and brought her closer still.

"Diana," he breathed, dropping a kiss on those tender lips. "Ah, love…"

She took in a breath and for an instant he feared she would reject him. But she soon welcomed him, opening her mouth as he kissed her deeply. Her hands worked their way behind his neck and she pressed against him fully. He stifled a moan of pleasure and turned, pinning her against the desk. Lifting her, he perched her there on the edge, and leaned into her. The tiny shudder she gave told him that she felt it too, this intense desire that he had never encountered in any other woman's arms.

He brought his lips to her throat, teasing the pulse there with his tongue.

"Robert," she sighed.

The tiny buttons at the front of her bodice, those that had yielded to his hands so easily last night as he readied her for bed, now frustrated him. He cupped her breasts through muslin and linen, her nipples pebbling at even this indirect touch. Last night he had struggled with her stays. There was no such encumbrance today.

"My God," he rasped.

He had to touch her. That evening at Shelby Manor, when he'd kissed her breast, came back to him in a rush. She might be innocent but she apparently caught his urgency. Delicate fingers worked the buttons free and she grasped his wrists. The next instant, her tender flesh filled his hands and he did moan then.

She arched toward him and he pinched her nipples through the chemise. "Oh!"

He watched her face as he caressed her. Her head bowed back and she closed her eyes, giving herself up to him. A glance at her breasts, their pink nipples hard beneath his fingers, told him that just one kiss, just one more caress, would ease her torment. *Liar.*

He grasped the ribbon holding her chemise closed and, with a flick of his wrist, he freed her breasts from their flimsy confinement and feasted. He drew one nipple deep into his mouth, holding on to her slender waist as she shifted beneath him. She was so sweet, so fresh. His hand caressed her other breast, kneading lightly and then with more insistence. When her hand cradled his head, holding him closer still, he inwardly rejoiced.

He turned his attention to her other breast and was rewarded with a gasp of delight as he lightly teethed that nipple. He gently leaned her back on the desk, pressing himself against her belly as she arched her back again. Her mouth drew him once more and he kissed her with a growing wildness.

Easing the skirt of her dress upward, he stroked her

leg, her thigh. Her center. She trembled and he grew harder.

Suddenly, she froze. He lifted his head and found her gazing up at him. She was spread beneath him, her lips slightly swollen, her breasts showing pink marks on that previously flawless skin. Her skirt rode high on her legs, her creamy skin beckoning. She appeared well-loved, and he ached to be inside of her.

"Robert," she whispered.

The sound was tiny, a plea and a cry both. He prayed for his experience to rein in the lust pounding through his body. After a long moment, he let out a breath.

Coming over her, he kissed her gently on the lips. "Yes, love?"

She licked her lips and he nearly groaned.

"What are you about?" she asked.

He bit back the most obvious answer and schooled his expression. "I do not understand your meaning, Diana."

Her eyes flicked toward her still-bare breasts and she eyed him meaningfully. "You cannot think to use me."

Robert straightened, irritation dousing his ardor. "I was not using you, Miss Ashley," he bit out. "And until a moment or two ago you were a most willing participant in what I was about."

Shame filled her eyes and regret stabbed at him.

"Bloody Hell," he spat.

She reclined on his desk, her dress gaping open, and he still wanted her. He helped her to a sitting position and averted his gaze as she covered herself.

"I shall go," she murmured.

"Where?"

She refused his offered hand of assistance and hopped off the desk. Her skirts settle over those splendid legs.

"I shall find Matthew on my own." She faced him, her chin raised. "You do not need to trouble yourself."

Carrying herself on shaky legs, she took a few steps toward the door. He reached out, catching her hand. He saw a wealth of meaning in her gaze as it settled on their joined hands.

"Do not go, Diana. You cannot know the danger."

She appeared to consider his words, and at last she inclined her head. "You have the right of it."

He dropped his hold on her, immediately missing her touch. "As to this," he began, indicating the desk. "I hadn't meant to… Ah, it seems that I am forever apologizing to you for my behavior."

"That may be true." She laughed softly and looked at him through her lashes. "But you are right."

"About what?"

"I was a most willing participant."

He drew her to him and kissed her again. When he lifted his head she once again wore her budding sensuality on her features. But he knew what he must do, despite the constant discomfort it would undoubtedly cause him.

"Stay here at The Hideaway, Diana. I promise to comport myself like the gentleman I am."

She raised a graceful brow in disbelief and he laughed aloud.

"Sit," he continued. "We will send word to your father that you reside here in safety."

He withdrew some foolscap from a drawer in his desk and began to write. "The constable will not have you to worry over in addition to his son," he said as he wrote. "I wish you to stay here until this matter is settled."

"Why, pray?"

He leveled a serious look at her. "If indeed your brother is innocent, then the true culprit—"

"Clive," she cut in.

"I believe that as well. But in any event, your father will be occupied with both the Hollis case and your brother's disappearance. I'll not have you there in Arundel, unprotected."

"But I am without chaperone."

He flashed a grin. "I shall serve the function of chaperone."

She gave a tiny snort. "Hardly."

He recalled all he'd done to that delectable body of hers and how she had welcomed his caresses until he'd frightened her. He would make a poor chaperone indeed.

"All right," he offered. "I will send for my sister. She will be glad to see you, I wager."

"Oh, I haven't seen Lady Thompson in ages!"

He grinned again and she returned it full measure. He bent his head and penned another note to his sister.

Chapter 13

The letters were sent and, while Robert worked in his office, she busied herself in the parlor set off the entry. A pretty space though small, it was outfitted with narrow bookshelves holding a few interesting titles. Diana chose a book of sonnets, as her nerves were still a bit overset and a novel wouldn't suit her sensibilities at present. She perched on a narrow upholstered bench done in pretty rose fabric that matched the wallpaper decorating the alcove.

Regret colored the relief she should have felt at Robert's vow to comport himself like a gentleman. Taken with the heat that flowed unabated between them, she doubted that they would be able to resist the temptation of such close proximity. He was a passionate man. That was certain. One thought to the scene she'd encountered last evening was all the proof she needed to that end.

When he'd sat himself across from her, the wide desk between them, she couldn't help but think about the smooth wood beneath her back as his mouth moved over her. Oh, the pleasure he'd given her with that beautiful mouth! Her breasts still tingled from his skilled attention. And pressing himself tightly against her? That had thrilled and frightened her both.

His smile as they spoke afterward, boyish and engaging taken with his still-tousled hair, had charmed her. She'd brazenly run her fingers through those golden waves and longed to do so again. She fisted a hand in her lap to still that unladylike compulsion.

The words on the page, those of undying love and comparisons of one's lover to flowers and the like, rang hollow to her. Never having loved save for her family, the nearest she could reckon to it was this new connection to Robert Shelby. Lust was not love. That was true. The light-skirts at the Inn at Arundel were ample evidence of that. For how could they fall in and out of love with such frequency as they served the gentlemen who patronized the place?

Matters appeared the same here at The Hideaway. She didn't believe Robert's heart was engaged with the buxom redhead, though certain parts of his anatomy were surely affected. She had seen that bulge in his breeches and, if she knew anything from Clive's horrid attentions, that was proof positive of a man's desire if nothing else.

Robert had called her, Diana, "love." Surely the lust he felt for her didn't mean he held her in tender regard despite his easy use of the endearment. And her wanton behavior in his office would induce nothing of the heart. Of that, she was quite certain.

"More's the pity," she murmured.

For her heart was very much in danger of being stolen by those very strong and graceful hands of Robert's. Her tripping pulse whenever she thought of him, let alone saw him, couldn't be solely due to her body's reaction to a fit and handsome man. No. It was Robert Shelby who held her passion. She would do well to guard her heart.

The sound of carriages and horses met her ears, through the small window in the alcove left open to let in the April breeze. It continued sunny, though in this part of Middlesex such couldn't be expected to persist. The door opened and shut with some regularity, and several of the patrons nodded in greeting to her as they passed on through to the dining room.

"'Tis almost time for luncheon, Miss Ashley."

Diana looked up to find Annie in the entry. Again she pictured the girl, her hands and lips on Robert's magnificent body. She swallowed and nodded.

The serving girl hesitated, then took a step into the alcove. "Might I have a word with ya', miss?"

"Oh!" She shook her head to set loose the image of the girl and Robert. "Y-yes, Annie."

"Ya' mustn't worry yerself over last evenin'."

She pressed a hand to her heated cheek and sighed. "I admit it troubled me, yes. Oh, but you mustn't worry yourself. I had no right to enter Mr. Shelby's room unannounced."

Annie laughed lightly. "He's happy to see ya,' that's the truth."

Diana marveled at that. She'd brought him nothing but trouble that would last for some duration. "Why do you say that?"

"I ain't seen him grin like he did this mornin'," she stated. "Not since before."

It was true that his manner this morning was far different than she was used to as well. She wouldn't think of that passion. She couldn't.

"He is a man with much responsibility, though."

Annie nodded, her red curls bobbing from the motion. "Aye. And ya' be one of 'em now, I daresay."

Diana couldn't argue that point, knowing full well the problems she'd placed squarely on his broad shoulders.

"Yes."

The girl turned to go, stilling once more and facing Diana. "Don't trouble yerself over last evenin'," she said again. "'Twas only a bit o' sport."

"Sp-sport?"

The girl grinned. "Aye. Mr. Shelby just needed a…" The girl blushed, a surprise. "He's a man, Miss Ashley. And I got no claim to him, nor do I be wantin' any. Well," Annie added in a bright tone. "Luncheon be ready when ya' like."

And with a curtsey the girl took her leave.

Diana tried to process the girl's words. A bit of sport? Was that what Robert considered their passionate play in his office as well? She swallowed a groan of disappointment.

No matter. She would keep her hands to herself and her distance from him. Let him find his "bit of sport" elsewhere.

She was there because of the horrible attack on Gertie Hollis, and the blame that fell unduly on Matthew's shoulders. Her own wants and desires mattered not a whit.

She returned the book of sonnets to the shelf and took herself into the dining room. Many of the tables were occupied, with an assortment of elderly couples, country gentlemen and travelers. The Hideaway did a brisk business for lunch, and no doubt the reason for that was the splendid nooning meal served by Annie and the two other girls. Those other two, brown haired and not especially remarkable in comparison to their fiery-haired friend, treated Diana to the courtesy afforded her station. Polite smiles ringed their round faces as they hurried to serve the diners.

More of Mrs. Mott's fresh bread sent its aroma through the room. Platters of cold roast beef and slabs of cheese made their way to the tables. Diana found a vacant table and sat herself.

"A bit of cider this afternoon, miss?" one of the brown-haired girls inquired.

"No, thank you. Tea, please."

The girl nodded and hurried back toward what must be the kitchen.

"Then get the lady her tea, Matty!" Diana heard a woman order, no doubt the gifted Mrs. Mott. "She be a guest of Mr. Shelby's and I won't have her waitin', ya' silly girl."

The door opened and the girl reappeared, a steaming teapot held in her hand. She poured a cup and Diana thanked her.

"I'll bring yer luncheon directly," the girl said, worry furrowing her brow.

"No hurry," Diana offered with a smile.

The girl smiled shyly then and hurried back to the kitchens.

"She's like our Lady Thompson," Diana heard the girl tell the unseen Mrs. Mott.

Diana treasured the comparison, for Taylor Shelby had been the nicest girl of Diana's acquaintance before she'd fled Arundel. Taylor kept to her baron now, in Sussex but far from the village that still spread those horrid lies about her. Diana longed to see her now that Robert had sent for her, and not only for the chaperone her childhood friend would provide.

Mrs. Mott, a stout woman with a mop cap and wide smile, peeped out from the kitchen. She bustled over to Diana's table and bobbed a curtsey. "Miss Ashley."

Diana smiled at the woman. "Hello. And you must be Mrs. Mott. I'd heard tell of your fine fare, but until this morning I believed the tales greatly exaggerated."

The woman's round face beamed from the praise. "I thank ya,' miss. And if ya' be wantin' anythin' special, ya' tell me."

"I will. And thank you."

The cook opened her mouth, shutting it with a snap as she glimpsed something just over Diana's right shoulder, a frown fixed on her face. Before Diana could turn to see the object of Mrs. Mott's attention, the woman bobbed another curtsey and hurried back into the kitchen.

"Diana."

She turned her head to find Robert standing behind her, a stern look on his face. Well. Where, pray, was the grin Annie had spoken of?

"Good afternoon, Robert."

"May I join you for luncheon?"

Diana nodded. "I take it your work is finished?"

"For the time-being," he said as he settled across from her.

"Ale, Matty," he said to the brunette who had served Diana. He said nothing until the girl came and went again. "I trust you are well?"

"Well?" she asked. "I continue on as I did a few hours ago."

Her words had an unintended effect and he winced.

"I'll not apologize again," he grumbled.

"But I was not… Oh, don't think you must, Robert. I merely meant that I am in good health and spirits. As I left you in your office."

He studied her, finally easing his expression. The girl, Matty, brought them each a platter of meat and cheese and bread.

"Mrs. Mott is a marvel with roast beef, as well," he offered.

A few bites proved his words.

"She holds your sister in high esteem."

Robert nodded. "She is one of Taylor's staunchest supporters, I daresay. She happily enforces each and every one of my sister's edicts."

Diana glanced about the pretty dining room, noting its brimming with happy customers. "The effect is unmistakable."

"Mrs. Mott takes too much upon her prying self, however."

She thought of the frown the woman had cast in Robert's direction, a clear sign of disapproval.

"The Hideaway was a far different sort of place before

Taylor's gentle hand," Robert went on. "Although when the hour grows late, you may not be so enamored of its patrons."

Diana wondered what he meant precisely, but nothing more came from him regarding the public house. She watched him as she ate, noting that he paid none of the serving girls any more attention than he paid Annie. Had he dallied with these girls as well?

Hadn't Clive boasted to her of his many encounters with the wenches at the Inn at Arundel? Surely he thought to impress her with such talk, but her low opinion of him only sank. Was Robert like those men, like Clive, taking his pleasure where he found it and treating it all like nothing more than a bit of sport?

"Pray, do not concern yourself," Robert said.

She raised her head. Had he read her thoughts? "Pardon?"

"I will find the truth, Diana."

Oh, yes. Matthew. "I know you will."

He wore that look of astonishment she'd seen earlier, then muttered something under his breath. Again she felt the weight of all that she asked him to do.

"I am sorry," she said. "Had I any other recourse open

to me? It is of no matter, as I do not."

"You misunderstand me. It is not your imposition that troubles me but the violent nature of this case. I do not know what I shall find in Arundel tomorrow."

"Tomorrow?"

"Yes. As soon as my sister arrives, I will take my leave."

Diana swallowed her disappointment. What had she expected? That he would keep himself to her and hold her hand in comfort? Now wasn't the time to trespass on his kindness any more than was practical. Matthew's safety, her father's good name. Those were of the utmost importance.

She nodded. "Of course."

***

A fine evening meal of fragrant stew and fresh bread sat untouched in front of Robert this evening.

"Bloody rain," Robert grumbled into his tankard of ale.

Last evening, after passing another meal with Diana and urging her abed before the rowdier patrons arrived at the pub, he'd gone into his office to occupy his mind with work. The late hours had at last caused his eyes to droop and he'd retired to his own chamber. How he'd ignored the delightful bundle curled in the narrow bed not more than two doors from his room, he couldn't fathom. And now he faced another night of bloody torture.

The day had started as gray as the previous had sunny. No doubt the driving rain kept Taylor from The Hideaway, damn the sky. He motioned for another ale. Acknowledging the serving girl with a grunt, he lifted the mug to his lips.

After taking breakfast with Diana—would he ever erase from his mind the look of pleasure on her face as she daintily bit into a sweet roll?—he had managed to avoid her for the better part of the day. Despite the foul weather he'd gone about the little town of Homerton to see to the bit of business that occupied him, asking after a minor case of stolen goods. The blasted case occupied him far too little, and he'd found himself looking for Diana as he reentered The Hideaway at luncheon. They'd passed another meal together, with the girl apparently oblivious to his discomfort over sharing so close a space.

The object of his distress sat across from him now, a pretty dress of blue wrapping her figure. Diana ate her supper with grace, doling worthy praise on the simple but savory stew before her. He had little taste for it himself, choosing instead to drink his evening meal. He reached beneath the table and rubbed his right calf. The wet weather had its usual effect on him, and walking about had done his leg little good. Bloody rain.

"Are you quite all right?"

Diana missed nothing, that much he knew. Her repeated snooping at her father's office door was certainly proof of that.

"I am fine," he muttered. "Do finish your meal, Diana. The revelers will no doubt soon arrive despite the blasted weather."

She looked about the dining room, interest clear on her features. Well, hell.

When she opened her mouth to protest his order, he held up one hand. "I will see you safely to bed."

Her eyes rounded. Ah, why had he said that?

She recovered and nodded her agreement. "I take it you have not heard from Lady Thompson?"

"No. The rain keeps my sister from Middlesex, I wager."

She blinked at his terseness. "What of my father? Has

he written?"

"His missive arrived this afternoon. He was most relieved to learn you are safe."

A hand on her bosom, she breathed a sigh. "I am glad of that." She leaned toward him and lowered her voice. "Did he say nothing of Matthew, then?"

Robert gave a shake of his head that set her image swirling for a moment. "Nothing."

Her lips turned down in a pout which he was sorely tempted to kiss away. She laid her napkin beside her empty plate and rose. He followed suit, grimacing from the pain the action caused him.

"You are fine," she quipped with a curl of one lip. "Hmm. I will bid you good night, then."

He bowed and she turned to make her way through the dining room. And not a moment too soon, in his opinion. Several of the male diners turned from their companions to eye her retreating figure with open admiration and more than a bit of wanting. His hands fisted and he lowered himself to the chair once more.

"Yer in a bad way."

He glared up at Annie. "Keep your opinion to

yourself."

"She's a fine lady."

He stared into his empty tankard. "I know that full well."

"And troubled."

A nod was all he would offer in answer. After a long moment the girl took her leave. Matty brought him another ale with no such comments.

"Leave the pitcher," he said.

Sometime later, he came awake. Slumped over his desk, he raised his head and peered through swollen lids. He vaguely recalled leaving the dining room, ignoring Annie's frown of disapproval as well as the pain in his leg. He stretched, rubbing his hands over his shirtsleeves. At least he'd removed his jacket and waistcoat before falling into his stupor.

A clap of thunder met his ears and he cast a quelling glance at the rain-soaked windowpane over his shoulder. Groaning from the effort, he pushed himself up off of the desk and straightened. More than his leg protested. "Blasted desk."

Unwittingly, the memory of Diana sprawled on the

desk beneath him, weak with wanting, sent a bolt of lust through his weary body. He cursed again and made his way out of the office.

The staircase appeared impossibly tall in the dim light given from the lone lamp set in the entry. Muttering, he lifted one leg then the other and slowly climbed.

Chapter 14

Diana awoke with a start, though she couldn't guess the reason at first. A low fire still burned in the small hearth and the rain still pelted the window. It seemed that nothing had changed since she'd gone to sleep.

She sat up and lit the candle in the holder on the bedstand, and that bit of light gave her a modicum of reassurance.

A strange sound came, no doubt what had awakened her. Dull, uneven thumping, accompanied by deep mutterings from down the corridor. The sounds came closer and she shrank back against the iron headboard, the linens clutched to her breast.

"Son-of-a-bitch!" Robert muttered.

A wave of relief crashed over her and she let out a breath. He apparently made his way past her door, though she could make out his odd gait as he did so. More dragging and thumping. More curses, some more creative than she'd ever heard, and he was past her chamber. A crash came next and she heard him cry out in pain.

Without thinking, she ran out into the corridor. "Robert!"

In the dimness she could make out Robert laying there in the hallway, his back propped against the wall, his right leg stuck straight out in front of him.

He looked up, the fierce frown on his face clearing as he slowly discovered her identity. "Ah, Diana," he breathed.

His voice was raspy and his words were thick. But the warmth in his red-rimmed eyes was undeniable.

Ignoring that bit of tenderness evident in his gaze, she stepped toward him. "Let me help you."

He shook his head and waved her hand away. "No. I can do this myself." He attempted to come to his feet, and slipped down the wall again to land on his backside. "Bloody Hell!"

"Easy," she soothed.

She grabbed his hand against his muttered protests and pulled. With a bit of help from him, she hauled him to his feet. The moment his right foot touched the floor his face screwed up in obvious pain. She placed his right arm over her shoulders and wrapped her arm around his waist, ignoring the heat of his skin she could feel through his thin shirt.

His booted feet all but dragged the floor as they made their plodding way to his chamber. Diana managed to ease his door open and she urged him inside.

An adequate fire burned in the substantial hearth, much like it had on that evening she'd discovered him with Annie. She wouldn't think of that. *Bit o' sport, was all.* She clicked her tongue at her wayward thoughts and shut the door with one bare foot.

She eyed Robert's big bed and dismissed it immediately. Not only did she wish to keep from tumbling around with him in the linens there, it was set so high she had little hope of assisting him up on it with any ease. She looked about the chamber. No, there was nothing else for it. The bloody big bit-o'-sport chair would have to suit.

She released his waist and came in front of him, her hands on his forearms. His body swayed toward hers and she sought to ignore his large masculine form as she danced him toward the chair.

"This way, Robert," she said, keeping her voice bright.

He stilled and stared down at her, his gaze clearing enough to show her his interest as he took in her scantily-clad body.

"Not the only way," he muttered.

What could his meaning be? Dismissing his words, she shifted and somehow got him settled in the chair. He spit out a curse as she straightened his legs. She stood, brushing her hair back from her face, and eyed him with worry.

His head rested on the back of the chair, but no passion burned on that handsome visage. No, with his features slack and nearly innocent, he almost seemed at peace. *Almost.* Lines bracketed his mouth and she guessed his right leg still pained him.

Ignoring the impropriety of the act, she straddled his left leg and began to tug off his boot. No protest came from him, and she only hoped that the shifting she sensed behind her was simply his getting more comfortable in the plump chair.

At last the boot released its hold on his foot. He had large feet. No great surprise there. The man was large all over. Giving a shake of her head, she turned her attention to his injured leg. Lifting with a tenderness borne of deep concern, she slowly worked the boot off of him. She removed his stockings and gasped. In the light of the fire she saw the outlines of scars too numerous to count trailing over his calf muscle. There was little wonder at the pain she read on his face.

"There we go," she soothed.

He moaned softly as she set his foot on the carpet. A glance toward him showed that still he kept his eyes closed, pain still etched on his face. She knelt at his feet and propped his right foot in her lap. It was a handsome foot, strong and graceful and much like Robert himself. His calf was all but ruined; in fact, she wondered that his limp only showed itself on rainy days. She began to work her fingers on the knotted muscles of his lower leg, humming to herself in an effort to ignore the indecency of being in his chamber clad in only her nightgown, her hands on his warm bare flesh.

Robert fell into quiet snores, and she took the opportunity to study him. His white shirt, opened deeply at the collar, showed his strong neck and broad chest to perfection. Tawny hairs peeped from beneath the gaping linen, and she followed the line of buttons to the waistband of his dark breeches. Still kneading his leg, she eyed the powerful thigh so close to her shoulder.

She reasoned that his strength must compensate for the injured leg, for the rest of him was more than adequate for the mysterious, courageous life he led. She brought her fingers to his thigh and gave a slight pinch. It felt like the granite of the columns of the church at the north end of High Street. A glance up at his face showed that he still slept. His leg tensed beneath her fingers and she began to massage his thigh as she had his calf, coming to rest between his outstretched legs.

Still humming, she stared at the fire as it sputtered and crackled. The intimacy of the moment couldn't be ignored. Should anyone learn that she passed even this brief time in his chamber, she would be ruined far worse than his leg. But he was to leave when Taylor arrived at The Hideaway, and the opportunity to steal this bit of closeness was too tempting to resist.

He slept on, so she indulged a notion that had come to her more than once these past few days. Reaching up she unbuttoned his shirt and ran her hands over his chest, just as she'd imagined when Annie's hands had been on him. It felt marvelous.

Diana knew how wonderful he made her feel when his hands touched her, and she brushed her fingertips over his small nipples. A tiny shudder shook him, but still he kept his eyes closed tight. Smiling to herself, she brought her cheek to his chest and rested there for a long moment.

What would it be like to spend their nights like this, so close and tender? It would be heaven. Never again would she have to give a care to Matthew or his clandestine activities. Never again would she have to hear the gossips in Arundel spreading tales of whatever poor soul claimed their blighted interest. She sighed aloud this time and dropped a kiss on his chest.

Shifting, she leaned into him. She tensed as she felt that part of him that both frightened and fascinated her grow hard against her belly. Gasping in surprise, she lifted her head to find him wide awake and staring at her. A flash of lightning lit the chamber, followed by a clap of thunder declaring that the little fantasy she'd woven for herself had come to an abrupt end.

"Do you have any notion of what you do to me, Diana?" Robert asked softly.

***

She placed her hands on his chest and held herself away from him. "I hadn't meant to. That is, your leg pained you and I thought to give you ease."

"My leg is not paining me at present, love."

Robert relished the expression on Diana's beautiful face as she grasped his meaning. True, he'd slipped into slumber for a few moments there, as she so tenderly massaged his aching leg. But her innocent exploration soon had him well awake and anticipating her next move with a combination of excitement and anxiety. He had feared that she would take her delectable self from his room at any moment. And he feared it still. But when she became blatantly aware of her effect on him, he had little recourse but to make his presence of mind known as well.

"I must return to my chamber," she whispered.

Regret colored her words however, and he managed to keep from shouting his triumph. Instead he drew her up the length of him, cradling her in his lap as he brushed the glorious tangle of dark curls from her flushed face.

"You must stay here," he ordered softly. "With me."

She shook her head even as he read the indecision in the depths of her incredible eyes. "It is not proper."

"Proper, love?" He laughed, low and deep. "I believe propriety flew out into the rain the moment you placed your delicate hands on my body."

She gaped at him and he happily kissed her open

mouth. Desire flared in an instant and he held her tightly. She shifted, her body teasing his through her nightgown. He brought his lips to her throat, delighted as she grabbed his shoulders and arched toward him. As if from far away, he heard the rain increase its pounding on the windows behind him.

Rasping her name, he brought his hands to her round bottom and urged her closer. The heat of her was evident even through his breeches, and he let out a low moan. He'd never felt so much, wanted so much, at once. She was pliant in his arms, and tiny sounds of pleasure escaped her as he rubbed against her. Straddling him now, her legs nearly bared as he lifted the hem of her gown, made him want nothing more than to bury himself deep within her. The ale still dulled his reason if not his response, and he abandoned any struggle with conscience as with her every movement she sweetly begged him for more.

Lifting her, he eased her nightgown from her shoulders and bared her breasts. The firelight lit her silken skin, and his besotted mind marveled at the perfection before him. Full and round, palest white and crowned with deepest pink, her breasts beckoned. And he gladly surrendered, sucking hard on one nipple as she cried out in bliss.

"Oh, Robert…"

His hands worked over her, baring her thighs as he sought the center of her. To his amazement she was wet for him. He eased one finger into her. She was so tight, so hot. Releasing her nipple, he met her gaze evening.

"I want you, Diana," he rasped. "And you want me."

She blinked those long lashes and looked deeply into his eyes. "Yes."

He caressed her again, deeper this time. She whimpered in response and he nearly disgraced himself. Her hands moved on him and he welcomed her every touch. She stroked his chest, his belly, and he prayed she would set aside her innocence and ease his torment. Her hand found him and he groaned aloud.

Fumbling with the buttons of his breeches, he released himself to her questing fingers. She leaned back from him then, her eyes round. She studied him with all of the interest he'd often glimpsed on her face as she snooped outside her father's office.

"Oh my," she whispered.

He managed a strangled laugh. "Now that is precisely

what a gentleman likes to hear."

She smiled at him, a knowing smile that seemed to belay her innocence. He set her hand around his shaft and showed her how to move. She stroked him with clumsy, wonderful movements that had him squirming beneath her.

"Ah, God." He set her hand from him and cupped her face in his hands. "I must have you, Diana. Now."

She nodded and began to climb off of his lap.

"No, love. Here. Now."

"Yes, but how?"

He grasped her bottom and lifted, pulling her down on himself as he finally let out a shout of triumph. She cried out as he impaled her, pain etched on her face. Bloody dolt!

"Easy, love," he soothed, holding her close. "You were pure. I… I know that you were pure."

She bit her lip and nodded, her eyes closed tight. He stroked her back, restraining the urge to plunge into her again and again until the lust pounding through his body at last subsided a bit. She was hot and wet around his shaft, and he prayed for control.

"The pain will ease, Diana. I promise."

She said nothing but cuddled closer. The tenderness

threatened to overwhelm him. Then she began to squirm, and the notion of finding completion for both of them overshadowed anything else at the fringes of his mind.

"That's it," he encouraged. "Yes…"

He lifted her, easing her up and down as she began to respond as before. The pain left her face and her body arched toward him. She caught his rhythm and braced her hands on his shoulders as they rocked together. Tiny tremors shook her and he nearly spilled inside of her.

When she tightened, astonishing in itself as she was so snug around him, he knew that she neared her release.

"Come to me, Diana," he said, kissing her throat, her cheek. "Come to me, love."

She trembled, at last giving a great shudder as she cried out his name in her climax. It was all he could do to hold her close, keeping his own pleasure in tenuous check. One more stroke, then two, then three. He lifted her just as his own climax tore through him, spilling his seed safely on her belly as he held her close.

Their bodies began to cool, and a decided wetness spread between them as she cuddled closer. The rain eased to a patter against the panes, the thunder a far off rumble now.

"Robert," she breathed.

He could say nothing. His heart lurched at the sweetness of her voice, her breath on his chest. She held him close and he felt…content.

Content as he had before Trevor's machinations, before he was kept from his family for those long months that changed more than his leg.

But soon his addled mind began to play an endless tune, one that urged him to see her safely away from him and far from his life. Thank God he'd had the presence of mind to withdraw from her before leaving them both with a consequence neither desired.

Or did she? He watched as she rubbed her cheek against his chest, bliss still evident in her every boneless sigh. Ah, to be worthy of love from a woman such as she. But he was tainted, and unfit for the kind of life she deserved.

"Let us get you to bed, love."

She lifted her head and gazed at him in adoration, shyness still evident even as she offered him a slight smile. "Yes, Robert," she said softly.

His body stirred again. Incredible. He eased her off of his lap and set her on shaky legs. She watched him as the inadequate nightgown settled over her exquisite body, and he hurriedly refastened his breeches lest she see the effect she still had on him. He had to get her out of there. Get her safely tucked into that narrow bed in the chamber far too close to his.

He led her into the corridor, unnecessarily checking the hallway for another occupant. The public house was quiet, the only sound the rain now softly falling on the roof above their head. They entered her room and he drew her to the bed. He longed to toss her onto those rumpled linens, to awaken that sweet response that only she had ever given him in all his adult life. But he wouldn't, and the recent yielding of her virginity was only one reason he held himself in check.

"Good night, Diana."

She stood beside the bed, that softness in her gaze now colored with uncertainty. He couldn't soothe her worries, not now. He couldn't offer her promises he lacked the strength of conviction to keep.

She reached up on tiptoe and dropped a kiss on his lips. He held himself tightly, giving her no more than what she offered at the moment. She slipped beneath the linens and he leaned over her, unable to keep from kissing those sweet lips one last time.

"Good night," he said again.

She stared up at him, looking for what? he didn't want to guess.

"Good night, Robert."

She turned on her side, giving him her slender back, and he hurried to escape the chamber. Soundly closing the door between the two of them, he rested his head against the wood panel and let out a harsh breath. Leaving her had been harder than he had imagined, since he had never given any piece of his heart as he gave his body to a woman before.

There was no one to give their secret away. No one to learn of their indulgence. Of his shame. But she was ruined. Why did that fill him with a cautious kind of hope?

"Because she is mine."

He reentered his room and kept his gaze from the plump chair beside the hearth. He would never look at the blasted thing and not think of Diana, of her tender care, her vibrant passion. Why hadn't he noticed her before Trevor had taken everything away from him? Why hadn't he listened to Blake and never gone down to the waterfront to try and capture the bloody bastard himself?

The whys and wherefores swirled in his brain as he sought slumber, but the most important question niggled at the edge of consciousness as sleep neared.

Could he have a future with Diana Ashley?

For the blighted life of him he couldn't think of one excuse not to as his body gave in to slumber.

***

Diana at last let the tears come, tears of confusion and tears of resignation. Oh, but the bliss to be held in Robert's arms, to take him into herself in a way she couldn't have imagined. She wouldn't think of the terse lines of his face as he bade her good night. She sniffed her tears away at last. They would only serve to dull the brilliance of the incredible moments spent in his chamber.

She shifted to stare at the door he'd closed so firmly between them. Was he thinking of all that had happened? Or was he all too soon regretting taking what she had so willingly given?

His sister Taylor would arrive on the morrow. Diana was sure of that as she listened to the rain now softly pattering on the roof above her head. She stared up at the low-beamed ceiling, her tears at last drying on her cheeks. She would put this behind her. She was no longer pure. Robert had said as much even as proof of his words pulsed within her. But there was nothing for her in marriage to some yet-unknown man.

The empathy of his embrace, the way she'd felt his pain even as she sought to ease it, was something even in her innocence she knew to be quite rare. And no one drew her heart in Arundel, let alone her passion. No one could touch her heart as Robert did. So she would end an old maid, with only memories of a single night of passion to warm her.

"Just wonderful," she whispered.

She closed her eyes and turned on her side as she had when Robert had given her his terse dismissal. Her body still echoed from all that he'd done to her, and she would revel in the memory until the cruel light of morning.

Chapter 15

"Good morning," Robert said as Diana reached the bottom of the staircase.

Diana returned his smile of friendly detachment with one of her own. "Good morning."

She ran her eyes over him then blushed and lowered her gaze.

"Fine morning," he went on.

He knew without following his gaze to the sunny front window that the weather this morning differed greatly from yesterday's gray deluge. His chamber had fairly glowed with sunlight as he'd dressed for the day, a shining clarity to illuminate his sins of last night.

"No doubt Lady Thompson will arrive this day," she observed.

His lips thinned. "Yes."

He indicated the dining room and she stepped before him toward the sideboard. As she filled her plate with a spoonful of eggs and one of Mrs. Mott's sweet rolls he regarded her closely.

"How are you this morning, Diana?" he asked softly.

"I am well, Robert." She faced him, her face

expressionless. “I was not ill.”

He glanced about the dining room and flicked his head toward an empty table nearby. She made her way and sat as he set his full plate on the table and folded his frame into the chair opposite. Annie served them both tea, which Robert took as much as an occupation for his hands as to quench his thirst.

When Annie left them Robert leaned closer. “I meant are you tender?”

Diana stilled, soon coughing as a swallow of tea apparently caught in her throat. “I am fine,” she whispered into her napkin.

Robert eased as he began to eat his very large breakfast. He caught her regarding his plate and flashed a grin.

“I fear I need to revive myself,” he confided. “An angel fairly stole all my strength last evening.”

A flicker of regret crossed her face and he inwardly cringed. She had been pure before his manhandling last night. Then her gaze warmed and he knew that she relived their interlude much as he did.

“Yes,” she choked out.

He watched as she picked at her meager breakfast. What had possessed him to tease her about last night? He had risen with little more intention than pretending last night had never happened. The most mind-splitting pleasure he'd ever known, the most tender sense of completion that had ever been his experience, had simply never happened. He could not be more wrong. He ate his meal without tasting it.

Diana's lovely black curls were coiled about her head in simple braids, several wayward tresses brushing her smooth cheeks, her slender neck. A pretty dress of white muslin, dotted with tiny blue flowers, showed off both her figure and flawless skin. He knew full well the incredible body hidden beneath the day gown, the sweet flesh hidden just beneath the modestly-scooped bodice. And the passion? He grunted and set upon his meal with renewed vigor.

They ate without speaking for a while, the pleasant murmur of conversation from the other tables accompanied by the clatter of china and silver adequately filling the void. Her head bowed as she ate, and he studied her graceful motions for long moments. Those delicate hands, so gentle on his flesh, so teasing on his arousal. The strength of desire held in that perfect little body.

"I will call on your father when I return to Arundel," Robert said at last.

Her head raised, her face alight with surprise and hope, and he swallowed audibly. Well, hell.

"I had not thought… That is, you never—"

"I need to know the particulars of the Hollis case," he rushed out.

Resignation took the light from her eyes in that instant. "Of course."

It was as if all of the color was sucked from the room with those two words. He studied the bottom of his teacup and ignored the little voice screaming inside his head to see matters set to rights. He had taken her virtue, and she was right to expect him to offer for her now. He couldn't seem to rouse the honor to do so at the moment.

"I trust you will be fine here with my sister."

Diana kept her eyes downcast now, and he felt relief at that. *Coward.*

"Yes, thank you," she said. "I am certain."

He was spared from any more inanity when she arose from her chair.

"I shall await her in the parlor," she said.

"Parlor?"

She waved one hand toward that silly little alcove near the front entry. Interesting, as Taylor also called the space a parlor. He stood and escorted her to the alcove, watching as she settled herself on the tiny upholstered bench within.

He glanced toward the entry and looked back at her. "I trust you will see Taylor when she arrives."

A faint smile curved her mouth. "I daresay it will be unavoidable."

For a moment he drank in her smile, sorely wishing it was half as bright as he knew her lovely face was capable.

"I bid you good day, then." He bowed and straightened stiffly. "Work awaits me and I must ready for my investigation in Sussex."

She nodded, her eyes unblinking. He turned on his heel and retreated to the sanctuary of his office.

Robert set aside the trivial cases here in Middlesex at present and began to puzzle over the identity of the monster who had hurt Gertie Hollis.

The butcher's daughter was simple and as trusting as a child. Robert would have believed her father was an adequate protector not a fortnight ago. Mrs. Hollis had passed away when Robert was a small boy and he had no recollection of any other person residing above the butcher's shop save for the man and his only child. The girl never walked about the streets of Arundel unescorted, or so Robert often observed. He thought of the pleasant girl, her wide trusting eyes, and felt nausea roil in his belly. What kind of man would dare to take a woman against her will, nonetheless one as guileless as Gertie Hollis?

He glanced at the closed door, mentally counting the steps it would take to bring him to Diana's little alcove. He could join her on that bench, though to accommodate both of them he would have to draw her onto his lap. That inevitably brought last night screaming into his consciousness. She had been so sweet, so giving. He hadn't taken her against her will. He could have used more tenderness, though. He could place the blame on the ale. That was certain. But he knew better. It was Diana and her innocent response that had sealed their tangled fate.

"We will not suit," he muttered.

It was no matter. Honor demanded he set things to rights. Her father would certainly press for such. He could offer for her, and put the reason squarely on that good man's shoulder. That he craved her touch, her smiles, was something he could deny in the light of day. He turned his back on both the door and the promise of a connection to the sweetest, most confounding young woman he had ever encountered.

"Focus on the case," he told himself as he gazed at the busy street visible beyond his office window.

Who would have access to Gertie Hollis? Was she taken from her home or had she been about darkened High Street, unwitting prey to the villain? The villain. He had a very strong notion of that blackguard's identity.

Clive Stilton was indeed the prime suspect in Robert's mind. But securing the evidence needed to prove that fact to Clive's pompous uncle would take skill. A smile curved his mouth. Ah, Robert welcomed the opportunity to employ his expertise in the matter. Thankfully within a few hours he would be in the blessed solitude of his carriage, able to concentrate on the case for more than fleeting moments at a stretch. Again, Diana entered his thoughts.

Would she welcome an offer from him? One truly from him and not forced upon him? The hope clear in her eyes when he'd misspoken earlier could be interpreted as such intent. But no. She deserved more than a blighted man like him, one who spent his time in dangerous pursuit or idle dissipation. His heart was not engaged. He once more gazed at the door wishing for what? he dared not imagine.

He would focus on the case and prove Diana's brother was innocent. Anything else was better left to future contemplation.

***

"Hello!"

Diana lifted her head to see Lady Taylor Thompson breeze through the entry of The Hideaway. Prettily attired in pale blue topped by a sapphire velvet spencer, the lady removed her bonnet and continued through to the dining room, oblivious to Diana's presence. "Robert!"

Diana set aside her book and came to her feet as Robert vacated his office, her heart catching as she watched him embrace his sister. Once more she felt the loss of Matthew keenly, not only his absence but the separation that her mother had unwittingly designed with her demand of the promise. But were her blasted brother before her now, she would hug him as tightly as Taylor did Robert, and with as little self-consciousness.

"Where is Miss Ashley, Brother?" Lady Thompson asked. Robert eyed Diana over his sister's golden head. "Pray, you haven't done anything to compromise her?"

Diana gasped aloud and Robert's sister turned with a jerk. Any discomfort the moment might have afforded was wiped away with the brightness of Lady Thompson's smile. The lady's dimple winked into view, so like her brother's, and Diana couldn't help but smile herself.

"Miss Ashley!" Robert's sister gushed, coming close to grasp both Diana's hands in hers. "How wonderful it is to see you."

Diana dropped a curtsey. "A pleasure to see you, Lady Thompson."

The woman gave a tiny snort and shook her head. "Pray, do not call me such, Diana. Didn't we run about Arundel together all those years ago?"

Diana smiled. "Yes."

"Then you must call me 'Taylor.'"

"Taylor."

The woman's eyes sparkled, eyes so like her brother's that Diana gave a start. But Taylor glanced at her brother at that moment, easing Diana's overly-tender sensibilities.

"When do you leave for Sussex, Robert?" Taylor asked.

"Directly."

Diana eyed him, hurt by his quick answer. The man wouldn't meet her gaze, blast him.

She turned her sunniest smile on his sister, genuinely delighted at the prospect of passing the time in the company of someone so cheerful. "I look forward to our visit, Taylor."

"As do I." Taylor smiled. "I trust you have sampled Mrs. Mott's fare to great enjoyment?"

"Indeed." Diana laughed. "Mr. Shelby has not exaggerated her talents, I daresay."

Taylor's blue-gray gaze slid to the man in question. "Though he can be decidedly close-mouthed on other matters."

Robert reddened, a curiosity to Diana. The siblings communicated on a level not privy to Diana, but perhaps that was most fortunate on this particular morning.

"My work awaits me in Arundel, Sister," Robert finally said.

Taylor watched him for another moment, her eyes flashing at her brother. "Your work." She sniffed. "How much like Blake used to speak before I reached his heart."

Diana cleared her throat and turned from the pair. "If you will excuse me—"

"Oh!" Taylor cut in. "Pray forgive me, Diana! My brother can rouse my ire like no other, I daresay."

Diana found a smile for her friend. "Believe me, my troublesome brother also knows precisely how to vex me."

Robert's sister came toward her and clasped Diana's hands once again. "Robert will find your brother, Diana," she promised. "I have never known him to turn away from duty."

Robert winced in response to his sister's words and Diana felt her own discomfiture grow in response.

She leveled her gaze on his face. "I am certain that Mr. Shelby gives the utmost attention to his cases." She smiled at Taylor. "I will leave you to get settled, Taylor. And thank you again for coming."

Taylor blinked at her and nodded. Diana carried herself up the stairs toward her little chamber, fuming.

If Robert wished to make something more from her words, so be it.

***

Robert watched Diana stiffly climb the stairs, her

body fairly trembling with anger. As if to confirm his suspicions, he soon heard what could only be the door to her room slamming shut with a bang.

"What a bloody mess," he muttered.

His sister whirled on him, her eyes ablaze. "What the devil have you done to that girl?"

Robert took a breath and faced Taylor's ire head on. "It is none of your concern, Sister."

He turned to the promised sanctuary of his office, Taylor dogging his heels.

"You will tell me all of it, Robert."

He cursed under his breath, but apparently not so far under that she didn't hear it.

"Your bluster will not frighten me," she said.

He turned to find a crafty grin on her face.

"You forget that I live with Blake," Taylor said. "And if that man could not frighten me away while you were missing, you have little hope to do so now."

Robert threw his hands into the air. "Very well, minx."

Taylor closed the door and perched herself on the chair facing his desk. Robert took his time and settled across from her, watching her warily.

She crossed her arms. “You’ve dallied with her.”

That was quite plain, he thought sourly. “I will not speak of this with you.”

“You want her, Robert. That cannot be denied.”

In this, Robert knew it best to give her a bit of truth. “Yes, I want her. But she is not— I will not keep her to me.”

Taylor’s eyes rounded. “But she favors you. I could read it in all her looks.”

Robert pulled his gaze from Taylor’s and sighed. “She does not know what’s best for her.”

“And you do?”

He fingered the edge of one folder, his eyes on the top of the desk. “I will not speak of this with you,” he said again, this time with far less conviction.

Taylor muttered an came to her feet. “I will yield on the point, then. At present.”

He raised his eyes to hers, pretending he didn’t see the conviction there.

“Leave Diana Ashley to me,” Taylor continued. “She has far more to worry over than your dour outlook.”

Chapter 16

"So my brother rides for Sussex," Taylor said.

Diana smiled as Robert's sister joined her for luncheon. "I am glad of it."

Taylor's eyes twinkled and Diana schooled her expression.

"Glad in a fashion, I imagine," Taylor observed.

Diana shook her head. "Mr. Shelby will find Matthew. And uncover the monster who attacked Gertie Hollis."

"Horrible, that." Taylor sighed. "Is there no notion of the man's identity?"

Diana thought for a moment, then leaned toward Taylor. "I believe it was Clive Stilton."

Taylor wrinkled her nose. "Oh, what a hateful pup!" She recovered. "Forgive me, but that young man is no gentleman. Why, he approaches my late cousin Trevor in his manners toward women."

"Indeed."

Taylor gazed at Diana with regret. "No doubt my awful cousin left a lasting impression in Arundel."

"They still speak of Trevor Shelby, yes."

Taylor smiled absently as Matty served their meals of

ham and vegetables, fiddling with her silver. "And of me, I presume?"

Diana nodded with regret.

"Hateful gossips," Taylor said.

"And now they convict my brother of this horrid crime," Diana put in. "With no proof, I'd wager. Robert will no doubt see the truth of it."

At her misspeak, she started. But Taylor apparently saw nothing odd about her calling Robert by his given name.

"Robert will, indeed," Taylor said.

They each nodded at the import of Taylor's words.

When talk turned to fashion and the like, Diana patted her simple hairstyle with a touch of regret. "My lady's maid is in Arundel, I am sorry to say."

"My maid is no doubt happily ensconced in the kitchens."

"The draw of Mrs. Mott's fare, no doubt?"

Taylor nodded with a smile. "That and the fact that she is Mrs. Mott's niece."

Diana must have shown her surprise for Taylor laughed lightly.

"When I came to Blake for help, the girl was looking

for employment." Taylor tilted her head to one side. "I daresay Sally could be persuaded to take a hand to that glorious hair of yours, Diana."

"Oh, that would be lovely. Thank you."

"Lady Thompson!" Annie called.

Diana looked up to find the serving maid beaming a smile for Taylor. Robert's sister stood and held the serving girl's hand in hers.

"Hello, Annie," Taylor said. "I trust The Hideaway has kept itself in my absence?"

Annie's red head flicked in the direction of the kitchen. "She makes sure of it."

Taylor laughed. Mrs. Mott peeped from the kitchen, her round face wearing a smile she sought to hide. She stepped from the doorway and brushed her hands over the apron covering her ample middle.

"Lady Thompson," she said with an awkward and genuine curtsey.

"Good day, Mrs. Mott. The lunch is delicious."

The cook blushed to the roots of her graying hair. "Thank ya', Lady Thompson." She turned her gaze on Diana. "Ya' find it to yer likin', Miss Ashley?"

"Oh indeed, Mrs. Mott," Diana said. "Your bread is delectable."

The older woman smiled and bobbed her head. "And where be that pretty little mite of yours, Lady Thompson?"

Taylor beamed. "Lily is residing in comfort in Sussex, not doubt putting both her father and grandfather through their paces."

Mrs. Mott laughed. "Seems like a lady what come here not so very long ago."

Taylor waved away the cook's comment, shaking her head.

Still smiling, Mrs. Mott disappeared into the kitchen once more.

"Wonderful to see ya', Lady Thompson," Annie said. She bobbed a curtsey first for Taylor and then Diana. "Miss Ashley."

The girl left the table, leaving Diana wondering at Annie's words just a day or so earlier. A bit of sport? Well, hadn't she herself just indulged in such sport with Robert? Suddenly, her meal looked less than appetizing. She leaned back in her chair and sighed.

"She is nothing to Robert, Diana."

Diana raised her head to find Taylor regarding her with sympathy. She wouldn't fall to tears. She wouldn't allow Taylor's earnest regard to turn her into a missish girl barely out of the schoolroom.

"I do not grasp your meaning," Diana said.

A soft smile ringed Taylor's mouth. "Robert lives as Blake did when first I came here. Taking pleasure in drink and women, and only concerned with the present. But I know his heart."

"H-his heart?" Diana stammered.

Taylor shook her head and let out a tiny sigh. "My brother was put through Hell at our cousin's hands. And I want nothing more than for him to at last become the man he once was."

The man he once was, Diana thought with longing. How wonderful it would be to see that bright, sunny smile every day. To pass the hours in tender passion every night. But it wasn't to be. She knew that in her heart. Robert had taken her virtue but that would change nothing between them.

"You should not speak to me of this, Taylor."

"I merely mention this because I sense something between the two of you."

Diana struggled to her feet. "There is nothing between us. And Rob—" She caught herself. "Mr. Shelby would be the first to say so."

Taylor came to her feet, regret on her face. "Diana, pray do not be overset."

"I am not," Diana said, hearing her own voice crack. "I… I must write my father, is all. Pray, forgive my absence."

"All right." Taylor took Diana's hand in hers. "I'll not speak of this again. You have my word."

Diana opened her mouth to protest, at last giving a weary nod and taking herself from the dining room. As before she closed herself into her chamber, though without the accompaniment of a slamming door.

"What the devil is wrong with me?" she muttered, dashing tears from her cheeks.

Mr. Robert Shelby preferred to act as if last night never happened, did he? Well, she would have to harden herself to the memory as well. And if Taylor's mere mention of a connection between her brother and Diana was enough to set her to crying, she would indeed have to strengthen her resolve in the matter.

No offer of marriage would come from Robert, and

she was a fool to tell herself otherwise.

***

"Welcome home, sir."

Robert nodded absently at the butler. "Sterns, are there any messages?"

Sterns shook his head, though his gray brow wrinkled. "Miss Ashley came looking for you, sir. I… I trust it was all right that I advised her of your whereabouts."

Robert stilled. Well. That explained that. "She traveled to The Hideaway alone, Sterns."

"No! Forgive me then, sir, but she was dreadfully upset. And after Mr. Matthew Ashley came here—"

"The boy came here? When?"

"Not three hours before Miss Ashley, I'm afraid. He didn't stay overlong. Merely asked after you."

Robert's heart began to pound, his senses heightened as the thrill of the investigation began to tease him.

"He said nothing? No words that would indicate his destination?"

"No, sir. Odd, but Miss Ashley asked the same question of me," Sterns said with obvious wonder.

Robert had no such wonderment. Diana would most

certainly seek to gain information about her brother. But Robert didn't wish to give any more thought to the girl who had plagued his mind on the trip from Middlesex. His sister's meddlesome words had certainly hit their mark. He still wanted Diana and feared that he always would.

"Thank you, Sterns."

He turned from his puzzled butler and headed out into the afternoon sunshine, bound for Constable Ashley's home. As he moved up High Street, he spied Squire Stilton outside the butcher's home. The man looked about furtively, his occasional smile of benevolence for a passing villager visible to Robert as he drew closer. The squire's usual air of fond Arundel benefactor was absent today. To Robert he seemed agitated and less than gentile. He regarded Stilton closely as he neared him.

"Blasted girl," the man muttered.

"Hello, Squire Stilton," Robert said in a clear voice.

The squire fairly jumped out of his slightly rumpled jacket and spun on his heel to face Robert. "Sh-shelby!" he exclaimed. The smooth mask slipped back into place. "Capital idea to involve you in this horrid business."

Robert said nothing but arched a brow in question.

Several villagers made their way past them on the cobblestones, allowing him to study the squire as he bestowed overblown greetings. Robert said nothing and the squire soon hurried to fill the silence as Robert had anticipated.

"Horrible act," the squire said. "Pity the girl's insensible,"

Robert filed that bit of information away and merely nodded.

"I do hope you'll not allow your attachment to Miss Ashley to keep you from bringing her brother to justice," the man added.

"My attachment, Squire?"

The man's face reddened and he greatly resembled his oaf of a nephew in that instant.

"Clive informed me that you've paid calls at the Ashleys," he sputtered. "I assumed you favored the girl." His brown eyes twinkled though Robert sensed no mirth. "She isn't without her charms, eh?"

Robert bristled at the man's words. The pup Clive no doubt inherited his penchant for lechery from his uncle.

"The constable and I have business, Squire," he said. "Matters which I believe are none of your concern."

Squire Stilton gulped. "Yes, yes," he rushed out. The pompous benefactor made its reappearance. "Pray, advise me of any developments. We cannot allow such awful acts to continue here in Arundel."

Robert watched as the man bustled away. Had he blinked he would have missed the squire's glance at the windows above Hollis's shop as he crossed the thoroughfare. That itch of intrigue niggled at Robert, his senses piqued. Interesting.

Gertie Hollis was insensible? Then perhaps she hadn't named Matthew Ashley as her attacker. Diana could have the right of it. The villagers put out the story condemning Matthew and readily believed their own tales.

"The gossips," he murmured to himself.

High Street began to empty of its usual bustling activity. The shops were closing for the day, the villagers on their way home for the evening meal. Few carts or horses traversed the thoroughfare as the sun neared its descent. He continued up the street, welcoming the growing solitude.

"Hello, Mr. Shelby," a girl called out, whom he recognized as one of the chits that often trailed after Clive Stilton.

"Hello," Robert returned with a smile.

The little blond stopped before him, her face upturned. Robert saw the intent there and hid his surprise at her forwardness.

"How are you this evening?" she asked.

"Well, Miss…"

"Miss Bates," the girl chirped.

He made a show of looking about the street before leaning toward her. "And how are you, Miss Bates?"

Her eyes widened a fraction before her mouth curved in a knowing grin. She placed her hand on his arm, her grip tight. "Oh I could be better, I daresay." She then sighed dramatically, brushing her bosom against his arm in the process. "Horrible business about Gertie Hollis."

Ah. Robert hid his smile. She'd given him a fine opening.

"Did you happened to see Gertie on the day of the attack, Miss Bates?" He turned and began to walk, the girl fairly hanging off of his arm as he slowly continued up High Street. "Were you in the village?"

Her gaze skittered away for a moment, and when she looked at him again her eyes were wide in feigned innocence.

"I didn't see her about, Mr. Shelby. But then, I would never go about Arundel without escort."

Odd that, as she was without escort this afternoon. Perhaps she was planning to meet a suitor in the waning daylight?

"May I escort you somewhere, Miss Bates?"

Regret colored her features as her gaze once more darted about the street. Robert followed her gaze and soon saw Clive making his way down the street.

"I must get home, Mr. Shelby." The girl giggled. "But you're welcome to call at my home."

That was never going to happen, even if the girl's wares held any attraction for him.

"I shall keep that in mind, Miss Bates." He swept her a bow as he watched Clive turn his gaze in their direction. "Good day."

The girl glanced between his own fine self and Clive Stilton, apparently torn. He turned and nodded in Clive's direction as he swept past, his ears cocked.

"Why were ya' speaking to Shelby?" Clive asked in a sharp voice.

The girl's response, accompanied by a fit of giggles,

was lost to Robert. But the girl knew her business, though he doubted she would gain the marriage she sought. Setting the cloying Miss Bates and her worthless suitor from his mind, he turned up the walk to Constable Ashley's house.

The man was in his office, and his appearance was far from the manner in which he usually presented himself. Diana's father looked bone-weary, his clothes rumpled and his hair on end.

"Do come in, Shelby," the constable said, pushing his fingers through his hair.

Robert did so, settling himself across from the constable. "No leads in the Hollis case, I take it?"

"The girl can scarcely move, let alone name her attacker." Ashley rubbed a hand over his face and sighed. "I admit, I am relieved."

"She could not have named Matthew," Robert stated.

Constable Ashley nodded. "Yes." Suddenly he brightened a bit. "You left my daughter well, I take it?"

Robert couldn't look the man in the eye at that moment, fully cognizant of precisely the manner in which he left Diana.

"She is well," Robert said. "My sister is there at The

Hideaway."

"Lady Thompson. Capital. I am glad Diana isn't here at present."

"What have you learned?"

"Gertie Hollis was apparently found on her father's doorstep two mornings past. She said nothing, but it was obvious what had transpired."

"What of her injuries?"

"The doctor was called, and confirmed to me that she was indeed compromised and beaten soundly."

Robert tamped down the bile churning in his belly. "Was she speaking then?"

"No, more's the pity. And so readily the town condemned my son."

"Had Matthew any contact with the girl prior?"

"Not to my knowledge. Though he hardly keeps me informed me of his actions. Not for the past several years."

No doubt the constable was still unaware of the boy's involvement with the smugglers. Well, Robert wouldn't be the one to broach that subject today.

"Have you any word from Matthew, sir?" Robert asked.

The constable shook his head. "Blasted boy! Leaves on the very morn of the horrible accusations. Little wonder they all pointed their fingers in his direction."

"He stopped by Shelby Manor before he took his leave."

The man's dark brows raised before he nodded sagely. "A moment of sanity, that. No doubt he believed you could somehow clear him of the crime."

"I would have taken the case in a thrice."

"I appreciate that." The constable's gaze softened. "My daughter holds you in great esteem, I daresay."

Robert shifted in his seat. "Well, I…"

"Didn't she readily go to you for help? Diana is a wise girl, if a bit imprudent."

Robert could say nothing. He had compromised the "imprudent" girl. He'd made love to her and it was the most pleasure he had ever felt. He'd made no mention of emotion, no offer of marriage after taking her virtue, as well. And now he sat before her father, speaking as if he had no real knowledge of Diana's personality or her passion.

"I will speak with Hollis in the morning, Constable." He came to his feet. "Perhaps the Hollis girl will have improved somewhat by then."

"Hollis lets no one near her, not that I blame the man," the constable said. "If anyone had dared to touch my Diana I would not be responsible for my actions."

Robert kept his expression blank at the man's words. He bowed and swiftly left for his home.

He couldn't erase the memory of the constable's trusting gaze, however. Nor his eyes so like his daughter's.

Chapter 17

Diana sat in the alcove again, joined today by Taylor. The two ladies worked on pieces of needlework, the squares of linen small by both desire and space. The day had passed for Diana in the usual fashion since she'd come to The Hideaway: walking about the small village of Homerton with Taylor, working on bonnets and handkerchiefs with mind-numbing stitches, taking their marvelous meals together.

By unspoken agreement, the ladies talked of neither Robert nor the heinous crime drawing his expertise to Arundel at present. Diana could scarcely wait for his return however, if only for the information he would bring. She doubted he would share it willingly. But she was in possession of one particular power of inducement. Not the fact that he had compromised her with her full cooperation, no. She would not hesitate to call upon his long-standing relationship with her father, however.

"The hour grows late, Diana," Taylor said.

Diana raised her head, barely aware that she'd been bending closely over her work until she felt the tightness in her neck. She set her work in her lap and rolled her shoulders, looking about the tiny alcove. Shadows stretched across the wide-planked floor, and her stomach grumbled in recognition of both the hour and the smells wafting from the dining room.

She turned a smile on Taylor. "Mutton tonight."

Taylor laughed. "And none other than Mrs. Mott can render it above palatable, I daresay."

Diana smiled and set her work aside. "I imagine I will miss her when I return to Arundel."

Taylor's eyes rounded. "Oh, pray tell me you do not plan on going back so soon?"

"Soon? I have been hiding here for nearly a fortnight, Taylor."

"But perhaps when Robert returns," Taylor began with a sparkle in her eyes, "he will have news to keep you here."

That flink of hope that dared to flicker within Diana when she thought of Robert flared a bit at Taylor's words. But aside from a terse note to advise her that her brother hadn't yet returned and her father continued in good health, there was little upon which to set such dreams.

"I shall rejoin my father," Diana stated. "There can be nothing to keep me here at The Hideaway."

Taylor conceded the point with a faint scowl. "My

brother can be a fool, Diana." She held up one graceful hand. "That is all I will say on the matter. Tonight, anyway."

Later, when at last Diana had no option but to return to her narrow iron bed in her borrowed chamber, she let her thoughts run their desired course.

Robert would undoubtedly return before much longer. His sister was right in that regard at least. But whatever would she, Diana, say to him? He had left under less than desirable conditions, in her opinion. Their last words had been terse, their last glances cold and remote. But icy disdain was the very last thing she could attribute to her feelings for the blasted man.

Annie's commiserating looks had not eased Diana's mind at all, though she no longer worried the girl held any tender regard for Robert Shelby. In fact, more than one gentleman appeared to partake of the red-haired girls charms over the past week, if the snippets of conversation Diana had overheard were to be believed. A bit of sport, she thought sourly. The phrase still rankled.

She donned her nightgown, thankful that the girl who did the laundry for the public house had washed away any remaining scent of Robert clinging to the fine lawn. If only she could erase her memories of that blighted night.

"Oh who, pray, am I fooling?" she asked herself in a whisper.

The memory of his body held against her, moving deep within her, still filled her with wonder. She couldn't bear to lose the only thing she would ever have to hold close to her heart when she resumed her dull existence in Arundel, her memory of Robert and their one night together. Caring for her father, seeing to her brother's affairs once all this trouble was behind him, would no doubt fill her abundance of time going forward. And should she pass Mr. Robert Shelby on High Street on some far off sunny morning, she would nod a greeting and continue on her way.

He had withdrawn from her at that last moment, she recalled. Spilling his seed safely outside her womb. So aside from her own knowledge that her virtue was truly gone, nothing would remain to mark that night save her memories. She'd had evidence of that just a few days ago, when her monthlies came as if on schedule.

Snuffing out the solitary candle on the bedstand, she cuddled into her bed and awaited another night of dreams haunted by a man with golden hair and blue-gray eyes.

And a smile, glorious despite its seldom appearance.

***

Robert alighted his carriage in front of The Hideaway, his head as clear as his convictions. No one in Arundel would confirm that they saw Matthew Ashley so much as speak to the Hollis girl on the day of the attack and yet they were strong in their belief that only Diana's brother could have done the horrible deed. The squire, his demeanor fixed now that he seemed to accept Robert's interference in the matter, pushed for him to hunt Matthew down and drag him back to Arundel for justice.

"And not Bow Street," the man had sneered. "We take care of our own."

The words had chilled Robert more than he was willing to admit. In the years since beginning his work with Blake, Robert had seen firsthand how some villages administered their own justice. While swifter than that in London, the wrong man was as often punished as the right one. Only when Robert could be assured of the person's culpability did he leave their fate in the hands of provincials.

Robert knew in his gut that Matthew Ashley wasn't guilty. And his intuition hadn't been this strong since before the business with Trevor. And thankfully Robert believed the constable now viewed matters as Robert did. A glimmer of hope had appeared in the man's eyes as Robert took his leave that evening. The Lord knew Robert had destroyed that touch of expectation in Diana's gaze. He was damned if he would do so to her father.

He hadn't shared with the constable the information he'd received late last night, but only due to an entreaty from the sender. The missive now stuffed into the pocket of Robert's jacket was from Matthew Ashley. Matthew apparently wasn't the fool Robert had readily believed. The boy wrote from Brighton, a fitting hiding place since it was fairly crawling with gentry on holiday this time of year. And Matthew could hide in plain sight there as no one in that circle had any contact with the rustics of Arundel.

Raw fear was evident in the note, along with the request that Robert not divulge his whereabouts to the constable. Robert supposed that the boy had reason to fear his father's dark opinion of him. Their relationship was so different than Robert's had been with his own excellent father. And Matthew's continued illegal actions would no doubt cause his father distress above and beyond these false and heinous charges.

Robert would allow Matthew a few days' time in seclusion, but once Robert forced the attacker to show himself he would happily drag the irresponsible boy's backside in front of his father.

The public house was quiet and Robert climbed the staircase with only a lone candle to light his way. His room beckoned, that door at the end of the hallway. But the one night spent alone after his and Diana's indiscretion had proven to him that sleep would be long coming in that chamber.

No ale muddled his thoughts tonight. No brandy dulled his senses. And yet he found himself before the door to Diana's chamber, staring at the wood panel as if he could gaze through it to the girl within. His hand reached for the knob and he smoothly breached the barrier. A rustling met his ears, his candle illuminating the tangled linens on the iron bed. And the perfect figure around which they twisted.

He closed the door and approached the bed, all the while his mind screamed its protest even as his body hardened in anticipation.

Diana shifted to face him, her eyes blinking open.

"What have you found?"

Robert stilled, at last breathing out a sigh. "Matthew is in Brighton."

Why he'd told her wasn't as vital as the expression on her lovely face. Relief and gratitude and something he couldn't name crossed her features as she sat up in the bed, her eyes shining more than the candle he set on the bedstand.

"Oh, thank God," she breathed.

Robert agreed with her simply-spoken statement. He came and sat down beside her, the bed's springs groaning under the unaccustomed weight. "I have not told your father."

"But why not?" She shook her head. "Oh, he doesn't still believe Matthew is guilty?"

"No."

Her relief was palpable to him.

"Your brother asked me not to divulge his location and I felt honor bound to follow his edict," he went on. "For the time-being."

"And yet you told me."

He shrugged one shoulder. "I felt compelled to allay your fears, Diana."

She blinked up at him, then curved her lips in a smile

that sent a shock through his body. Throwing her arms around his neck, she kissed him with all of herself. Robert deeply tasted her, catching her urgency, and pulled her tightly to him.

Suddenly Diana stopped, holding herself away from him with braced arms. “Not again.”

“What is it, love?” he asked.

She bit her lip, and lowered her lashes. “I will not be a bit of sport, Robert.”

He touched her chin. The tiny bit of contact sent a tremor through her he felt to his soul. “Diana.”

Still she said nothing, keeping her eyes downcast.

“Diana,” he said again. When she lifted her gaze he locked on to it. “You can never be a bit of sport. This is… Ah, I do not know precisely what this is, but it is far from simply a way to fill my time.”

“It would have to be enough, then.”

“What?”

She shook her head but he couldn’t deny himself a moment longer. He could withdraw again. He could leave her safe if not pure. Just the pleasure of her touch…

She was right. It would have to be enough.

***

Molding her body to his, Diana pulled him down on top of her. He shed his jacket as she tore at his cravat and waistcoat. Soon he wore nothing but his shirt and breeches, and her eager hands sought to free him from those as well. He leaned back from her and removed his shirt, tossing it onto the floor. His boots fell with two thuds and he faced her. The tiny bit of candlelight he'd brought into the chamber was inadequate in her opinion. She longed to see him, although using her hands would be very exciting compensation.

"You are beautiful," she breathed as her hands ran over his chest, his shoulders.

He shook his head and grinned, tugging at her nightgown. Diana raised her arms to free the garment, earning a wonderful boon in the process. Robert stretched on top of her once the thin lawn joined his clothes on the floor, his chest moving against her breasts in maddening circles as he held her arms over her head.

"Robert!"

"Shh, love."

He kissed her again, his tongue deep in her mouth, then shifted. His tongue flicked over her nipple and she bit back a moan. When his mouth closed over her she did moan, softly in the quiet chamber. Her hands still held over her head, the pressure was exquisite as he teased and suckled first one breast then the other. With one free hand he caressed her. Long strokes that went from thigh to bottom to belly until he found the center of her. He teased her with his strong fingers, mimicking the enticing motions he would soon perform. She began that ascent he had given her before, but she froze as his thighs settled between hers.

Robert raised his head, bringing his face to hers. Those eyes of his, dark and stormy in the half-light, bore into hers. "There will not be any pain this time, Diana."

She could barely think, could only give him a jerky nod. He worked the buttons of his breeches and peeled them from his body. Her hands now free, she stroked his smoothly-muscled back, his bare buttocks. My, he felt incredible. Like solid fire.

Before she was aware, his manhood pressed at her. She parted her legs willingly, biting back a scream as he surged into her.

"Ah God," he rasped. "You feel so good."

She squeezed her eyes shut and held on to him as he moved deep within her. It was so different from their last time together. There was no pain, just a deep sense of connection sorely lacking the first time he took her. He flexed and moved and she wrapped her legs around his waist. Feeling quite wanton, she bit his shoulder and earned a shout of delight from him.

"Minx," he chided, a bit out of breath.

He kissed her, his tongue delving into her mouth as his body continued its incredible motion. Pressure built within her, that bliss that had washed over her before. She knew now he could give this to her. She also knew that she was the one causing those provocative sounds to come from his lips as he moved faster still.

"Come to me, Robert," she urged, echoing the words he'd given her on that night.

"I… I cannot," he gasped.

She wanted to ask why, to soothe his worry. But she was soon lost in her own spiral, soaring high as he thrust deeper still. Her climax struck her, and she clutched him tighter to her as she gave herself up to it. As if from afar she heard him groaning, felt him begin to shudder. Then he burst within her, his big body shaking as he poured into her.

He cradled her to him and she reveled in the closeness

for however long it would last. At least he didn't have to bring her to her room tonight. She closed her eyes and snuggled closer. But he would leave. And she would face the night alone again.

He shifted and drew her close. "I am sorry, Diana."

She opened her eyes and gazed at him. His eyes were a bit clouded, his features relaxed save for the furrowing of his brow.

"Sorry?" That was not she longed to hear at this moment. "Oh."

"No, love. Not that we were together. I should have withdrawn from you."

Realization dawned on her. He had taken himself from her their first time, leaving both her and himself a bit sticky. But this time he had kept himself within her and she found it so much more to her liking. "I do not mind, really."

"There could be consequences."

Sighing, she shook her head in bemusement. She could hardly think with his beautiful body still pressed so close to hers.

"You could have a child," he went on.

She froze as if dunked in the River Arun. "Oh!"

His frown cleared and he held her close again. "You will tell me and we will handle the matter should it arise."

"The matter?"

Her brain could scarcely function and he talked of matters and consequences? She said nothing of it, knowing only that she lacked the emptiness that had filled her after the first time he'd taken her. And if there were indeed consequences?

"How, pray, would you handle such a matter, Robert?"

Resignation colored his features and he gave her a curt nod. "We would marry, of course."

Not the glowing proposal she might have once hoped for, but that dream was tossed to the floor beside his big boots. "Of course."

A smile curved his lips. "But there is no need to trouble ourselves at present, love."

"N-no."

Silence settled on them and Diana began to set aside the awkward conversation. Awkward indeed, for they were both as naked as the day they were born and in a close embrace. Oh, but it felt utterly wonderful to lose herself for even this fleeting moment of bliss.

"I must return to my chamber," he said.

She glanced down at them, at their naked limbs tangled in the linens on the narrow bed. He filled the space and there was hardly room for her to breath.

"Yes."

He turned and pinned her beneath him, dropping a kiss on the tip of her nose. "But I do not want to leave."

Then stay! But she said nothing, merely watching as he took his warmth and strength from her and hastily donned his clothes. Shifting, she pulled the rumpled linens over herself as he straightened.

"Diana, I…" He raked his fingers through his hair and faced her. "I will speak to you on the morrow."

Again she uttered not a word as he left the room on silent steps, his boots and jacket held in his hands. She placed a hand on her brow and let out a long breath. They might have made a child tonight. So much for the assurance of no lasting repercussions when she returned to Arundel. Oh, but their child would surely be a lovely thing with his golden hair and her strength of conviction.

"And where, pray, was your conviction when he

tumbled you yet again?" she murmured.

She closed her eyes and sought slumber as her body slowly gave up the heat from their passion. Was Robert as affected as she? Perhaps not.

At least the memory of his contented smile would fill her dreams tonight.

***

Robert entered his chamber and deposited his clothes in a pile for his valet to attend. Let the man wonder at their state. Lord knew Robert himself had no notion what had possessed him this night.

First he informed Diana of her brother's whereabouts. That was a befuddlement in and of itself, as it was not his custom to share information on a case no matter the person's connection to the parties involved. Then he'd indulged in a passionate exchange the memory of which would haunt him for the foreseeable future. And what if there was a child?

He stripped off his breeches and fell onto the bed. A child of Diana's, with her deep blue eyes and his spirit of adventure. Adventure, indeed. What, pray, had he done but compromise a girl of gentle birth for his own lustful needs? And hers, he allowed with a grin. My God, she was incredible in her release, begging him to take his own pleasure deep within her. Had she thought to…? No. He ceased that line of questions before it could begin. The surprise on her face told him that she had given little thought to the consequences of their joining so completely. She was not a girl who would think to trap a man so.

He would have to face Diana tomorrow, her every emotion clear on her features. And his sister. What, pray, would Taylor say should she learn of his actions tonight?

"Fine mess, Shelby," he said to himself.

But when he fell into slumber, it wasn't regret that filled his dreams but a cautious hope that flickered in the distance like a signal light on the river.

Chapter 18

"You will marry her."

Robert looked up from his desk, his refuge for the whole of the morning, and met his sister's glare dead on. The tray at his elbow, bearing a plate of cold eggs and sausage, bore testament that he hadn't dared to brave the dining room this morning.

"I trust you speak of Diana?" he asked, keeping his tone light.

Taylor closed the door with a resounding click and advanced on him. He fixed his features in as even an expression as he could manage.

"She is not meant to be trifled with, Brother."

"I am not trifling with her."

Taylor arched a brow and crossed her arms over her chest. "What, pray, do you say you did with her last night?"

Robert stared at his splayed fingers on the desktop. "What does Diana say I did with her?"

Taylor snorted. "Diana has not said anything. The condition of her room speaks volumes, however."

He glanced up at her with trepidation. "Explain."

"My maid sees to her care, Robert. And the rumpled

linens and general distraction of the lady in question bears evidence."

"Slim evidence indeed. Has your husband taught you nothing of investigations?"

"Do not jest, Brother. Your cravat, laying beneath the girl's bed, is evidence enough."

That gave him pause. "Damn."

"Indeed."

She stared at him and he rubbed his hand over his face.

"I cannot marry her," he said.

"Whyever not? She is a gentleman's daughter. And a wonderful young woman."

"I am aware of all of that, Taylor. Diana would make any man an excellent wife."

"Then, what is the matter?"

"She is too good for me."

"Nonsense! You are good, Robert. Any young woman would count herself lucky to marry you."

Robert let out a reluctant laugh. "How quickly you go from defending Diana to defending me."

Taylor shrugged one shoulder. "Well, you are both

excellent creatures in my considered opinion."

He fixed a gaze on his sister and fisted his hands on the desktop. "I am not meant for marriage. Not to anyone." His throat tightened. "And certainly not to Diana."

Taylor placed her hand on his, her eyes soft. "Pray, let it go, Robert. You have dwelled too long in the horrid past."

"I dwelled too long in that prison, Sister."

She straightened. "You are free now," she declared. "Physically, at least. And you must fulfill your duties regarding Diana."

Robert stood and turned his back on her to stare out the window at the bustling street beyond. Taylor was suspiciously quiet behind him, but he knew what he must do.

"I cannot send her back to Arundel now," he mused aloud. "Her father would surely kill me."

"There is that," Taylor intoned, at touch of humor in her voice.

He faced her once again. "Send Diana to me."

Taylor smiled and gave him a firm nod. "About time you saw your way to my way of thinking."

His shook his head at her. "Hardly. But I shall do my duty."

"Good," she said, walking toward the door.

"Taylor."

She turned back to him.

"Do not come to me when she is heartbroken," he stated. "I warned you that my heart cannot take a woman like Diana in it. There is no room for her."

To his surprise Taylor crossed to him, standing on tiptoe to kiss his cheek. "You are coming back to us, Robert. Back into the light."

She left him and he stared at the door closed tight behind her. Sitting once more behind his desk, he thought about all he had to do now that he had set his course of action.

He was certain a special license would be no trouble. The vicar in Homerton would contact the bishop and see to the ceremony. A note written to Constable Ashley would secure that man's approval. And Robert would then be bound to Diana. What should have frightened him to the core filled him with a kind of reluctant satisfaction, however. He would return to Shelby Manor with a bride, of all things.

He felt a smile curve his mouth. "A beautiful bride."

He began to work his mind around the exact wording of a proposal to win the girl, if not her heart, to him.

***

"Diana," Taylor said softly.

Diana looked up from yet another piece of nothing in her lap to fix a smile on her face. Taylor stood in the entry, leaning into the little alcove with an expectant cast to her features.

"Yes?"

Instead of answering right away, Taylor glanced about the room. Her friend seemed a bit ill-at-ease, immediately putting Diana on her guard.

"Is something wrong?" Diana asked.

"Oh, no," Taylor said, giving a shaky laugh. "My brother has asked for you to join him in his office."

Diana froze. Whyever would Robert wish to see her? Oh, surely he would send her back to Arundel, alone and ruined. She gave a quick shake of her head. *Pitiful girl.*

"Well then," she said, coming to her feet. "There is no sense delaying the inevitable."

"Oh, indeed," Taylor teased.

Taylor's eyes, so like Robert's, sparkled with merriment. What was going on? She made her way to Robert's office and rapped sharply on the door.

"Come in, Diana," he called from the other side of the panel.

She stilled again. He almost sounded eager. No doubt he *was* eager to see her well and gone from The Hideaway. She pushed open the door and stood there, loath to step any closer. Thankfully Robert stood behind his desk, giving her adequate protection for the coming discourse.

"You wished to see me?" she asked, keeping her tone light.

He regarded her closely and she held herself rigid there in the doorway. How wonderful he looked on this, the last day she would likely see him. The sunlight behind him illuminated every golden strand of hair on his head and lent him the carefree look she hardly ever glimpsed. She squared her shoulders and forced her mind to the coming dismissal.

"Please sit, Diana."

She took small steps and perched on the edge of the chair facing his desk, folding her hands in her lap to keep from worrying the skirt of her yellow day dress.

"I have something to tell you," he said.

She raised her eyes to his and she focused intently on him.

He cleared his throat. "Well, ask you, really. That is…"

He stopped, his cheeks reddening. Diana blinked at him. She had never seen him in such a state, as he apparently searched his gifted mind for the exact words to kindly set her from him forever. Anger pricked at her and she fisted her hands. It would not serve!

"Pray, tell me to go and be done with it!" she said.

He pulled back at her outburst. "Go? Why do you think I would tell you to go?"

Tears choked her throat but she persevered. "Surely you want me well and gone after last night, Robert." He said nothing to that, certainly nothing to confirm or deny her words, and simply stared at her. "Do you deny that fact?"

He shook his golden head, dismay clear on his face. "I have only one recourse after last night, Diana. To ask you to marry me."

The breath left her body in a rush. If he had told her he was involved with the smugglers of Arundel she couldn't have been more surprised.

"W-what?"

He fumbled with the folders set on his desk, at last

fixing his gaze on something over her right shoulder. "I compromised you, Diana. I will not have the gossips in Arundel tearing you apart when they learn of it."

"The gossips." She shook her head. "No, I suppose that would not suit. It would surely kill my father after what Matthew has put him through."

He met her gaze. "It is settled then?"

At her nod, he let out a breath.

"Good. I will write your father. I do not foresee any difficulty there."

Diana agreed on that point. Her father held Robert in high esteem, but then he couldn't know Robert had taken what his daughter had freely given long before any mention of marriage had been made.

"I shall see to the license and we shall marry three days hence," Robert said.

She gaped at him. "Three days?"

A shrug of dismissal followed that. "Why delay the inevitable?"

Such romantic words. "Why, indeed?"

Not precisely the marriage proposal of her childhood dreams. But then again, she hadn't thought to go to her wedding bed a ruined woman.

Robert walked around the desk, took her hands and pulled her to her feet. She sought to ignore the spark his touch sent through her.

"I will try my best to deserve you, Diana," he said. "Pray, do not expect much from my blighted heart."

Diana gazed up at him, choosing to take what little tenderness could be gleaned from his words.

"Three days, then," she said.

He kissed her, first softly and then with growing ardor. She surrendered to his caress. At least they had this. But would it be enough?

That evening the public house grew crowded, the diners slowly replaced with revelers. Diana sat with Taylor, taking dinner without Robert's company.

His proposal that morning still had the power to stun her when she dared to give it thought. The glimmer of happiness that suddenly came upon her at odd moments today couldn't be discounted. Yet she knew theirs wasn't a love match. On his part, certainly. On hers, she wasn't so ready to make such a decision.

She fiddled with the silverware beside her plate,

barely hearing the melodious tinkling in the increasing noise in the pub.

"We should get to our chambers, Diana," Taylor offered.

Diana nodded as she watched Annie and Matty serve the gentlemen crowding the tables. The more sedate patrons would soon number precisely two.

"That would be best," Diana sighed, moving her fork over the smooth linen.

Taylor covered Diana's fidgeting fingers with her hand. "What troubles you?"

"Nothing." Diana withdrew her hand and folded them in her lap, staring down at the tablecloth. "There is nothing amiss in a hurried wedding taking place far from my home with a groom who cannot bear to be in my company."

Silence met her ears and she slowly raised her gaze to Taylor's. To her credit, Taylor barely blinked at her hushed outburst.

"You are good for my brother. He will see that."

Diana attempted a shrug of indifference, but could muster no more than a pitiful attempt. "No matter. I will marry him and he will solve the Hollis case and all will be as it was before."

Taylor laughed lightly. "Hardly that."

Diana did shrug then. "Very well then. I will move into Shelby Manor and keep to myself. He can go about solving his cases and finding his bits of sport and no doubt we will be content."

Thankfully, Taylor didn't argue the point despite the slow shaking of her head. Rising from her chair, Diana bade her good night and climbed the stairs to her little chamber.

"Diana," Robert said softly.

She whirled at the sound, her heart tripping as she saw Robert in the growing shadows of the corridor. She pressed her hand to her bosom. "Robert. You startled me."

He stepped toward her. "I wished to bid you good night."

"Good night?" She snorted at that. "You've managed to keep from my sight all of today and now you wish to bid me good night?"

He moved closer. "I thought it fitting I give my betrothed a good night kiss."

"I am hardly your betrothed." Her voice sounded curiously small to her own ears. "I am merely another consequence."

He frowned down at her. "You will be my wife."

She forced a light laugh up at him. "How fierce you look, Mr. Shelby! Do you intend to frighten me as you did that night on the bluff?"

Another step brought him achingly closer. She could smell him, that scent of soap and brandy and Robert, and felt her heart trip again.

"I recall what transpired after that fright, Miss Ashley. In my parlor." His eyes glittered as he brought his face to hers. "Ah, you were not frightened then."

Yes his lips on her flesh, her body yearning for something she couldn't imagine then.

Diana sought to put the provocative memory from her mind. "Had I known what your true intentions were—"

"Had you known what my true intentions were, Diana, I daresay we would be married already."

She gasped and he touched his mouth to hers. His tongue surged past her lips, smothering either shout of protest or sigh of pleasure. He laughed low in his throat and turned, pinning her against the wall with his body as he brushed his lips over her throat.

"Ah, I admit it will be no hardship kissing you every night."

Her thoughts bent in that very same direction, scattered though they were from the skilled work of his delightful lips and tongue. He reached behind her and opened the door, urging her inside. That brought her back to herself.

"You should not be in here, Robert." She stepped away from him. "Not again."

He grinned and pulled the door closed. "You are mine, Diana. Whatever muddled manner in which it came about, you are mine."

Diana slowly nodded, unable to deny the thrill his words gave her. She might never have his love, she had no illusions in that direction. But his desire… Oh, that was hers. And she wanted him, damn her to Hades. She wanted him and would have him again.

"And you are mine, Robert," she whispered.

He stared for a long moment, at last touching his forehead to hers. "Ah, this marriage will have its advantages."

Chapter 19

Diana finally graced him with a smile, one that spoke of carnal pleasures only she could give him. He loosened his cravat, suddenly stilling to bark out a laugh. She arched a brow in question. He walked over to the narrow bed and reached underneath, withdrawing a length of linen. He relished the realization dawning in her deep blue eyes.

"Oh!"

He let out another laugh. "I believe I shall have to be more careful with my neck cloths."

She nodded, watching avidly as he at last removed his cravat from his neck. She should let out a missish cry of outrage. She should demand that he keep himself from her until they were good and wed. But by the expectant light in her eyes and the manner in which those lovely eyes raked over him, he knew she wanted him here in her room.

In her bed.

"I am surely ruined," she murmured.

Both dejection and bemusement colored her voice.

He came to her and took her hands in his. "You are not ruined." He dropped a kiss on her chilled fingers. "In your future husband's considered opinion, you are what you always were." He quirked a smile at her. "Perhaps a bit more."

Apparently mollified, she returned his expression.

In a very short while he had her out of her pretty yellow dress, though he possessed the presence of mind to see to its careful placement on a chair beside the privacy screen. The stays held him up a bit. She shared Taylor's maid in all things, apparently. But soon she stood in only her chemise.

As to his own clothes, he found he couldn't be so cautious and most of them soon littered the floor. But by the time he stripped to his breeches, her reticence had returned.

Her mouth thinned to a line even as her eyes flitted over his body. "We are to be wed."

To hear her utter the words, laced though they were with astonishment, made it all the more real for him.

He sobered, his fingers frozen in the act of unbuttoning his breeches. "Yes." She faced him, shivering in her chemise, but he couldn't bring himself to bridge the distance as before. "Do you now regret your promise?"

Diana squared her shoulders in an obvious show of bravado. "I have no other option, do I?"

Her decided lack of enthusiasm struck him.

"Well, that is plain speaking," he said.

Hurt flickered in her eyes, yet he couldn't force a smile. Just a moment earlier he'd been hot, hard-pressed to go gently with her, to keep from throwing her upon that ridiculously narrow bed and taking what would shortly be his forever. But now she stood there, regret clear on her lovely face as she trembled in her near-transparent chemise, and he felt the chill of her resignation to his very core.

He gathered his discarded clothes and gave her a bow. "I shall see you on the morrow."

Her eyes shimmered as her succulent lower lip quivered.

He forced himself to turn away from her. "Good night, Diana."

As he pulled the door shut behind him he heard her response.

"Good night," she said, her voice small.

Bloody wonderful start. He stalked to his chamber and threw his clothes in the vicinity of his dressing room. Diana had appeared so innocent, even though he knew for a fact that she had welcomed him wholeheartedly more than once before. And in three days' time they would be bound to each other. Forever.

She most certainly felt nothing tender toward him, despite Taylor's insistence to the contrary. Passion? Most assuredly, though she was still innocent at least in mind to that fact. Regret? More than likely, since she had never sought his suit. Odd that, as she had been pure when he'd taken her that first night. Had she thought to ever marry? If so, how would she have explained away the decided absence of her maidenhead on her wedding night?

Possessiveness gripped him. That was his gift. His prize as her husband. Husband-to-be, to be truthful.

"It is done," he growled.

He would go to the vicar soon after sunrise tomorrow to assure the legal binding to his prospective if reluctant bride. Though the hour was early for him he hid away in his chamber and forced Diana from his mind as he stared long and hard at the beamed ceiling above his very large, very lonely bed.

Perhaps it was better if Diana didn't form an emotional attachment to him. She would have less risk of disappointment that way.

It was only a matter of time before she realized he had

nothing to give her in return.

***

"Where is my brother?" Taylor asked, her hands on her hips.

Diana looked up from her late breakfast of sweet rolls, eggs and ham. Mrs. Mott had seen to the accompaniment of preserved plums as a treat for both her and Taylor but Robert's sister had not eaten with her. And judging from the frown creasing Taylor's brow, wherever she had been hadn't brought her much enjoyment.

"I cannot begin to guess Robert's whereabouts, Taylor." She didn't add that she hadn't seen him since that awkward exchange in her room last night.

Taylor let out a sigh of exasperation. "Well that is fine, isn't it? The vicar's wife wishes to meet you and Robert."

"The vicar's wife? Whyever…? Oh."

A smile brightened Taylor's face. "Do not fret, Diana. Mrs. Gaines is quite kind."

Diana feigned nonchalance. "I assume her husband will see us wed, then?"

Taylor met her gaze evenly. "And it will be a very

lovely ceremony."

"That is something."

Taylor sat in the chair opposite and leaned toward her. "The ceremony will be fitting, Diana. As will the marriage, I daresay."

Too tired of the subject to argue the point, Diana merely nodded. After Robert's escape last evening, sleep had been elusive. What had happened to change his demeanor, she couldn't guess. But she'd missed his presence keenly, only illuminating her own sorry condition. She'd missed his touch, his kisses.

"Mrs. Mott will wish to speak to you regarding the wedding breakfast," Taylor went on.

Annie stopped at their table and, with a curtsey, set a plate before Taylor bearing the same food with the precious plums.

Diana drew her fork through the purple plum juice swimming on her own plate. "Whatever you and Mrs. Mott deem proper."

"Do rally a bit of enthusiasm at the prospect," Taylor teased. She ate one of her plums. "Mmm. You are marrying my brother, after all. And you would be hard pressed to find a better man. My husband excluded, of course."

Diana thought of Blake Thompson, that good friend of Robert's whom she scarcely saw out of his company before Robert's imprisonment. The gossips had only glowing reports of the baron of course, choosing instead to focus their venom on unmarried young ladies who couldn't readily defend themselves.

"Your excellent husband must sorely miss you."

Her friend nodded, a glow on her cheeks. "I miss him as much, and our sweet little baby." She lowered her voice. "And Blake's kisses. Oh I daresay I do not have to tell you about passion, Diana."

Diana's heart began to beat furiously as her cheeks heated. "Passion?"

Compassion filled her future sister-in-law's eyes. "I know of your indiscretion, but it does you no discredit in my eyes."

Diana's heart ceased its pounding, thudding dully as her head pounded in rhythm. "At least I will not return to Arundel in shame."

"There is no shame in love," Taylor stated simply.

Diana opened her mouth to protest, closing it with a

soft sob. "I do love him. More's the pity."

Robert's sister smiled at her, the expression full of warmth that began to thaw Diana's chilled soul.

"Then all will be well," Taylor said.

To that, Diana couldn't so readily agree.

"My father will be pleased, I admit," Diana said.

"Your father is a wise gentleman. And fair-minded, if my memory is true."

"He is," Diana said with a sniffle. "Oh, I do not know what is wrong with me."

"There, there." Taylor patted her hand. "Pray, do not trouble yourself where my stubborn brother is concerned. Consider your own happiness in the matter."

"My happiness?" Diana took up her reticule and withdrew the prettily-embroidered hanky that had filled her first days at The Hideaway, dabbing her damp eyes with it. "Oh, I will endeavor to find peace, Taylor." She crumpled the hanky in her hand. "Peace is all I can expect."

"Peace. Hmm. Then we shall go into the village this day and see how much damage we can do to my brother's credit accounts."

"What do you mean?"

Taylor grinned. "You need a trousseau, Sister."

"You may be a bit premature," Diana said. "I am in no spirit for such an outing, I fear."

Taylor gave a vehement shake of her head, stilling as she peered over Diana's shoulder. "Robert," Taylor called. "Do join us."

Diana worried the hanky, twisting it as she cocked her ears for the unmistakable sound of his booted feet. He stopped somewhere close behind her, the heat from his body scorching the bit of bare flesh at the back of her neck. An answering flush spread over her body.

"Good afternoon, ladies."

Diana inclined her head, keeping her back to him, her posture rigid.

He took a few steps and faced both her and Taylor. "I trust you are enjoying your meal?"

She glanced at her barely-touched plate and gave him a nod.

"I have your father's answer, Diana," he went on. "The constable gives his consent."

She had expected as much, though she would have liked to see her father and gauge his true reaction to Robert's request. "So soon?"

He simply nodded.

"We were just discussing the wedding breakfast, Brother," Taylor said, her tone bright.

"Mrs. Mott will prove more than capable to the task," he nodded in return.

"Yes," Diana put in.

"The day should be pleasant, I wager," he continued.

So this is to be the level of discourse? And after last night, she had grave doubts regarding the only aspect of their relationship upon which she'd had any confidence.

"I am sure the ceremony will be pleasant," she said a bit archly.

A raise of one of his brows told her that he more than grasped her meaning.

Taylor bit her lip, no doubt to keep her opinions within though her eyes twinkled merrily.

Diana rushed to her feet. "Excuse me. Taylor I will be down directly."

Without waiting to get her friend's agreement, she hurried up the stairs and away from the Shelbys for the time-being.

Not more than an hour after that stilted conversation with her betrothed, Diana walked the streets of Homerton with Taylor. The thoroughfares were much narrower than those of Arundel, but in the spring sunshine the village was quite pretty. Little shops, their storefronts a bit shabby to Diana's eye, lined the thoroughfare. Dusty cobblestones muffled her and Taylor's footsteps as they made their way toward the dressmaker's.

"You will love Mrs. Smythe's shop, Diana," Taylor assured her. "She is a lovely woman with excellent taste."

Diana nodded, unable to keep from feeling a flicker of excitement at the prospect of choosing a gown for the wedding. "I admit it will be pleasant to pass a bit of time on the pattern books."

"Oh, you will not find this shop as enchanting as the dressmaker's in Arundel," Taylor pointed out. "But she has quite a selection of elegant gowns for a spot tucked in this particular corner of Middlesex."

Diana glanced at the crowded street, seeing little of fine vehicle or fancy dress. "Are there many of the gentry that live in Homerton?"

"Hardly that. One can perhaps find the odd squire

about, but my husband is the only peer to keep even occasional residence here."

Diana nodded and loosened the ties of her cloak. The day was growing warm, and her flower-sprigged muslin day gown was adequate if tiresome to her by now. "Perhaps she will have a few day dresses."

"Oh yes! Pray, charge them to my brother's accounts. Goodness knows he gives little business to these struggling shopkeepers."

Diana let out a sigh. "Oh, I suppose I should accustom myself to my husband's keeping."

"The loss of independence is really a small price to pay. And if you marry the right gentleman, you scarcely lose much of it."

Diana's heart sank a bit. "I daresay Robert will infringe on little of my time or occupation."

Taylor stilled her just outside the dressmaker's. "What do you mean?"

Diana met her gaze evenly. "Robert will no doubt keep to his present course, Taylor. He will take his cases and escape Arundel for The Hideaway with little provocation, let alone thought to my wishes."

Taylor pursed her lips, no doubt holding back yet another glowing opinion on marriage and its power to change all for the better.

"I believe you are wrong." A sunny smile lit Taylor's features. "But I will allow you this point, if only to speed our coming assault on Mrs. Smythe and her surprising array of gowns."

Diana did smile then, and it very nearly felt natural to her.

Mrs. Smythe, a pleasant-faced woman who appeared to be ten years older than she and Taylor, greeted them with a smile. Her pristine white mop-cap couldn't contain the light brown sausage curls framing her face.

Mrs. Smythe did indeed seem a bit out of place in tiny Homerton, and her inventory boasted of more than enough to tempt Diana. In the end she chose a few simple day dresses, done in cunning fabrics the bright colors of spring, and a gown that took little convincing on Taylor's part to urge Diana to agree upon. It was pale blue, almost white, and trimmed with tiny satin roses and deep rows of ruffled lace.

As she stood in the back room of the dressmaker's she was unable to mask the delight in both the gown and Robert's anticipated reaction to it.

"Oh, Diana!" Taylor sighed. "You look a vision. And Sally will no doubt perform some sort of magic on that glorious hair of yours." She clicked her tongue. "It is a shame that we must hide that hair with a bonnet."

"But such a bonnet," Diana said with a grin.

The article in question, for which Taylor had escaped to the milliner's next door, was a shade darker than the dress, to match precisely the satin pelisse that Mrs. Smythe insisted must be worn with the gown.

"Just the thing for this spring weather," the dressmaker chirped. She draped the cool satin over Diana's bare shoulders. "It will keep your shoulders warm and allow the skirt of the gown to sway unrestricted."

With the ensemble carefully boxed for delivery to The Hideaway at last, Diana allowed Taylor to choose the finest underthings and a special nightgown and wrapper. The last two pieces should have scandalized Diana, but she felt her cheeks heat with something other than embarrassment.

"The fabric is nearly transparent, Taylor," she offered in weak protestation.

Taylor merely grinned. "And these, Mrs. Smythe."

The dressmaker shared a smile with Taylor and Diana's face burned hotter.

"Very good, Lady Thompson."

Diana and Taylor headed back out into the sunny morning, Diana's steps decidedly lighter than before they entered the dressmaker's.

Taylor wound her arm through Diana's, her eyes sparkling. "Aren't you growing the tiniest bit excited for the wedding now, Diana?"

Diana laughed softly. "I admit I cannot help but happily anticipate wearing that gown."

"It suits you quite well."

Diana allowed her friend's kind words and her own growing excitement to buoy her spirits as she returned to the public house.

Would Robert think her a vision in that gown? And what of the nightgown and wrapper? She flushed again as she thought of his reaction.

If passion was truly all they had, she would make certain to get her fill on their wedding night.

Chapter 20

"Thank you, Mr. Gaines."

The vicar nodded to Robert. "I will see you and your bride on Friday then, Shelby. Mrs. Gaines has lovely decorations procured."

"Do give her my thanks."

Robert gave a short bow and took his leave from the vicarage. With a few well-chosen words the man would see to the speedy procurement of the special license and, with his wife's expertise, a speedy wedding ceremony.

He glanced in the direction of The Hideaway, catching a glimpse of two familiar female forms locked arm-in-arm. Two bonneted heads bent close, sharing what? he dared not guess as they entered the public house. He once more thought of the horrid gossip that still kept Taylor and Blake from Arundel and wished there was some way to draw Diana's friend and soon-to-be sister for more than the occasional visit. The Lord knew that Diana would need a such a particular friend if he turned out to be the husband he much feared he would. He passed the dressmaker's, and was a bit startled as the woman peeped out to greet him brightly.

"Good morning, Mr. Shelby!"

He bowed his head to her. “Good morning.”

He didn’t know the woman’s name that was certain, having never frequented this particular shop.

“And congratulations on your upcoming nuptials,” the mop-capped woman smiled.

Ah. Now Diana and Taylor’s conspiratorial air made sense.

“Thank you.”

He continued to the pub, his mind still refusing to accept that marriage awaited him in two days’ time. A brief note to Blake would bring him here, and that gave Robert a bit of solace. His best friend’s glowing opinion of matrimony would most assuredly set his own doubts aside if only for the length of the ceremony and wedding breakfast. He entered The Hideaway.

“Good morning, Robert.”

He froze, at last turning to face his sister in the alcove. A glance over her shoulder showed Diana, her flickering expressions indicating both her pleasure in seeing him and her apprehension that he would once more act the dolt.

“Good afternoon,” he intoned with a smile.

He was rewarded with a glimpse of delight on her

lovely face.

"Good afternoon, Robert," Diana said.

He stepped into the ridiculously small room and stopped before the two ladies. "Did I see the two of you about the village a short while ago?"

A pretty blush stained Diana's cheeks and Taylor nodded with enthusiasm.

"Oh yes, Brother. Both the items and the bill will no doubt arrive shortly."

He arched a brow the instant before recognition settled one him. "Ah. The dressmaker's. The woman seemed most pleased to see me this morning and wished me felicitations."

Diana and Taylor both laughed lightly.

"And Mrs. Smythe was most pleased to help Diana with her selections," Taylor offered.

He looked at Diana, who worried the skirt of her flowered frock.

"I hope you do not mind."

So, it has come to this?

"You will be my bride, Diana," he said. "Certainly you are entitled to whatever you need."

She blinked up at him but said nothing.

The tiny room grew smaller and he backed out into the entry with a bow. "I will see you for luncheon."

"Well, that was prettily done," Taylor said as she caught up to him in his office.

Robert let out a harsh breath. "Pray do not start again, Taylor."

"She is not happy, Brother."

Robert glanced toward the doorway, longing to seek out Diana and apologize for his strange behavior in her chamber last night as well as his coldness today.

He turned to his sister, bracing his hands on his desk. "I warned you. I do not have it within me to make her happy."

"Nonsense! You will keep yourself to her and the happiness will follow."

Irritation simmered. "Of course I will remain faithful to her," he snapped. "But all of us are not as fortunate as you and Blake. You would do well to keep that in your meddlesome mind."

Taylor met his gaze with her own, her blue-gray eyes opened wide. "You cannot frighten me, Robert. You never could."

Taylor's brand of bravery and strength of character was what he had first recognized in Diana Ashley. He now suspected that his bride was no longer in possession of the same brave nature he had seen when he'd found her there on the bluff, however. Damned if he didn't want her precisely as headstrong and passionate as she had been then.

Last night, when he'd fled her chamber, guilt and frustration had warred within him. And now, she could scarcely bear to be in his company. Those eyes of hers showed everything, her expectations and her disappointments. He longed to tell her what he felt for her, if he knew what the bloody Hell that was.

"Diana will be safe, Taylor. And that is the most I can promise."

Taylor narrowed her eyes at him, at last giving him a slow nod. "Then that will have to serve." She turned and glanced at him over her shoulder. "At present."

Robert watched as his sister left him in peace at last. He settled himself behind the desk again, focusing not on Diana's reticence but the genuine delight that had lit her eyes for that brief moment in the alcove.

He prayed that marriage to him wouldn't dim that

expression forever.

"So you're caught well and good," Blake said from the same doorway not three days later.

Robert looked up from his desk to find Blake eyeing him closely. "Do not look so smug."

Blake closed the door. "My wife is pleased with your choice of bride."

"And you?"

Blake shrugged and stretched out in the chair facing him. "I value Taylor's good opinion. And yours."

Robert thought of the girl who had become so important to his life in so short a time. "Diana is… Ah, I do not deserve her."

The concern that had so often filled Blake's eyes following Robert's rescue made its reappearance. Robert had had enough of it for the length of his recuperation and was loath to see it now.

"Put it behind you, Robert," Blake said. "You are not to blame for Trevor's actions any more than I."

Robert couldn't face his friend. He turned to gaze out the window at the twilight sky beyond. "Trevor does not signify."

Silence pressed at his back, followed by a soft string of curses.

"Do not worry over this, Brother," Blake said softly. "Diana Ashley has accepted your suit, short though it was. Turn your attention to that."

Robert turned to face him at last.

"Her hand was forced more than mine." He raked his fingers through his hair. "I compromised her and now we must wed. It is as simple as that."

Blake barked out a laugh. "Ah, that is precisely how I imagined my marriage to your sister would be. Simple."

"Your suit was different."

"You do not know that. You were in that stinking room under Trevor's thumb while Taylor was here under my so-called protection."

Robert quirked a smile at him. "Are you saying that you compromised my sister?"

Blake met his gaze evenly. "A little late for such talk, I daresay. Given your towheaded niece's existence. But yes, I hadn't thought to marry at all before your lovely sister dropped into my lap."

It was Robert's turn to laugh. "You might want to

rephrase that."

Blake grinned unashamedly. "And the day after tomorrow you will wed and take your bride back to Sussex. That should put them on their guard, I wager."

Robert sobered. "Diana will be safe, Blake. And I will find the bastard who hurt the Hollis girl."

"You will return directly, then."

It wasn't a question. "Justice demands it. And Diana will want me to drag her brother back to Arundel."

"You do not believe him guilty."

"I do not. The boy wrote me, amazing as that is. He is in Brighton."

Blake nodded. "Fitting place to hide this time of year. Do you have an inkling of the true culprit?"

Sour anger simmered in Robert's belly. "Diana believes it to be Clive Stilton."

"The squire's nephew?"

Robert wasn't surprised by Blake's knowledge of the place despite his long absence.

"Young Stilton has a history of violence toward women," he told Blake. "More than one serving wench at the inn bears his mark."

Blake's face mirrored the disgust Robert felt at present. "Bastard."

"And he dared to touch Diana."

Blake's mouth gaped open. "He hurt her?"

Robert thought of the purple marks on Diana's delicate flesh. "He marked her arm and I nearly throttled him when I learned of it."

"Little provocation to see him dragged to justice, then."

Conviction settled in Robert's breast. "Justice would be too good for Clive Stilton should I prove him guilty of the Hollis assault."

***

"Your answer, Miss Ashley?"

Diana froze, staring blankly into Mr. Gaines's round face. The vicar smiled with encouragement and she spontaneously returned the expression. Robert cleared his throat and she glanced over at her groom. At his intense gaze she gave a tiny nod and lost her silly grin.

"Y-yes."

Was that relief in Robert's gorgeous eyes? Or resignation?

After a too-brief brush of Robert's lips on hers they were surrounded by the well-wishers and ushered out of the little church. People Diana didn't know called out their felicitations as Robert draped her pretty blue pelisse over her shoulders.

"That is done, then," he murmured.

She turned her head to find him smiling down at her.

"Yes," she said again.

What the devil ailed her? A half-remembered ceremony followed by a tiny kiss now bound her to this man. Astounding.

"Welcome, Sister," Taylor cried, wrapping her arms around Diana.

Diana returned the embrace, the reality once more striking her. Lord Thompson gave her a brotherly kiss and grinned in Robert's direction.

"I am famished," Blake said. "Our cook at Thompson Hall pales in comparison to Mrs. Mott."

Relieved at the turn of topic, she permitted Robert to take her arm and escort her down the street toward The Hideaway. The slight pressure of his fingers on her bare arm made her long for a more insistent hold, one that she hadn't encountered since that last night in her borrowed chamber. She was surely ruined. No, not ruined precisely, she corrected. Wed.

"It was a lovely ceremony, Diana," Taylor said. "The flowers filled the space and the people were most pleasant."

Diana nodded. "I do miss my father and brother."

"We will return to Arundel on the morrow," Robert said.

That brought her vague musings into sharp focus and she looked up at her husband. "I wonder how poor Gertie Hollis fares."

The hard look on Robert's face told her that he hadn't lost his outrage or his conviction. "The villain will be held accountable, love. Depend upon it."

She trusted him to see to the conclusion of the case, and knew in her heart that Matthew would be cleared of the heinous charges.

If only she could face her marriage with like conviction.

Robert matched his stride to her even ones, time and again letting his gaze flit over her. "Your dress is lovely, Diana. Tell me, is it blue or white?"

The inane start of a conversation muddled her for a moment, then she gave a nod. “Blue.”

“Your skin…” He smiled and for a moment she was blinded by his beauty. “Forgive me, but you look quite fetching.”

Her cheeks heated and she dipped her head. “Every bride is lovely, Robert.”

“I shall have to take you at your word.”

“Mr. Gaines had been most efficient there in the little church,” she put in.

“You hesitated.”

She bit her lip. “Pray, do not take offense. I admit I was a bit overwhelmed.”

“Still, it was a relief to hear your answer in the affirmative.”

She took him at his word in return, and allowed herself to feel relief herself that he had been as affected during the ceremony as she had.

He took Diana’s elbow and she realized it was the first time he’d touched her since running from her chamber that night.

“Are you happy, Diana?” he asked.

Her surprise turned to astonishment as she stared wordlessly up at him. What had prompted him to ask such an question? Happy? She truly had no notion.

"We will suit, Robert. For a time."

"For a time?" he repeated. "What do you mean?"

She lifted her chin. "After we return to Arundel, all will be as it was." She stared forward. "As it should be."

"You will reside at Shelby Manor, Diana," he said in a low voice. "That will not be as it was."

She shrugged. "No matter, as you will live at The Hideaway."

He stopped her, grasping her arms. "What are you saying?"

Her gasp stopped him, thankfully. She glanced over at her new sister and brother-in-law and saw that Taylor and Blake feigned distraction. But the sturdy people of Homerton didn't take such pains to hide their interest in the newlyweds.

He dropped his hands and took her elbow, his grasp firm. "Are you telling me we will not live together, Diana?"

She worried her lower lip. "You will have the marriage you crave, Robert. One in name only."

He gave a snort and she eyed him with obvious

trepidation. “I assure you, wife, our marriage will be far from one in name only.”

She didn’t argue, but kept her face forward as they made their return to The Hideaway.

Diana looked about Robert’s sumptuous chamber hours later, taking her time to ready for her wedding night. The decadent nightgown and wrapper awaited her in the dressing room, where Sally had put Diana’s new dresses as well. Well and gone from her own borrowed little chamber, she eyed the large bed. She had never shared such a space with anyone, let alone a man. Against her will, her gaze was drawn to the plump chair beside the crackling fire. No longer did she imagine Annie’s red head bent toward Robert’s manhood. No, none other than the image of herself riding him like a wanton flitted in her mind’s eye. Her virtue and her shyness had fled the instant he’d breached her maidenhead.

A flush of heat filled her, centering at her core. Tonight Robert would take her again, legally and completely. Her body quivered and her fingers fumbled as she removed the mint green dress that had replaced the beautiful wedding gown for the afternoon. Her husband had been anywhere but in her company after their strange conversation upon leaving the church. That ought to have struck her as odd. But aside for a slight frown marring Taylor's face, apparently none other than she believed it so out of fashion.

"Diana?" Robert asked from the other side of the door.

Her head jerked at the sound, her hands frozen on the buttons on her bodice. "Yes?"

Silence persisted for a long moment.

"May I enter?"

A glance down at herself assured her respectability. "Certainly."

Robert opened the door and peered inside. Light from the sconces in the corridor poured into the room. A flick of Robert's gorgeous eyes, followed by a slight frown of disappointment, told her that he had hoped to find her readied for bed. That flutter of heat came once more and she swallowed a gasp. He'd insisted they would have a marriage far more than one in name only. *Oh, my.*

"Do you want me to leave?" he asked her.

She shook her head, mute for a long moment. "Pray do not go, Robert," she rushed out. "I shall change in the dressing room."

Before he could do more than nod, she escaped and closed the door between them. She leaned against the panel for a moment, willing her heart to cease its pounding and her hands to quit their shaking.

"Silly chit," she muttered.

She removed her pretty dress and set it aside for Sally to ready for the trip to Arundel tomorrow. She wouldn't think about her father or Matthew or the Hollis case or anything else tonight.

Letting her chemise fall from her body, she turned to put on the lovely nightgown and wrapper. Froths of lace fell from the sleeves, caressing her as the rest of the gown settled over her body. A tremor of excitement couldn't be ignored. So lovely a garment could surely elicit more from her husband than had her chemise-clad figure two nights past.

She hurriedly ran her fingers through her curls and let them fall free of any pins. She tied the belt of the wrapper around her waist and left the dressing room, stepping with a combination of eagerness and anxiousness toward her husband. He had removed his clothes while she'd taken her time changing, and she noted the change with appreciation. He looked so fine in just his breeches, so strong and virile in the flickering light of the fire and the few candles on the bedstand. And he was hers.

Forever.

Chapter 21

"Good evening, Robert."

Robert let his gaze rake over Diana's form, disguised though it was in the pretty nightgown and wrapper. But he knew the bounty hidden beneath, and that caused his body to swell in anticipation.

"Good evening. Wife."

She gasped in response to his use of the word, her deep blue eyes fathomless. Her glorious hair, that mass of inky curls that shone in the firelight, swayed about her shoulders as she took halting steps toward him.

Praying inwardly for calm, he bridged the scant distance separating them. "Diana…"

She leaned toward him and he happily caught her in his arms. Her breathing was a bit rapid as she smiled up at him. The abstinence of the past few days had taken its expected toll and he took her mouth with his. The thin garment covering her body couldn't shield her response from him and he let out a growl as her puckered nipples rasped against his bare chest. The pretty wrapper fluttered to the carpeted floor with a soft rustling sound as he pulled back to gaze at her. The nightgown did little more than showcase her exquisite figure. Lace teasingly played across her breasts, her hips. The thinnest lawn nearly showed her rosy nipples, and he could just see the dark curls at the juncture of her thighs through the fabric.

He swallowed audibly. “This nightgown.”

“I admit I favor it as well.” She shrugged and the nightgown slipped off of one shoulder. “It feels heavenly against my skin.”

“That is a shame.” He reached for the thin ribbon of blue satin attempting to hold the garment closed over those breasts, but at last fisted his hands at his side lest he rip it in two. “Take it off,” he softly ordered.

She complied, and with enough enthusiasm to set his own apprehensions aside. She would welcome him with her incredible body. The heat in her eyes told him that much. Lord, he was a lucky man tonight.

“I have missed you, Robert.”

That struck him dumb. He hadn’t given thought that she had miss their passion as much as he.

“I daresay it is embarrassing to say so,” she added.

He found his voice. “No. We are wed, Diana. And the Lord knows I’ve missed you sorely these past days.”

"But you… You left."

He raked his fingers through his hair. "I was a bloody fool. Pray, believe me, Diana. I have not stopped wanting you."

Her gaze lowered to settled on his manhood, which throbbed in response in his breeches.

She licked her lips nervously and faced him. Her cheeks colored and she took a step closer. "You want me now."

"Ah… yes."

A laugh tumbled out of her, the sound full of relief. He caught her up again and fell with her onto his bed. Their mouths met and she tasted sweeter than he'd remembered. That woefully brief kiss after Gaines tied them to each other paled in comparison to the hot exchange at this moment.

He kissed her mouth, her cheek, her throat. She purred with pleasure and he brought his lips to her breasts. As he flicked his tongue over one nipple, she arched toward him.

"Yes, Robert…"

He suckled and teased her eager flesh, his fingers pinching her other nipple with just enough pressure to cause her to let out a whimper of frustration. As she tangled her fingers in his hair, he came up and kissed her parted lips.

"Do you want me, Diana?"

Robert's fingers kept up their magic and she opened her eyes. He couldn't keep the grin from his face.. Not a grin of triumph, no. One of shared desire.

"Yes, Robert," she breathed again.

His mouth began their descent again and she waited in obvious anticipation for him to once more kiss her breasts. But he dropped a kiss on her belly and before she could guess what he was about he parted her legs and placed his mouth on her center.

He felt her tremble as she fisted her hands in the fine linens. His fingers trailed over her belly, her breasts, as he murmured vague sounds without abandoning his decadent task. When his tongue entered her, so like his taking of her with his very self, she rose toward that pinnacle he'd shown her before. The intensity, the pressure, was exquisite. Crying out, for what? he dared not guess, she trembled again and gave herself up to him.

He came up and covered her with his body. "Did you like that?"

She nodded mutely, her eyes still shut. He chuckled

and she smiled weakly. He kissed her and parted her thighs with his. Her tender flesh, still quivering from the climax he gave her, seemed to open solely for him. Drawing him within her, she let out a shout of completion. This was what she was made for, his mind whispered. She was made for him.

"My God, Diana," he rasped. "You are so wet, so tight."

His words must have registered, but she seemed to focus instead on his kisses which fell on her brow, her cheek. His shaft was deep within her, pounding with growing strength, as he drove her once more toward that peak.

"Oh, my!"

"Yes, love." His breathing was harsh. "Come to me again."

She did, at the precise moment he poured himself into her and shook mightily. Clutching him to her breast, she sobbed from the release. He murmured words of praise and cradled her in his arms.

"Oh, Robert."

To hear her say his name in that way, sweet and reedy and so damned satisfied, pleased him to his core. When he at last lifted his head, she opened her eyes to him and he smiled.

"Ah, Diana," he teased.

She let out a breathy laugh which sounded most wanton. His own breath caught and he kissed her again.

"It is done then," she said.

"Done?" he returned. "I daresay the night has just begun."

"I only meant…" Her cheeks flushed pink as her fingers play over his bare shoulder. "I meant that now our marriage is…"

"Consummated? I suppose." He struck a thoughtful pose. "Though our bodies were wed before Mr. Gaines ever pronounced it so."

Instead of the embarrassment his words should have elicited, she nodded with enthusiasm.

"Our marriage will be more than pleasant," he vowed. "And a damn sight more than only in name."

His words must have pleased her sensibilities as well, for she threw her arms around his neck. "Love me, Robert."

At her demand he grew hard within her.

"Anything to please my wife."

And please her he did.

***

"We shall see you soon, Sister," Taylor said the next morning, hugging Diana tightly.

Diana returned the embrace. "Thank you for everything, Taylor. The ceremony was lovely, and…"

The ladies shared a look of understanding not lost on Robert. He knew full well the strength of their attachment, visibly grown since Taylor had come to The Hideaway.

Facing Blake, he clasped his brother-in-law's hand. "Blake. You cannot come to Arundel?"

Blake glanced toward Taylor and shook his head. "No. Thompson Hall and our Lily awaits. But we shall plan a visit to Shelby Manor soon. Perhaps by Michaelmas."

Taylor turned sharply, worry etched on her brow. But she smiled gamely and nodded. "That is less than three months hence. Surely not overlong."

"No," Diana returned, relief in her tone.

Robert recognized that she only felt comfortable in his bed, not in his company. How he would change that, he couldn't begin to guess.

"September, then," he said. "I hope to have this foul case wrapped up and all back as it was by then."

"But what of the smugglers?" Blake asked. "Do you

think to set that matter to rights?"

"Hardly. If the guard can do nothing, what am I to do?"

Diana's worry was evident as she fingered the fine kid gloves dressing her delicate hands. "Matthew had best find himself free of them."

Blake arched a brow.

"Matthew will be safe, Diana," Robert put in. "That is all you need believe."

Blake caught Robert's meaning and asked nothing of the boy's involvement with the free traders. Blake's moral character would no doubt insist bringing all the nasty truth out for inspection, and Robert couldn't allow that to happen. Not with Diana already skittish where her brother's welfare was concerned.

"We bid you farewell, then," Blake said with a nod.

A kiss from his sister to Diana's cheek, following by one to his own, and Lord and Lady Thompson took their leave from Homerton. Robert's carriage, parked behind Blake's, awaited his and his bride's boarding. He handed her up into the vehicle and she settled herself prettily on the front-facing seat. He joined her, noting her slight look of surprise.

"We are wed, Diana. It is completely proper that we share a seat."

She said nothing, that resignation fixed on her face as she gazed out the window at the completely unremarkable streetscape of Homerton. He stretched out his legs and turned his own gaze out his window, his mood souring. This would be a bloody pleasant ride.

After nearly an hour of silence, she let out a sigh. He turned to see her stretching and couldn't help but imagine the supple way she'd moved last night. With him. Beneath him. Around him.

"This is a far more comfortable ride than when last I traveled," she confided.

The same was not true for him, he allowed as he shifted to ease his growing discomfort.

"You prefer my carriage to a hired hack, I take it? Such a compliment."

She smiled, her ease returning. "There is that. And I was quite disturbed at the time."

He nodded. He took in her appearance, clad in a lovely gown of rose topped with a spencer of red velvet. She had removed her bonnet while he'd been seeking to divert his attention out the window, and now the straw and fabric thing rested on the seat opposite. The breeze coming through the opened window ruffled the dark tendrils at her cheek, her nape, and he fought the urge to catch them between his fingers. He knew her hair to be silken to touch, sweet to smell. He shifted again.

"Are you uncomfortable?" she asked.

Innocence rounded those eyes, and he couldn't help but dispel it, if just a bit.

"I believe you drive me to distraction, wife."

Recognition dawned and with it a smile he hadn't foreseen. Though her lashes lowered to pinkened cheeks, she leaned toward him. "As you do me."

A glance out his window showed their location, and he mentally calculated the time left for their arrival in Arundel. Ample time, in his considered opinion.

"Is that so, Diana?" he said, leaning across her to shut her window tightly.

She watched him, her breath coming as fast as his. Tiny buttons marched up the front of her spencer and he deftly worked them free.

"Robert," she gasped, only anticipation in her voice.

"What are you about?"

A grin told her his answer. And her answering sighs told him that the ride was about to get much more comfortable.

***

"I daresay I have never done that in a carriage," Robert observed as his thoughts began to settled along with his pulse.

Diana let out a breath and cuddled closer to him, still firmly ensconced on his lap. Aside from her spencer and drawers, no other clothing had been removed and she felt incredibly wanton. She leaned back to regard him. Except for his slightly-rumpled cravat and tousled hair he looked the proper gentleman. And if she didn't still feel his tremors deep within her she wouldn't have guessed anything amiss.

"I hadn't thought that after last night we would do that again so soon."

He let out a lazy laugh. "I shall never grow tired of your loving, Diana." He lifted his lids, his blue-gray eyes cloudy. "Even after the rigors you put me through last night."

She should feel a touch of shame, shouldn't she? But if this was to be the one place where she could feel certain of his interest, so be it. Perhaps in time… No. She wouldn't hope he would come to love her as she did him. She would be content to have his polite regard during the day as long as she had his passion at night. She glance out the window toward the bright afternoon sun. Or during the day!

Stunned by her thoughts, she extricated herself from his embrace and concentrated on righting her clothing. She loved him, and he must never know. True, Taylor knew. Robert's sister had guessed it with alarming ease. Would Robert soon know her heart, too?

"How long before we arrive?" she asked.

He took his time buttoning his breeches and gave a lazy shrug. "Another hour. Perhaps two. The road is fairly dry and we are nearly in Sussex."

Her stomach growled and he shot her a knowing glance.

"I will signal the driver to stop for luncheon at the next inn." He opened his window once more and peered outside. "Should be Horsham."

She nodded and took great pains in fixing her spencer. Her breasts were still tender from his kisses and she sought to ignore the delicious tremors the fitted jacket elicited as she worked the buttons. Robert seemed at his ease, his big body languid on the seat beside her.

"I am eager to see Father," she said, turning her thoughts to a safer subject than that of her beguiling husband.

"The constable will welcome you, no doubt. He has missed you sorely, I daresay."

"And Matthew, Robert. When will you go for him?"

"After I capture Gertie's attacker it will be safe for his return."

"Capture?" Her heart stuttered. "Oh, Robert you will not put yourself in danger?"

He quirked a smile at her. "I hadn't thought to, love. But I believe I will employ a trick that Blake and I have found useful in the past."

"A trick?"

He must have sensed her interest, though it hardly vexed him as it would have before her flight to The Hideaway. She recalled his words when he'd caught her snooping outside her father's office and hid her smile. Amazing what a bout of lovemaking could do to ease a man's irritation.

"Yes," Robert began. "We will arrange for Gertie

Hollis's travel to a safe house far to the north, though we will not disclose that fact. Then we will let it be known that she has regained her wits and will soon name her attacker."

"Oh! That will make Clive most desperate."

"The attacker, in any event. We cannot assume it is that blackguard. And you, my sweet, will be safe at Shelby Manor."

"But Robert, I could most assuredly assist you. Perhaps if I disguise myself as Gertie—"

"No!" His eyes were dark now, as was his scowl. "You will not put yourself in danger, Diana. Never again."

She pulled back at his vehemence. He had seemed worried that night on the bluff, that was true. But this? He must care a bit for her.

"I will endeavor to keep myself out of it."

He let out a breath and visibly relaxed. How very interesting.

"When do you do this?" she asked him.

"We begin to set matters in motion tonight. Blake sent word to the north and the girl will be moved directly."

"Then she will be safe." She took in a breath. "Have you told Mr. Hollis?"

Robert shook his head as he fixed his cravat. "Only that she will be safe. The less the man knows beforehand, the better. His nerves are stretched taut."

"Poor man. And poor, poor Gertie."

She shivered when she imagined the horror his daughter had endured. Robert placed his hand over hers and gave a squeeze, warming her flesh through her gloves.

"Arundel will be safe again, Diana."

The image of the child flashed through her mind then, that poor mite left like so much refuse on the riverbank.

"What of the boy, Robert?"

His lips thinned. "I have not abandoned that matter, love. Merely set it aside."

"Do you think the two cases are connected?"

"I cannot imagine how." His fair brows furrowed for a moment. "Though both crimes were exceedingly violent."

She rubbed her wrist, the marks from Clive gone from her flesh if not her memory. As if sensing her thoughts—was there nothing she could conceal from her husband?—he lifted her hand to his mouth and placed a kiss on her wrist.

"I haven't forgotten Clive's actions, Diana. He will pay for hurting you."

She gazed into his stormy eyes and felt his certainty deep within herself. Oh, she had his passion and his protection. She was a very lucky woman.

"I never doubted it, Robert."

A raise of his brows told her that her words both surprised and pleased him. He gave a nod and entwined her fingers with his, and the slide of their skin as their hands fit so closely together was much more intimate than even the carnal pleasures they had just shared. Diana closed her eyes and said a silent prayer that they would always have this as the carriage rolled on toward Arundel.

Toward home.

Chapter 22

Sterns took Diana in hand as they entered Shelby Manor, and Robert was grateful for once for the butler's supercilious air and deference.

"I have some matters to see to in my office, Diana. Pray allow Sterns to show you around the house?"

She glanced about the entry, peering down the corridor toward his office, but she gave him a nod of agreement and removed her bonnet and spencer.

"This way, madam," Sterns said with a bow.

Robert didn't miss the gleam of satisfaction in the old man's eyes and he shook his head. Surely the man was most pleased to have a mistress to serve in addition to his own surly self. Robert withdrew to his office and removed his jacket.

The ride from The Hideaway wasn't far from his mind, and only one reason was the incredible release he'd shared with his wife in the close confines. He had also shared his plans with her, the strategy he would employ to catch the bastard who'd hurt the Hollis girl. As when he'd shared information regarding her brother the words had spilled from his lips, surprising him. He couldn't blame either spirits or sexual temptation for his loose tongue this time. That was certain. Diana's guileless blue eyes had merely turned in his direction and he found himself drawn as surely as that light on the river had drawn him to the bluff.

Turning to the correspondence waiting on his desk, he withdrew the letter from Matthew Ashley. He swiftly penned an answer, directing the note under a false name to the boarding house currently serving as Matthew's refuge. He set it aside for Sterns' attention and opened another missive awaiting him. Blake's solicitor had secured a temporary place for Gertie Hollis to the north. Good.

He stood and donned his jacket. When he opened the door he found his wife standing in the hallway outside, her hands clasped before her as she gazed up at him with hesitation.

"Robert?"

"Yes, love?"

"I am sorry to bother you, but I thought to visit my father."

He smiled then and she returned the expression so quickly he wondered if she was aware of the fact.

"Capital notion. Have you instructed Sterns to see to

bringing your lady's maid here?"

"I hadn't given that thought. I will tell the girl myself when we reach my house. That is, my father's house."

He caught her misspeak but wisely said nothing of it. So much had changed for her since last she was in Arundel.

"Come, love," he said. "I daresay we have much to meet this day."

She nodded and allowed him to take her elbow and lead her to the entry.

"Will you and madam return for dinner, sir?" Sterns asked as he helped Diana into her spencer.

"I am not at all certain, Sterns. Pray have cook prepare something cold."

"Certainly, sir. Madam."

The butler beamed another smile in his new mistress's direction and Robert rolled his eyes. The man was well on his way to becoming besotted with the new lady of the manor. Diana faced Robert then, and he thought that he was in as much danger. The beautiful girl was now dependent upon him, and no longer her father's responsibility. No, her safety was completely in his care, of both her person and her heart.

"Your father will be pleased to see you, Diana," he

said as they made their way up High Street. "I daresay he has had much to trouble him these past weeks."

She nibbled her lower lip as she gazed at the bustling shops. He followed her gaze and spied the villagers eyeing them closely. Let them stare. Village gossip wouldn't touch her, not if he had anything to say about it.

"Hello, Miss Ashley!" a stout matron called from the dressmaker's doorway.

Diana stiffened but met the woman's greeting with a small smile. "Hello."

"Out and about with Mr. Shelby, are you?" The lady bounced and jiggled as she made their way toward them. "I told Nan just the other day that the gentleman would do well to escort one of the fine girls here in Arundel."

Robert bent his head to Diana's. "Now is as good a time as any."

"I know," she whispered in answer. "At least we know this particular bit of gossip is true."

The plump matron stopped before them, her round cheeks red from the exertion and the anticipated information, true or false.

Robert bent in a bow. "Good day, Mrs…"

"Mrs. Sparts," the woman happily provided. She glanced toward Diana. "Miss Ashley, do not tell me you and Mr. Shelby have business of some sort?"

"Of the best sort, Mrs. Sparts," Robert put in. "Miss Ashley and I are wed."

The color in the lady's cheeks intensified and her dull brown eyes nearly bugged from her face. "Wed? You and she?" She rounded on Diana. "Miss Ashley, is this true?"

"Mrs. Shelby," Diana returned smoothly.

The woman's fat lips flapped but no real sounds came forth.

"If you will excuse us, Mrs. Sparts," Robert intoned. "We have an appointment we simply must keep."

With that he urged Diana along at as reasonable a pace as he could manage without outright running from the meddlesome bird.

"I suppose that within the hour all will know of our nuptials," Diana said softly.

"As it should be. I am pleased with my choice of wife."

She stopped and faced him, one graceful brow arched. "Choice?"

He gave her a crooked grin. “I chose you, Diana.”

No argument came from her, though doubt still colored her face as they neared the constable’s home.

As Diana and Robert entered the Ashley house, she paused.

“Diana, I assure you, your father was for our match.”

“Diana!” Constable Ashley called.

Diana’s father exited his office and stormed into the entry. He caught himself and clasped Diana’s hands in his, beaming down at her with a look that spoke of both worry and relief. “You are well, then?” He glanced in Robert’s direction before studying her face once more. “Shelby wrote me. You are well? Happy?”

“Yes, Father,” she assured him.

Another pointed glance in Robert’s direction urged Robert to nod his head.

“Constable,” he intoned.

“My heartiest felicitations, then.” Her father’s smile dimmed as he grew more serious. “Shelby. Have you heard nothing of the case?”

He saw the worry lines that seemed more numerous than when last he met with him.

"I have no new information, though I anticipate the girl's safety to be secured as of this evening."

The man nodded. "Capital." Once more he threw a worried glance in Diana's direction. "The nuptials were suitably lovely, I suppose?"

"Yes, Father. Lady Thompson saw to them."

The constable nodded again.

"I thank you for your acceptance of my suit, Constable," Robert said. "Diana is indeed a treasure."

Diana and her father both eyed him, the former wearing a look of disbelief, the latter one of satisfaction.

"And what of Matthew?" her father asked.

Robert and Diana exchanged a look, and he conceded to her with a nod.

"Matthew is in Brighton, Father," Diana said. "He wrote to Mr. Shelby."

The constable rounded on Robert. "And you did not tell me? When will he return? I demand you drag his sorry hide back here!"

Diana placed her hand on her father's arm and the man visibly calmed.

"Matthew cannot return as yet. Mr. Shelby and I

believe him innocent, but the people of Arundel are another matter entirely."

"Yes, yes." Diana's father nodded, his brows drawn together. "You have the right of it."

"When all is safe for his return, sir," Robert began, "we will bring him home."

The constable dismissed Matthew from his mind with obvious reluctance as he faced Robert, his eyes as intent as his daughter's. "Tell me your plans."

Robert look over at Diana. She took his cue and climbed the stairs as he followed his new father-in-law into his office to share his plans for the Hollis girl and her attacker.

***

Diana went up to her chamber—no, not her chamber any longer—and rang for her maid.

Jane dropped a curtsey. "Yes, miss? Er, ma'am?"

Diana smiled at the maid. "Hello, Jane. Pray, ready my belongings for Shelby Manor. And yours, of course."

The girl curtseyed again. "Yes, ma'am."

Jane hurried into the dressing room to do her mistress's bidding and Diana sank down in the chair before the vanity. Gazing into the mirror, she regarded her reflection. She was so changed since her flight to The Hideaway. She was now wed to Robert, the man who had filled her dreams just weeks ago in this very room.

A glance at the pretty rose and gray colors which made up her chamber caused a stab of melancholy. Everywhere she saw her mother's influence. Her mother's hand was in more than decoration. That bloody promise had sent her tumbling into Robert's arms on the bluff, and ultimately into his bed at The Hideaway.

"You can hardly blame your mother for that," she muttered. She stood and brushed her hands over her skirt. "Jane?"

The maid reappeared from the dressing room. "Yes, ma'am?"

"When you are finished, Jane, pray send word to Shelby Manor and Mr. Shelby's man Sterns will see to their transport."

"Yes, ma'am."

The girl returned to her task and Diana left the chamber. Intent on joining her husband in her father's office, she descended the stairs only to find Robert waiting for her at the bottom.

"You are finished here, then?" she asked.

"Yes. All is in readiness." He crooked his arm for her and she placed her hand on it. "I want you safely at Shelby Manor before tonight's work, love."

"Father will help you?"

"Yes. He will put it forth that Gertie is close to naming her attacker."

"And for once the gossip will work for the good," she said.

He patted her hand and leaned close, a teasing smile on his lips. "In the space of a few hours everyone will also know we are wed, Diana. And that is surely for the good as well."

"The marriage or the news of it?" She nearly bit her tongue as her words penetrated. Their marriage would keep Clive away from her, giving her Robert's lauded protection.

Blessedly, Robert did no more than blink at her. "Come." He turned her toward the door. "We must return to the manor."

To keep from once more speaking foolishly, she clamped her mouth shut and followed him out into the waning daylight.

"Shelby!" Clive Stilton shouted from the street

She turned and saw Clive hurrying toward them, his face red and his eyes wild as he puffed. To his credit, Robert assumed that air of calm she had noted before, a calm she now knew hid a keen mind intent on investigation. She assumed a similar stance, though she tightened her fingers on Robert's sleeve.

"Young Stilton," Robert said with condescension.

Clive skidded to a halt before them, his beefy hands in fists at his side. "Tell me it's not true!" He put his face very close to Diana's. "Tell me you didn't marry him."

She had glimpsed such anger on his face before, the time he'd dared to put a mark on her arm. Endeavoring to hide her fear of him, she raised her chin. "I did."

Clive's mouth gaped open and he pulled back. "You're mine." Recovering, he took a step closer and raised a fist. "And you let him have you?"

In a flash Robert had him by the rumpled cravat encircling his thick neck.

"You will speak to my wife with respect, Stilton," he said in a low rumble. "Do not bother her again."

Clive reddened further and smiled, the effect anything but placating. "I'm surprised is all, Shelby."

Robert released him and took Diana's hand again, deliberately placing it on his arm once more. "A lot has happened since we were gone," he observed.

"Eh?" Clive sputtered.

Robert fixed a stare at him. "The Hollis girl."

Clive's mouth worked again. "What of her?"

"My father says she is much improved since even two days ago," Diana put in, her voice holding what she hoped was the appropriate note of excitement. "Surely she will tell who really hurt her and my brother will be vindicated."

"I ain't heard—" Clive's eyes narrowed. "The constable talked with her?"

Diana cast a look of adoration up at Robert, a bit overdone in her opinion, but she reasons that it would do its intended work. "Mr. Shelby says that soon she will divulge the horrid truth, Clive. And then all will be well."

Clive glanced about the street. "I… I'm late for dinner at my uncle's."

"Good day, Stilton," Robert said.

Clive had not lost his fierce expression despite his

jerky bow of respect. He puffed out his chest and fixed a cold glare on Diana before facing Robert. "Good day, Shelby," he sneered.

He stalked off in the direction of his uncle's home. Robert's arm was still rigid beneath her fingers and she placed her other hand on him.

"Robert?"

He flicked his eyes over her, their blue-gray depths steely in the dwindling light.

"The son-of-a— He nearly touched you, Diana. Goddamn him, he nearly hurt you again."

His protectiveness, his possessiveness, was clear to her. Oh, she was lucky to be held in such regard by this man, even if she didn't have his love.

"Clive will never hurt me again, Robert. You told him not to, and I believe that bully is very afraid of you."

Robert's expression eased. "Come, love." They walked toward the bluff. "That was inspired, Diana. You delivered the lie with the perfect blend of excitement and awe."

She took the praise he offered. "I thought that particular tack would prove effective."

"You appear gifted at the task." He slanted her a look. "A gentleman would do well to guard his secrets around you."

She halted and turned toward him, her heart racing. "Do you have secrets, Robert?"

Chapter 23

Robert froze, swiftly reviewing all he'd told her. And all he hadn't. That year in Hell, the worst of the cases he'd handled since… He couldn't tell her. Not now and perhaps not ever.

"My secrets are my own. And too dark for your delicate sensibilities."

She looked away, but he didn't miss the lines bracketing her mouth as she held back whatever she was thinking in that quick mind of hers. But nothing she could say would sway him from his course. She didn't need to know of the darkness still within him, that core of his soul that stayed so cold despite the warmth of her closeness.

"I do not know how I shall pass the time this evening," she mused aloud.

Robert let out a breath. Good. Better to focus on the resolution of the Hollis case and not on matters best left alone.

"It will not be overlong, love," he said. "You have my word. Pray, distract yourself with the arranging of your effects. I assume Sterns showed you to our chamber?"

"Yes, though I hadn't thought of it as such. We will

share it?"

Ah, sharing his remarkably large bed with his remarkably passionate wife. Did she not wish to?

"Would you prefer your own room?" he asked. "There is a smaller one adjacent if you prefer."

"Oh, no," she said quickly, pleasing him more than she could know. "Whatever you deem proper is quite agreeable to me."

He let out a short laugh. "I do not know about propriety, but I know that I want you with me each night. All night."

A becoming blush stained her cheeks though she nodded her agreement. "Then I shall instruct my maid."

To his relief, no more questions of his secrets arose as they continued toward the manor.

After sharing a meal of cold roast beef accompanied by fresh bread and salads, Robert left Diana to the diligent watch of Sterns and the manor staff. Like her father had that afternoon, Diana wore her worry on her face. Robert prayed he could remove the specter of guilt around her brother before tonight was through. It was the least he could do for her.

Entering the Inn at Arundel, he waved to one of the

maids for service and settled himself at a table in the back of the dining room. The noise of silver clattering and glasses clinking reached his ears and the scents of hearty fare and tallow candles filled the space. The men populating the room, those he knew on sight from his years in the village, nodded greetings to him. One man, a loud-mouthed oaf of little account, rose to his feet and sauntered over to Robert's table as the serving maid placed a tankard of ale before him. The maid, the dark-haired girl who had suffered at Clive Stilton's violent hands, offered him a timid smile and hurried to wait on the other patrons.

"Back in Arundel are ya', Shelby?" The oaf, Thom or Thad, Robert wasn't certain, settled his broad frame in the chair opposite.

"Yes," Robert answered. "My wife wished to visit her father."

"Wife? Ah, the Ashley chit. Fair lass." He leered as he obviously imagined Diana's face and form. "We didn't know of yer regard for her, but she was always a temptin' piece."

Robert wouldn't rise to any bait the man foolishly offered. "She is most overset at present," he put in, drawing a deep drink from his tankard.

"Her brother took off, he did." He gave a nod and a snort. "Guilty as sin, that one."

Robert eyed him evenly. "My wife believes differently. And perhaps soon we shall all know the true identity of the villain."

"What's this?" another man said from a nearby table. His long face bore keen interest ringed with growing inebriation. "The Hollis girl be struck dumb."

Robert shrugged. "Apparently no longer."

The men shared a look that spoke of surprise and a good dose of skepticism.

"We ain't heard nothin' of it, Shelby," horse-face said. "And you been gone to that public house o' yours."

"You do not know my actions, I daresay," Robert said. "My investigations have never drawn much notice from Arundel."

"True, true. Yer work be yer own," his fat tablemate quickly said. "Yer's and Lord Thompson's."

"But ya' can't ignore the Ashley boy's guilt, Shelby," horse-face pointed out. "Don't matter he's yer brother now."

"I ignore nothing," Robert said. "And familial connections have never swayed me."

Robert's lingering anger with his cousin Trevor must have shown in his eyes for the man gulped, his Adam's apple bobbing. "That's right, Shelby. Ya' be a crack investigator."

"Never paid mind to the smugglers, though," came from across the room.

Robert was only mildly surprised to see Clive reclining there, the dark-haired serving maid perched on his lap. Apparently the man's coin made her forget any mistreatment.

"Excuse me?" Robert asked.

Clive's fat lips spread in a smile. "You don't do nothin'… anything about the smugglers."

"It is not my job, friend."

"But you poked your nose into the boy's death."

Robert gave him an arrogant arch of one brow. "Are you linking the poor child to the smugglers, Stilton? Pray, enlighten me with information I might have missed in my investigations."

Clive seemed to choke on that. *Interesting.*

"Do you know something of the child, then?" Robert pressed.

"N-no," Clive rushed out. "I was only talkin'."

Robert took a long deliberate drink of ale before fixing a glare in Clive's direction. "Perhaps, then, you should keep your mouth shut."

Silence blanketed the dining room, soon broken by the scrape of Clive's chair on the scarred wooden floor. He lumbered over to Robert, who held himself rigid in his seat.

"My uncle is squire, Shelby," Clive sneered. "He runs this village. More than ya' know."

"More than I know?" Robert slowly came to his feet to stand very close to Clive. "Pray, enlighten me."

Murmurings now filled the space, and the heady anticipation of a good, hard brawl. From the angry red blotches high on young Stilton's round cheeks, the pup's intentions most definitely bent in that direction. Robert would give them none of that, no doubt to their acute disappointment.

"Ya' can't just come back here and take over, Shelby!" Clive shouted. "Ya' were well and gone those months, and as well as gone this past year."

"I am firmly fixed in Arundel, Stilton. And believe me, I am going nowhere."

"Ya' came back here and took everything!" Clive

sputtered.

"What's he talkin' 'bout?" Robert heard someone wonder aloud.

"Stilton looks ready ta blow," another laughed.

Robert had too much to do this evening to waste his time with the lout. He placed his hand on Clive's broad chest and pushed. "See here, Stilton—"

"Ya' took her, damn your hide," Clive said. "And Diana was mine!"

Robert ducked the man's meaty fist and drove his own into Clive's broad middle. With a whoosh of breath, Clive doubled over.

Robert tossed him into a nearby chair and straightened his own jacket. "Do not think to so much as mention my wife's name again."

Without a word to the gaping crowd, he took his leave of the inn.

"That was pleasant," he muttered as he walked through the darkness.

The bastard believed Diana belonged to him? Ah, if only Robert could be certain that the pup was up to his fat neck in all of it. The assault, the dead child, the smuggling.

Robert came to a stop. Smuggling? Was that what Clive had meant when he'd alluded to the squire's running the village? Perhaps it was at long last time to involve himself in the matter of the free traders. And if it led to ridding Arundel of both the bothersome Clive and his condescending uncle, all the better.

Robert continued toward the Hollis home to await the arrival of the person with the most to lose should the girl divulge her attacker's name. He said a silent prayer that Clive Stilton would be the one to show his guilt.

***

Diana couldn't bear to wait for Robert any longer. Her effects were well situated in Robert's beautiful chamber, her dresses and the like arranged in one half of the spacious dressing room. She perched on one of the large blue chairs bracketing the wide hearth in the sitting area.

The room was indeed quite lovely, yet it still possessed the masculine stamp of her husband. Oversized furnishings done in warm elegantly-carved woods, draperies and linens in golds and blues, she could easily imagine the gentleman of the manor reclining in the space. Or striding about, his strong legs occasionally visible through the opening of the brocade dressing gown she saw hanging at the ready in the dressing room they would now share. Mmm.

She rose and entered the dressing room, running her fingers over the satin as she imagined the cool fabric heated from his body, the slither of sound as it slipped from his form to pool on the floor.

She left the dressing room, her pulse pounding from the mere image of her husband's fine figure, his smoldering eyes. The memory of the way he made her feel, inside and out. Alarm trilled through her. Her body was as attached to him as her heart soon would be. What if this evening's task didn't go as smoothly as he'd assured her? Would he put himself in danger to see the villain captured?

In an instant, she knew the answer. He would indeed. He was brave and good and would see the case through to its conclusion. Her stomach twisted sickeningly. Hadn't such diligence led to his horrid imprisonment at his own cousin's hands?

"I will not lose him," she vowed.

She once more looked through her effects in the dressing room, finding that Jane had indeed been most thorough. Diana's ugly oversized cloak stood at the ready, though the evening was hardly chilly. She would use it this last time however, and for a cause more important than ensuring her blasted brother's welfare as he worked with the smugglers. Tonight she would know what, precisely, Robert's work entailed.

She was soon outside the butcher's shop, hiding well away from the lamplight that fell on the cobblestones in the narrow alleyway to one side. She didn't see Robert about, though that was no surprise. This was his trade and his talent. And if she couldn't see someone for whom she was searching, however would someone not expecting him make him out? Pride mixed with the niggling certainty that danger awaited just beyond the shadows.

Voices reached her, nearly right behind her. She stilled and shrank against the rough stone wall of the shop, training her ears to catch each sound.

"You bloody fool," a man grumbled. "Why did you goad him?"

The voice was familiar, though holding a roughness that confused her.

"He took her," the other man whined. "She was mine."

Without a doubt, the whiner was none other than Clive.

"The chit doesn't signify, you clod. *This* one needs silenced, not Shelby's doxy."

Her eyes went round. Was this the squire, talking so crudely? Her eyes narrowed in the next moment. He called her a doxy? She bit back a retort.

"You shouldn't have taken the simpleton, Clive," the squire said. "Once again you're thinking with your prick. And now she's going to give your name? No. Not if we have anything to say about it."

"I'll shut her yap, Uncle," Clive went on. "Don't I always do what ya' tell me?"

Something unintelligible passed the squire's lips. "I won't have the Stilton name sullied, nephew."

"What'll ya' do? Do me like ya' did the child?"

Diana swallowed a gasp, covering her mouth. A slap sounded, as loud as thunder to her ears.

"Don't talk about the boy. The same fate could befall you."

"All right, all right!" Clive whined again.

"Now get in there and take care of the chit. I won't

have her telling anyone that my family is anything other than what I deem proper."

"What of the goods?"

Another slap.

"Shut up about that," the squire said. "Bloody Shelby and his investigations. The trade has suffered, as has my purse."

Nausea pulled at Diana's belly. *Oh my Lord.* Squire Stilton was the venturer? He was the one responsible for Matthew's danger? For the smuggling operation itself and for reaping the benefits for these past years? Her heart pounded in her ears. Robert was in more danger than even she imagined.

Squire Stilton passed very close to her as he stalked away from his nephew, his steps furtive and unlike anything she'd seen him exhibit before. He paused, his head cocked to one side, and she feared he could hear the very pounding of her heart. To her great relief he continued toward his stately home at the top of High Street, no doubt to enjoy the fruits of the labors forced on the young smugglers.

Clive came within a hair's breadth of her as he turned to climb the backstairs to the Hollis home. Robert would see

Clive captured. That was certain. And her father would be present to hear the man's confession that her husband would encourage.

She had to tell Robert about the squire.

She hurried back toward the bluff. She had even more serious evidence to present her gifted husband, and she would do so in the safety of the beautiful chamber at Shelby Manor as soon as he returned to her, safe and whole.

***

Robert eyed the narrow bed, thinking the pile of blankets made a fair impression of Gertie Hollis's prone form. A mop-cap solved the dilemma of Gertie's hair, and to his trained eye the girl's attacker would indeed believe she was in the cozy room. And that she merely slept, not persisted in stupor.

Thankfully the butcher was to the north, seeing to his daughter's welfare as she settled in the safe house. The worry on Hollis's face had been clear. Robert could only imagine his own turmoil were Diana ever in such danger. He managed to set that chilling thought aside and focused on the task at hand.

The house was quiet and Constable Ashley waited in

another dark corner of the room. A sliver of moonlight fell upon the bed, the effect more than Robert might have hoped. The blankets appeared to move under the shifting light through the clouds, seemingly rising with breath. His leg protested the position held, crouched there in the corner, but he fought the pain. Waiting was part and parcel of his occupation. And hadn't he always soothed its discomfort afterwards? More than brandy and bed awaited him at the manor when his task was completed this night. Diana was there, as well.

The sound of footfalls ceased his musings, heavy and clumsy despite their stealth. The back staircase. Good. The hinges of the bedchamber door creaked with protest as the wood scraped the floor.

"Gertie?" came a man's harsh whisper. "Gertie, my girl?"

No sound came from the bed, of course. This seemed to enrage the hulk now fully in the room, for the figure shook itself and stepped further into the room. "Gertie, ya' worthless bitch."

Ah. Clive Stilton.

Clive froze for a moment to look about the chamber,

no doubt belatedly thinking that Gertie would have someone watching over her.

"Are ya' alone, sweet?" he then cajoled, the words and tone sickening Robert. "Ah come on, Gertie. Ya' ain't truly gonna tell I did this, are ya'?"

He neared the bed, stepping into the moonlight. The big fists at his side belied the placating nature of his voice.

"Wake up, ya' simpleton!" Clive shouted, charging at the bed. "Wake up or I'll give ya' more of the same!"

Robert momentarily relished the comic surprise on the lout's face as he held up the mop cap clutched in his hands.

"What the bloody Hell?" Clive muttered.

"Clive Stilton," Constable Ashley said, his voice clear in the darkness.

Clive whirled to face the man as Robert lit the candles to his right.

"C-constable!" Clive stared at the mop cap in his hand before throwing it down on blankets. "This ain't what it looks like." His eyes rounded when he spied Robert. "Shelby!"

"The constable heard all of it, Stilton," Robert said. "Your uncle will have nothing to say about the true villain in this matter seeing justice."

One last burst of bravado puffed the clod's chest. "She asked for it, she did! Silly girl, followin' me around. Beggin' for it."

That was it. One blow to Clive's fat face silenced his foul mouth.

"No woman deserves such treatment," Robert growled.

"Shelby," came the constable's even tone.

Robert reined in his anger, his hands in fists at his side to keep from wringing Clive's fat neck.

He stepped back and gave Diana's father a nod. "I'll leave this to you, Constable." He cast another quelling gaze at Clive, who rubbed at his jaw as tears poured down his cheeks, before facing the constable again. "Call on me should you need my testimony."

"Certainly."

Robert left him to his work. Justice would indeed be served. It was a pity the butcher wasn't here to employ the tools of his trade tonight. Gertie's father deserved his own bit of justice, and slicing Clive from stem to stern would be too good for the bastard.

Chapter 24

"Oh, you're home!"

Diana flew at him as he entered the chamber, and his arms encircled her as if of their own accord. She pressed her cheek against his chest, murmuring words he could almost imagine were a prayer.

"It is done," he assured her. He rubbed his hands over her back, the fabric of her wrapper whispering in response. "Clive confessed in front of myself and your father."

She nodded. "Good. Good."

He held her for a moment longer, then reluctantly eased her arms from around his waist. She clasped her hands and stared up at him, worry still clear on her features.

"No more worries," he offered with a smile as he removed his jacket and waistcoat.

She shook her head wildly, her loose curls a cloud around her flushed face. "But there is so much you do not know, Robert."

"What is this?" He looked about the chamber, seeing nothing amiss to his trained eye.

She shook her head again. "No, I…" She clamped her mouth shut, and stared up at him once more. "Tell me you will not do anything more this night. Promise me."

Her agitation struck him. He had never seen her this upset, even when she'd first come to The Hideaway for his help.

"What is troubling you, love?"

She hugged him again and he felt her trembling to his soul. She lifted her face to his and kissed him, her lips quivering and sweet as her fingers worked at his shirt and neck cloth.

"I cannot bear to lose you," she murmured. "Pray, stay with me."

He placed his hands on her cheeks and held her face close to his.

"Always, wife," he vowed.

She offered him a shaky smile and resumed her sweet assault on his person. Almost before he was aware, he was prone on the bed. Diana ran her hands over him, a bit wild now. She kissed his bare chest, flicking her tongue over his flesh as she moved down over his stomach. He reacted as to be expected, with that urgency he only felt with his wife. She worked the buttons of his breeches free and held him. Licking her lips, she glanced up at his face. He sensed it, the hesitation, the state in which she'd found him with Annie just a few weeks ago.

"You do not have to do this, Diana."

Her head tilted to one side, the effect innocent and lovely. "But I want to."

He couldn't stifle the groan that issued from his lips. She licked him, her soft lips teasing and arousing him as never before. Her dark hair caressed his thighs and belly as she hesitantly and perfectly made love to him with her mouth. His pulse thundered in his ears and with supreme control he grasped her hair and drew her face to his.

"Did you not like that?" She lowered her lashes and blushed. "I know I am not skilled."

"My God, Diana. Could you not feel how you affected me?"

She gave him a smile then, pure and bright, and he kissed her. Turning to pin her beneath him, he worked her wrapper free and sent it fluttering to the floor. She arched as he caressed her through her nightgown, begging for what she now knew he could give her. He brought his mouth to one nipple, tugging and teasing through the thin fabric until she gasped.

"Robert!"

He eased her nightgown from her body and kissed her. "Yes, love?"

She closed her eyes and bit her lower lip as he ran his hands over her smooth skin. With hushed words and eager hands she urged him inside of her. She was ready for him and he surged forward. She was so close to her release. As was he. Easing up on his arms, he sought to slow down. To make this last. But she wouldn't allow it. Her hands on his back, his buttocks, urged him on until he was rocking hard into her and she was taking all of him.

In a moment it was over, her body bowing back as he poured himself into her.

"My God," he rasped.

She didn't open her eyes, just let out a sigh of satisfaction that threatened to arouse him again. He kissed her smiling mouth and settled beside her.

"That was a most wonderful welcome home," he mused aloud.

Amazingly, she let out a soft laugh.

"Oh!" She colored and ducked her head against his shoulder. "I should be embarrassed, I suppose."

He brushed her hair from her face and grasped her chin. At last she raised her gaze to his.

"Never, Diana." She began to shake her head but he stilled her. "We are married. I am yours and you are mine."

She gazed at him, her eyes shining. "I lo—"

Then she stopped herself, but not before he knew in his heart what she'd been about to say.

He blinked, dropping his hand from her. She seemed to sense his reticence and pulled away from him. But he couldn't bring himself to bridge that distance. She donned her nightgown and returned to their bed, though no part of her touched him. Astounding, for not two minutes earlier they were as close as two bodies could be.

He thought to turn the subject from matters of heart and love.

"You said something of another worry, Diana," he said.

She flicked a glance at him, at last nodding. "Squire Stilton."

Robert shook his head and sat up in the bed. "What does the squire have to do with Gertie's attack?"

"He was there tonight, Robert. Instructing Clive to

silence the girl."

"He was where?" He glanced about the room, spying the big ugly cloak that had escaped his notice earlier. "Pray, do not tell me you left the manor."

"I could not sit here and worry over you, Robert," she cut in. "I had to know that you were safe."

Anger flared within him, and he welcomed it. "My work is my own, Diana. Do not ever think I need you to see me safe."

She sat up and faced him. Her lush lips, still swollen from his wild kisses, thinned to a tight line. "I do not think you need me for anything, husband," she bit out. "Not my concern, and certainly not my love."

There it was, bright and shiny and hanging in the room for him to see. She loved him. Damn it.

"See here—"

"Squire Stilton killed the boy, Robert," she said quickly. "The boy at the river. He threatened to do likewise to Clive if he did not silence poor Gertie."

"The boy at the river?" Robert pulled back. "My God, the squire killed the child? But, why?"

She crossed her arms and shrugged. "I have no notion.

But there is more."

His head spun for a moment. She'd gone out against his wishes, had eavesdropped on the squire and his nephew? The danger she'd dared to put herself in caused his stomach to clench sickeningly.

"What else did you overhear?" he asked.

"I believe the squire is the venturer."

That stunned him speechless.

"He complained of your investigations keeping the free traders away from Arundel," she went on.

"Of course." He raked his fingers through his hair and bit out a curse. "Ah, I've been a bloody fool."

"The smugglers are not your concern. Did you not tell my father so?"

He slanted her a look. "I had forgotten your snooping."

She shut her eyes and settled back down on the bed. "Forgive me." A sob, soft and almost silent, came from her lips. "You now have a snoop of a wife who loves you."

He stiffened, relieved and guilty of it when she didn't say anything more.

"Diana."

"Good night, Robert. In the morning, I shall see my things settled in the pretty pink chamber Sterns showed me yesterday."

The chamber that had been his mother's? Away from his side each and every night? Not bloody likely.

But before he could think to argue the point, the sound of her even breathing reached him. A tear glistened on her cheek and guilt slashed through him.

"I am a bloody fool," he grumbled to himself.

He curled his body around hers and sought the slumber that was her escape at present. She loved him. He knew she wasn't the fool, not by any stretch of his imagination. But to give her heart to him, that was the epitome of foolishness. Why then did he feel like he was on the verge of something so perfect, so wonderful, he would be a fool to let it go?

***

Diana managed to remain still as Robert held her, feigning sleep. He didn't love her. That was certain. He'd taken her information even as he still held her behavior in disdain. Impossible man!

Soon Matthew would return to her father's house and,

if she wasn't mistaken, she wouldn't be long absent from it either. The pretty pink chamber might suit her at Shelby Manor, but to pass long stretches of time with Robert at The Hideaway wasn't how she wanted to spend her life. No. She would move back to her father's house before living with that indignity.

Her behavior upon Robert's return should have embarrassed her. She had never been forward in their intimate exchanges, but taking his passion in hand had struck her as right in that moment. But she had the sense to admit to herself that she loved her husband, and his words after their making love at least bore some truth. She was his, even if he would never truly be hers.

She sighed and relaxed against him. The caress of linens covered the two of them in the next moment and a kiss, as soft as a whisper, fell on her temple. Relishing the bit of tenderness from so hard a man, she let another tear slide from beneath her lashes.

"Do not cry, Diana," he soothed, his voice holding a sweet note she had never heard before. "Pray, do not cry."

She shuddered and he held her tighter, murmuring soft words in her ear as he stroked her hair. She heard three words then, the declaration he would never dare utter if he knew she were awake. He loved her?

She trembled again as the truth struck her. She had his heart, even if he wished to keep that particular truth a secret.

"I will see the squire shown for the villain he is," Robert said the next afternoon.

Diana looked up from her luncheon plate to eye her husband holding himself so rigid there in the doorway. Of course. There would be no mention of last night save for his cases, then. The Lord knew he had kept from her sight since waking that morning.

"Yes, Robert. I have the utmost faith in you."

He arched a golden brow and settled across from her. He looked so strong and handsome this afternoon. After the maid set his dish before him he offered Diana the smallest smile, causing Diana's heart to lurch.

"I will need to know all that you, um, heard."

It was her turn to arch a brow in question. "You mean 'overheard,' don't you?"

A crooked smile curved his lips, though he schooled the expression once he faced her fully. "Yes. I sent word to your brother and he should join us shortly."

"Dear, exasperating Matthew." She covered her heart with her hand and took in a breath. "Safe and home again. Did you speak with my father?"

Robert took a long sip of his tea and set the cup in the saucer. "Clive Stilton was read the charges, love. I suppose that while his uncle still wields power the reprobate will merely be sent to Australia."

"Instead of hanging?"

Robert eyed her. "Do you believe he should be hanged?"

"Oh, yes. Horrid man."

She covered her mouth but Robert only smiled.

"Bloodthirsty chit, though I agree wholeheartedly."

She waved away his mock-censure. "What of Matthew?"

"Cleared, thanks to Clive's confession. But I need to speak with him."

She fingered her napkin, her gaze on the edge of her fine china tea cup. "I suppose he knows of the squire's involvement. That he is the venturer. I suppose Matthew has known all along."

"Do not take this upon yourself, Diana."

"But I watched, Robert." Raising her gaze to his, she shook her head. "For so very long, I watched. I did nothing."

"And I did not see what was before me. What type of investigator was I, pray? I am to blame far more than you are for the trouble in Arundel."

She opened her mouth to protest when Sterns appeared at the doorway of the dining room.

"Mr. Matthew Shelby, sir."

Robert and Diana exchanged a glance.

"Take him to the parlor, Sterns," Robert said.

The butler bowed and left them. Diana at last relinquished her napkin and stood.

"This is it, then," she sighed.

Robert nodded. "We shall know all of it." He stood and crossed to her and took her elbow. "Unless you wish to keep out of the interrogation?"

She gave a tiny sort. "Hardly."

He laughed. "Surely you would just listen at the door."

She felt her lips curve in an answering smile.

***

Robert read Diana's regard as she cast a glance up at

him. Ah, he was indeed in danger of betraying his own regard for his lovely wife. Last night, as the tears had dried on her smooth cheeks, he'd known it fully. He loved her. His blighted heart held her in it, and would not soon relinquish her.

Thankfully, the work that would occupy him over the next few days would set aside any opportunity for conversations about love and the like. He suspected he would make a muddle of it should he try to tell her of his feelings.

"Come, Diana. Your bothersome brother awaits."

They entered the parlor to find Matthew Ashley pacing within. His hair was overlong, his clothes a bit rumpled. But he was whole, which would no doubt please Diana. She stilled beside Robert, then flew to her brother as she had to him last evening.

"Oh, Matthew!" she cried, clinging to him.

"Easy, Sister," young Ashley returned with a grin. "You will do me a grave injury."

She pulled back to slap him soundly and Robert winced in response.

"I should do you an injury, you bloody fool!" she said. "Do you know the danger your simpleminded actions caused?

Do you know what happened after you ran away?"

Matthew rubbed his cheek and frowned at her. He glanced at Robert, who kept his expression even.

"Tell us all you know, Ashley."

The boy's eyes flicked in Diana's direction, curiosity in them.

"I know all about it, you dolt," Diana snapped.

Robert eyed his wife, at her deep blue eyes sparking with anger, and never found her more beautiful. Or formidable. Pleased that he wasn't the one under her sharp scrutiny at present, he permitted her to take the reins for the moment.

"Y-you know?" her brother stammered.

She sighed, her shoulders slumping. "I have watched you, Matthew. For so very long. Since Mama passed, I've watched you on those cold nights by the river."

Matthew's cheeks reddened and Robert was reminded of just how young Ashley was. Had he himself ever been that young?

"Your sister looked after you, you ungrateful cur," Robert said. "And you gave your alliance to the Stiltons?"

"I believed that Clive was…" Matthew made a sound

of exasperation. "I did not know what he was truly like until the Hollis girl's trouble."

"Where you there, Ashley?"

He sat his lanky frame down on the closest settee and rubbed the back of his neck. "No. But Clive boasted of it to me. And coming so close after the child's murder, it proved nearly too much to take."

"Did Clive kill that poor boy, Matthew?" Diana asked.

"I do not know, Diana. Perhaps. But the squire saw to the dumping of the body. I was there." The boy swallowed audibly. "It was horrible."

"Why didn't you go to your father?" Robert asked.

Matthew shrugged one shoulder, a gesture Robert had often seen his sister display.

"After all the years of escaping his very notice?" Matthew asked. "Not likely."

"You were a fool," Robert stated.

No one in the room voiced an argument.

"But I will not work for the Stiltons any longer," Matthew said. "Not after what I learned in Brighton."

"What is this?" Diana asked. "What could you have possibly learned?"

Robert shook his head to silence her, surprised to see the gesture worked. For the moment.

"Tell me," Robert said.

"Well, my investigations—"

"Your investigations?" Diana cut in.

A smile tugged at Matthew's lips. "Yes, Sister. I did not go to Brighton for the sea bathing."

Diana snorted in response.

"Go on," Robert urged.

"It seems the squire had a mistress," Matthew said. "One Clive had boasted about on several occasions. Well, I discovered that the woman bore a son some years past. And that she died not two months ago."

"Two months?" Diana murmured.

Knowledge struck Robert soundly. "The boy." Diana and Matthew stared at him. "Of course. He was the squire's son. The constable mentioned that the boy seemed too soft and clean to be one of the smugglers' boys despite his clothing."

Matthew nodded and raked his fingers through his black hair. "I am afraid so. The squire wanted Clive as his heir, though I can scarcely fathom the reason now."

"Nothing so simple," Robert observed. "Clive knew all of his secrets. It was wise of the squire to keep him close."

"But to kill a child," Diana breathed.

Diana's heartbreak was clear. Dismissing the subject for the moment, Robert went to her and urged her to sit on the settee across from her brother.

"This is horrid, love. That is true. We will lay this crime on the guilty person, as well."

She sniffed and gave him a reluctant nod. "But how, Robert?"

"I have proof," Matthew said.

"What?" Robert asked.

"His mistress was not the addle-pate the squire might have hoped," Matthew went on. "When she fell ill, she sent correspondence to an elderly lady friend. She named the squire as father, and indicated that upon her death the boy be sent to live in Sussex with him."

Diana swallowed audibly. "Good Lord, she sent him to his death."

Robert stepped closer to her. "She could not have known, Diana."

She buried her face in her hands. "How horrible."

Ignoring her brother, Robert knelt before her and wrapped his arms around her. She cuddled against him and he rubbed her slender back.

"Mr. Shelby!" Matthew said in obvious shock.

Robert shot Matthew a look of irritation. "We are wed, Ashley."

That quieted the boy. "Wed? When?"

"Two days past," Diana said.

Robert lifted her chin to smile into her eyes. "Has it only been two days?" he teased.

She let out a little laugh and nodded. Robert stroked her cheek before standing once more.

"Fine bit of investigative work, that," Robert said to Matthew. "Well done."

That prompted a smile from Diana's brother. "I believe I may have a talent for it."

Robert threw a glance at Diana, who lowered her gaze to her lap.

"Why does that not surprise me?" He faced his new brother-in-law. "I wager you have this incriminating paper on your person, Ashley?"

"Not at present, though it is well hidden. I spoke to the

lady and she told me she would be willing to make a statement should it be necessary." Matthew's face set. "She was shocked to hear of the boy's murder." He took a breath. "There is no evidence to truly link Squire Stilton to the smuggling, though."

"No," Robert agreed. "There wouldn't be, would there?"

Diana blinked her confusion.

"The free traders owe their livelihood to the blackguard, Diana," Robert said. "The squire fronts the capital to the landers down on the coast."

"So he will simply continue?" she asked.

Robert and her brother gazed at each other. Robert knew Matthew read the intent in his eyes when he gave an almost imperceptible nod.

"Without Clive and his best boy in your brother, I think not," Robert told Diana. "But the matter at hand is the child."

The three of them nodded in agreement, and set about planning the best way for Robert to approach the squire with their evidence.

Chapter 25

"Are you out alone so soon after your wedding?"

Diana whirled to find Squire Stilton standing before her. She glanced down the road, her heart skipping a beat. High Street wasn't as crowded as she might have hoped, as it was the dinner hour. And the Inn at Arundel was far up the street. Robert and Matthew were with the constable, and had she not grown tired of inactivity at the manor she would still be awaiting their return in safety if boredom. No. Instead she'd set out alone for her father's house. She had foolishly thought the village safe, with Clive locked away.

The squire eyed her closely and, knowing now what she did of the man, she struggled to keep her expression serene as she wrapped her cloak more tightly about her.

"Mr. Shelby had business to attend, Squire. With my father."

A look of shame settled on the man's face, as false as his congeniality had been all these years.

"I am heartbroken, Miss… er, Mrs. Shelby. For my own nephew, whose praises I sang to the very clouds, to sully the Stilton name so. I am indeed heartbroken."

She swallowed and nodded, searching the

thoroughfare for some escape. Why did Fran or Nan not come and antagonize her? Even the dress shop was closed.

"Clive was not a nice young man," she said, taking a tiny step back from him.

Rolling his eyes heavenward, the squire gave a shaky nod. "Mrs. Stilton is quite beside herself. We had such high hopes."

He flicked his gaze over her, his expression far different than one she had ever glimpsed on his face prior. Her skin crawled at the dark intent in eyes she now saw were quite like Clive's.

"Clive should have pressed his suit with you, I wager," he said. "You are a catch, to be sure."

Once more, she glanced up and down the quiet street. Wherever was Robert? Or Matthew, for that matter? Why had she not listened to the wise and assertive Sterns and simply waited for her husband and brother to return?

"I never believed we would suit, Squire."

He took a step closer. "No," he said in a low voice that sent a tremor through her. "That dolt would never appreciate you the way a more experienced man would."

She didn't miss his meaning. Stiffening her spine, she

brought her gaze to his. “My husband appreciates me.”

A slick smile curved the squire’s lips, an unpleasant expression that rivaled his prior lascivious one.

“Ah, he is experienced then,” the squire said. “Has he taught you any doxy’s tricks?”

She sucked in a breath. “Squire Stilton!”

He chuckled, though to Diana’s ears the sound lacked any joviality.

“You are a picture, Diana.” He placed a hand on her arm, firm and tight in a grip nearly identical to Clive’s. “You are so indignant now, when I know full well you teased my nephew time and again.”

She said nothing, her throat tight. Fear gripped her, icy cold at the back of her neck. There was no sign of assistance in the growing gloom. And no sign of her husband.

“The dinner hour approaches,” she said. “I am wanted at my father’s.”

A grin slid onto the man’s face, chilling. “You will eat at Stilton House.”

She shook her head as he turned her toward his home. He began to take long strides, dragging her along with him.

“I cannot,” she said, her kid slippers having no

purchase as they slid over the damp cobblestones. "My husband is expecting me."

"That is of no consequence," the squire said with a shake of his head. "He shall have to do as he did before."

"Before?"

"Yes, my dear." Squire Stilton stopped and faced her, his head tilted to one side. "He will keep to himself in that great house of his. Alone, as he should be for all of his meddling ways." He began to drag her along again. "You do not lend credence to his false tales, I wager."

Diana dug in her heels. "Those 'false tales' are truer than any gossip heard on High Street, Squire."

He narrowed his eyes on her face. "Your husband has no proof of my activities, Diana."

"What of your child?"

His eyes grew round and his nostrils flared. *Oh, no.* She bit her tongue, but the damage was done.

"My child?" His tone chilled her. "The river rat? Nothing ties me to that boy."

"Nothing," she quickly agreed.

Something must have shown on her face to belie her agreement, for he yanked her closer to him. "Your husband has proof, doesn't he?"

She mutely shook her head as Stilton House loomed before her. Its windows were dark and suddenly she knew true terror. Nights spent on the bluff watching the smugglers or walking alone in the village now seemed as safe as sitting in her father's parlor. Good Lord, she was a great fool.

"Ah, it seems that Mrs. Stilton is visiting relatives. Clive's downfall has affected her greatly." The squire sighed. "We shall have to make do with each other's company." He faced her, his dark eyes glinting in the fading light. "Diana."

***

"It is settled, then," Robert said as he came to his feet.

"Yes," the constable agreed. "The direct approach is the best way to handle this."

"I still disagree," Matthew Ashley said. "You do not know him fully, Father."

"Yes, Son." The constable's face wore a dark scowl. "Pray, remind me for how long you worked for that reprobate?"

Robert held up a hand to still them. "Now is not the time for this argument."

Matthew and the constable nodded with reluctance.

"Matthew has the right of it, however," Robert continued. "The squire is not the man he presented to Arundel all these years. He will no doubt be extra careful now that Clive has been apprehended, at least for the time-being. This would be the opportune time to approach him, before he can cover his tracks or destroy any evidence. Had the lady in Bath ever had contact with him, Matthew? Is she known to him?"

"No. I believe she is safe."

"Good." Robert nodded. "I am off for the manor, then."

"Pray bid my daughter good evening, Shelby."

"Of course." He bowed his head. "Good evening, gentlemen."

With relief, Robert took himself from the tension boiling in the constable's house and headed for Shelby Manor. High Street was quiet, though the inn's windows glowed brightly. The night was dark, the moon wreathed in clouds. No doubt a good night for smuggling, not that Diana's brother would ever take part in that again. And the snooping smugglers' watch girl would never put herself in danger again, thank God.

As he neared the bluff, he saw no signal light, no flash

of a beacon from the river's edge. Ah, the free traders didn't ply their trade this night. Their venturer must be too preoccupied to see to the distribution of goods at present, what with the tangle ensnaring his nephew.

"Bloody bastard," he muttered.

To kill a child was as reprehensible an act as Robert could imagine. Diana's distress that afternoon struck him again. It had been so natural to wrap his arms around her and give comfort, even as her brother had looked on in surprise. Hell, he had been surprised himself. Him? Giving comfort to another? My God, he was surely daft. Or in love with his wife.

"Sterns," he called as he entered the manor.

"Yes, sir?"

The butler appeared swiftly as always. The man then peered over Robert's shoulder, his gray brows raising a notch.

"What is it, Sterns?"

"Is madam not with you?"

"Whyever would she…?" Robert's pulse began to trip. "Isn't Mrs. Shelby here?"

"She left, sir. Without her maid, though I urged her to wait here for your return."

Robert tensed. "Where did she go?"

"To Constable Ashley's residence, sir. Said she was tired of pacing about the parlor."

"But I just left there. She wasn't there, nor did I pass her on my way here." Dread settled in his belly. "Bloody Hell!"

Robert left the butler staring after him as he hurried back to Diana's father's house. He had seen no sign of her on High Street, that was certain. She was undoubtedly not at the inn. If something happened to her… No! He wouldn't think of that now.

"Constable!" he called, brushing past the housekeeper and into the dining room.

Diana's father stared up from the dining table, his eyes round. "Shelby?" Concern wrinkled the man's brow. "Whatever is wrong?"

"Is Diana here?"

"No."

"What is going on?" Matthew asked, coming to his feet with his hands in fists at his side.

"Diana is not at home," Robert quickly explained. "She told the staff she was coming here."

"When?"

Robert raked his fingers through his hair. "I do not know. Sometime while we were discussing Squire Stilton."

Diana's brother stilled and Robert's alarm increased.

"Matthew," he began, his blood pounding low. "Pray, say what you're thinking."

Matthew shook his head. "Squire Stilton."

The boy didn't have to finish his thought aloud. Robert let out a string of curses, echoed by both the other men, and headed back out onto High Street.

***

Robert pounded on the door of Stilton House, ceasing only as Diana's brother grabbed his arm.

"Easy, Mr. Shelby."

"He will tell me where she is, Matthew."

"You do not know he took her."

Robert shot a look of exasperation in his brother-in-law's direction. "Do you doubt it?"

Matthew was silent for a beat. "No."

That little word brought all of it into clarity. Robert raised his fist again.

"A bit late to be making calls, isn't it gentlemen?" the

squire said from behind them.

Robert spun to face him. "Where is my wife?"

"Excuse me?" The man gave a jovial laugh and glanced over at Matthew. "Pray tell me, Ashley, has your new brother-in-law lost his wife already?"

"Do not push me, Stilton," Robert snarled. "I'll not be trifled with."

"You find me alone this evening, gentlemen." The squire clicked his tongue and turned the key in the lock. "Mrs. Stilton is away visiting relatives," he explained. "Quite distraught over Clive's downfall, I'm afraid. So I gave the staff a few days off as well."

Robert entered the house before the squire, his gaze taking in the dim place. No sign of Diana, damn it to Hell!

"Where is she?" he asked again.

"I do not know what you're talking about, Shelby. If you are unable to hold on to your wife, perhaps—"

"Enough!" Robert cut in. "I want to know where she is."

"Perhaps we both have something the other wants," the squire said.

Matthew let out a low whistle. "Why you cunning

bastard. Though I shouldn't be surprised."

Robert eyed Matthew, suddenly guessing what it was the squire wanted.

"You are not as stupid as you appear, young Ashley," the squire said. "I want the proof tying me to the boy."

"We will give you nothing, Stilton," Robert said.

Squire Stilton gave a careless shrug, which lost some of its effect as a bead of perspiration dripped down one of his cheeks. "Then we have nothing to discuss."

"Where did you take my sister, you blackguard?"

Robert shook his head. "Come, Ashley."

"But, Mr. Shelby—"

A wave of his hand silenced Diana's brother. They left the squire's home, a sputtering Matthew close on Robert's heels. Their booted heels struck sharp reports on the cobblestones.

"Why did we leave?" Matthew asked, a bit out of breath.

Robert took several long strides before giving him an answer. "Because he wants something from us. That gives us an advantage for the time being."

"But what about my sister?"

Robert clutched Matthew's arm then, stopping his forward motion and his endless questions.

"I will find my wife, Ashley. Count on it."

***

Diana paced about the dank space, her slippers making almost no sound on the dirt floor. The meager moonlight piercing through a slit above her at street level showed as much of her prison as she wished to see. Casks of brandy and crates of tea both sent up their scents, the odors mingling with decay and dampness causing her nose to tingle. The smugglers tools of the trade, creepers and grapnels for dragging the barrels, spout lanterns for sending signal lights, lay strewn about the place. She guessed that the smugglers didn't work tonight despite the perfect cloudy sky. Maybe that was because their venturer was off planning something more foul than the distribution of ill-gotten goods on this particular night.

No more than two hours could have passed since the squire had locked her below in this chamber, yet she could scarcely stand the confinement. How the devil had Robert endured those long months in captivity?

At least the lecherous squire had not placed his hands

upon her since leaving Stilton House. She'd told him nothing of the letter in Matthew's possession, but the man was cunning. Her fear for Robert's safety grew even as she acknowledged the danger surrounding her like the damp walls of this chamber.

She knew that she was beneath the Inn at Arundel, and the stench of the river was evident through the stone walls of the low-ceilinged chamber. She huddled within her cloak. She had no idea what the squire would do with her. But she wouldn't wait to find out. Not as long as she had a breath in her body.

The squire believed to ransom her, perhaps? That made no sense, though. The squire was wealthy, more wealthy than she had ever imagined now that she knew he was the venturer. But how long could he continue that occupation? He would get desperate. And a desperate man was all the more dangerous. Her arms still ached from his rough handling, which had been worse than even Clive's bruises to her wrist weeks ago.

She rested her chin on her hands, working her mind around her confinement and a possible means of escape.

"Dinner, ma'am." A dark-haired serving girl entered,

a tray held before her.

The aroma of the stew almost overpowered the collection of scents in the chamber and Diana's stomach rumbled. The girl brought the candlelit tray closer and bobbed a curtsey. Odd, taken with the situation.

"Won't you let me abovestairs?" Diana asked.

The maid shook her head and set the tray on an overturned crate near Diana's feet. "Squire says yer to remain belowstairs."

"Why?"

The girl shrugged and turned to go.

"Wait," Diana said.

She stilled and turned back to Diana. "Aye, ma'am?"

"Pray, do not leave me here alone."

"Squire says I'm needed upstairs, ma'am."

"Why are you helping him?" Diana asked the serving maid.

The dark-haired girl turned and looked at Diana like she was daft. "He pays me."

"But, you know what he did. What he is."

"Squire says he didn't hurt the boy. Squire says Clive's the one what did 'im."

"And you believe him?"

She shrugged. "Clive hit me."

Diana stared at her for a long moment.

"The squire hits me sometimes, too," the maid went on. "But he don't hit me where it shows."

Diana swallowed the sadness she felt at the girl's words. There was no arguing with her. Diana would simply bide her time and gather her strength for when the squire returned. And Diana was certain he would. Let him attempt to harm her as he obviously had this serving maid. She would make certain he never hurt another child or woman again.

The girl took up the tray, and Diana placed her hand on her arm.

"Can you leave the candle?" she asked sweetly.

The girl's eyes darted about as her mind worked.

"I don't know 'bout that, Ma'am. The squire, he didn't say nothin' about the candle."

"Then you can leave it!" Diana said in a whining tone. She wrung her hands, and pity flared in the maid's eyes.

"Oh, pray do," Diana went on, applying a bit of dramatics at this moment. "This room is dismal enough with that bit of light. Do not leave me in the dark!"

After another hesitation, the girl nodded. She shuffled over the dirt floor and climbed the wooden stairs beyond Diana's vision. But Diana didn't care. She still had her candle.

And the flink of an idea.

Chapter 26

Robert limped along the bluff, his mind working. Matthew had at last returned to the constable's house, leaving him in relative peace. The boy wanted to storm the squire's house, and Robert was hard-pressed to find a reason for him not to. But the squire wouldn't divulge Diana's location, no matter the threats to his person. The bloody bastard wanted the mistress's letter and for nothing less would he divulge Diana's whereabouts.

He stared up at the shrouded moon, following its meager light down to the river. No smugglers worked the currents tonight despite the ideal conditions. No lights flickered or voices called through the dark. The night he'd found Diana on the bluff came back to him in a rush. The surprise, the desire. Where was she?

She loved him, damn his own fractured soul. She loved him and he loved her and he would tell her so as soon as he held her in his arms again.

Turning, he made his way up the shifting sand toward the manor. His leg protested, but he welcomed the pain as a sort of penance. Why had he fought his feelings for Diana? He had faced Trevor on that fog-shrouded night over a year ago, only to find himself injured and held prisoner. But he'd survived, damn it. The weeks of captivity and the months of convalescence and rehabilitation afterward until he was nearly whole, at least in body. The thought of being vulnerable to someone as sweet and good as Diana had frightened him. Why? He was a coward to hide from the truth for so long.

A flicker of light caught his gaze, drawing his eyes toward High Street. It was gone in an instant, and he thought he might have imagined it. But there it was again, a tiny wink of light coming from street level near the inn.

"What the devil?"

A flash of a signal light far from the riverbank had to be from a smuggler's lantern. He had seen the lights countless times before, bobbing on the river. But how could a beam shine from town? Realization struck him. There must be storage beneath the inn, a place for goods to be kept before taking them further toward London and other points of purchase. And the only reason there would be a light, a beacon shining out toward the bluff, was Diana.

His pretty little snoop used the lantern to signal to him! He grinned as he ran up the shifting sand of the bluff toward High Street.

Toward Diana.

***

"You're far smarter than I gave you credit for, my dear."

Diana dropped the lantern, extinguishing its small point of light but not before the squire had seen it. He approached her.

"Let me out of here," she said.

He gave a harsh laugh, accompanied by a shake of his head. "I think not." He set the candle he held on the crate nearest him. "And unless your husband gives me what I want, you will perish down here."

"What could Robert possibly have that you want?" She shut her mouth. He had to mean the letter Matthew had procured. "My husband is a seeker of justice, Squire Stilton. Your wait will be in vain."

"So you say." He walked over to her and sat on an overturned crate. "And as I recall, your husband works for the money the cases bring him, does he not?"

"What money did the case of the child bring?"

She bit her tongue, but it was too late. Anger flared in

the squire's eyes, more chilling than Clive's most dastardly glare. She backed up against the rough wall behind her, praying that for once she could keep her mouth shut.

"You think you know of my troubles, do you?" He came closer. "The bitch never should have sent the brat here."

"But you—"

"Killed him? Had to."

Oh, dear Lord. His voice was flat. She watched as he warmed to the subject, her stomach clenching.

"Clive was to be my heir, fool that he was. Mrs. Stilton's wealth assured that her blasted nephew inherit my lands. And no by-blow was going to get in the way."

She eased away from the wall, unable to keep from voicing the obvious. "But he was your son."

"What of it? His mother was a doxy, and I'll not mourn her passing. As for the boy, he fell easily to a bump on the head."

"You left him by the river like… like…"

"Like the bit of trash he was."

She slapped him. No doubt the surprise on his face mirrored her own, and she backed away from him.

"Think yourself above me, my dear? You thought

yourself well above Clive, that dolt, and perhaps you had the right of it. But me?" She saw the flash of a slick smile as he brought his face to hers. "You cannot outthink me or outtalk me." He closed a hand, a very large hand, around her throat and began to squeeze. "And you cannot outfight me."

She placed her hands on his wrist, fighting to ease the pressure. Darkness fluttered at the edges of her vision, and she opened her mouth to cry out. As her pulse pounded in her ears the earth floor seemed to rise toward her.

In her mind at least, she called out for Robert.

***

"The storeroom," Robert said to no one in particular as he threw open the door to the inn.

Shocked looks from the patrons met his request. No answer came from that quarter. He glimpsed a flash of dark hair and turned. The serving girl, the one used so poorly by Clive Stilton, sought to escape the dining room.

"You there!"

She stilled, keeping her gaze on the floor.

"Where is the storeroom?" he asked her.

"Ain't be no storeroom here, save for the back, sir."

He crossed to her. "Belowstairs, my girl. Take me

there."

Alarm rounded her eyes and she began to shake her head. She must have read the intent in his gaze, for she soon gave him a shaky nod. Robert followed her to the back of the inn and through a hinged portion of wall set behind the larder. Narrow steps and a low ceiling didn't hamper his progress as he followed the maid. He'd left any pain in his leg back on the bluff once he'd seen Diana's beacon.

A flash of light caught his gaze. Candlelight, from a spot somewhere around a corner to the left. As they neared a shuffling met his ears.

"Close that pretty mouth for good, I will. And those prying eyes."

Diana!

Robert rounded the corner, his mind swiftly processing the scene before him. Diana, cloaked in shadows and so still beneath the squire's hands. The hulk stood before her, his wide shoulders working as he shook her.

Robert flew at him with fists raised. "Release her, you bastard!"

The squire glanced over his shoulder, unwittingly turning his head to precisely the right angle for a killing blow against his temple. The man fell like a stone to the dirt floor, Diana's limp body settling down atop him.

"Diana!"

"Oh!" The serving girl hurried over to them, twisting her apron in her hands.

Robert shot her a look. "Go get the physician."

She stared at Diana and the squire, her mouth agape. "Go!" he shouted.

She nodded and hurried abovestairs. Robert moved Diana gently, cradling her against his chest as he settled on the cool floor. "Diana, love. Pray, open those beautiful eyes." His leg pained him now, from both the run up the bluff and the odd position he held. It didn't matter one bit at the moment. "Diana."

He couldn't tell if she breathed, the room was so bloody dark despite the lone candle, but one touch to her throat gave him hope. A tiny pulse beat there, a faint but even flutter.

"Diana, open your eyes." His eyes stung with tears and he swallowed thickly. "I cannot bear to live without you."

How long he sat there in the dark he didn't know, one minute or one hour. But as he pressed his lips to hers for what seemed the hundredth time, he was rewarded with a tiny intake of breath. His own heart began to beat again and he squeezed her in his arms.

"Ah, thank God."

"Mr. Shelby, is she all right?" Matthew Ashley placed a candle next to the other on crate and fell to his knees beside his sister. "Diana!"

The combined light flickered over Diana's lax features, nearly causing Robert's heart to break. She was so still.

"How did you know to come here?" Robert asked Matthew.

"I remembered the squire's storeroom, though I wasn't often here. I stopped at Shelby Manor to tell you of it but your butler told me you were gone. Is she all right?"

Diana's brother reached for her and Robert pushed his hands away, holding her closer.

The boy let out a soft moan. "This is all my fault."

As much as Robert longed to set Diana's fate on Matthew's shoulders, he couldn't.

"No," he said. "True, your foolishness played a hand in all of this. Working for that blackguard."

Matthew noted the squire then, lifeless on the floor, and Robert couldn't arouse a bit of concern over that man's demise.

"But I kept my heart from her, Matthew. She doubted me." His throat grew tight. "She doubts me still."

A murmur drew Robert's eyes to Diana's pale face. Her lips opened, a breath as soft as a whisper escaping.

"No," she rasped, her voice scraping softly.

Forcing himself to stay calm, he bent closer to her. "What is it, love?"

"I do not…" She swallowed, visibly wincing from the action. "I do not doubt you." She stirred, her deep blue eyes gazing at him from lowered lashes. "You love me."

The warmth in her eyes, bright like the beacon that had drawn him to her this night, flooded his very soul. The tightness in his chest loosened and he let out a breath.

"I do love you, Diana. With all my heart."

He hugged her tightly and was rewarded with a soft kiss before she fell slack in his arms again.

The physician was summoned to Shelby Manor, for Robert couldn't bear to leave Diana in that chamber one moment longer. She soon rested on their bed, her appearance worrying him. The constable would see to the removal of the vile squire's body from the cells beneath the inn, along with countless ill-gotten goods which would be handed over to the Landguard. Robert had no doubts in that regard.

"How is she?" Matthew asked.

Robert glanced over at Matthew Ashley, taking in his smudged dishevelment, and guessed that he most likely wore even more dirt on his own person. Apprehension was clear in Matthew's blue eyes, eyes so like Diana's. About bloody time the boy showed some concern for his sister.

"How the devil should I know, Matthew?" Robert asked wearily.

Robert then dismissed the boy and stared at Diana once more. Since waking for that brief moment in his arms she had not stirred again. Her hair was tangled, her face smudged and pale. Angry purple marks ringed her slender throat, and if the squire wasn't already dead Robert would have happily killed him again.

"Where is that physician?" he grumbled.

"Here, sir."

Once again, Sterns reappeared at precisely the moment Robert needed him. He brought the physician with him, a thin bald man some years older than the constable.

"Mr. Shelby," the physician said.

"Dr. Todd."

The man stepped closer to the bed and Robert moved to accommodate him, though not too far from Diana's side. He held her chilled hand in his, and watched for any sign of wakefulness as the doctor palpated her chest and stomach. As he ran his bony fingers over her throat Robert winced as if pained himself.

"Nasty injury, that," the man observed.

Robert said nothing, nor did Matthew. Diana's chest rose and fell beneath the linens with regularity, though still she continued unconscious.

"She seems fine, Mr. Shelby," the doctor said, straightening. "Aside for her throat, I do not see any other injuries."

"Then why will she not wake?"

The shrug from the physician did little to set Robert's mind at ease. "Perhaps the events of this night have left her overset."

Robert opened his mouth to berate him for stating the obvious, but Diana stirred at last. He clutched her hand tighter. “Diana, thank God.”

She opened her eyes and blinked in puzzlement. Her gaze flitted about the large chamber as she licked her pale lips. “Home?” she asked him, her voice rough.

“Yes, love. You are home.”

She gave him a tiny smile and nodded. Her brow furrowed. “Squire?”

“Dead.”

She narrowed her eyes. “Good.”

He laughed lightly, the tension in his body at last easing. “Bloodthirsty chit.”

A touch of mirth danced in her eyes.

“How do you feel, Mrs. Shelby?”

Diana dragged her gaze from Robert’s toward the physician. “Hard to talk.”

“I do not doubt that,” he said with a smile. “I will leave a bit of laudanum.” He set a small bottle on the bedstand and looked at Robert. “She may well need it for the pain in her throat.”

Robert nodded as the man readied to take his leave.

“She’ll be all right, Doctor?” Matthew asked.

“Yes, son.” The man looked at Diana as Robert kissed

her fingers and stroked her hand. "Mr. Shelby has matters well in hand, I wager."

Diana smiled, making Robert's heart trip.

"He does," she rasped.

Matthew left soon after the physician, and Robert relished the privacy with his wife.

"Say… again," she said.

He kissed her gently and smiled. "I love you. My God, Diana. When I saw you lying there I nearly died."

She took glass of water he offered her, laudanum mixed with it, and winced as she swallowed. "Just scold me."

"For what, pray?"

An arch of a brow was all the answer she had to make. Robert grinned, knowing full well what she meant.

"You left the manor," he began, fixing a mock scowl on his face. "You went out alone, throwing yourself in the worst kind of danger. Worse than the nights on the bluff, worse than the night of Clive's confession."

"There," she breathed. "I am… snoop."

Robert laughed and hugged her in his arm and wonderful embrace. He stretched out beside her, hoping his warmth penetrated the chill he could still feel clinging to her from that chamber below the inn.

"Yes, love. A pretty little snoop. But you're *my* pretty little snoop."

She sighed and closed her eyes. The drug seemed to take effect quickly.

"Pray, confine your investigations to matters of far less danger?" he asked.

"Help… cases?" she asked on a whisper

He groaned. "All right, if I deem it safe. No more smugglers, no more thieves or blackguards." He caught her chin and ever so gently tilted her face to his. "Promise me."

She blinked up at him for a moment, then yawned and cuddled against his chest. "Promise."

Epilogue

Sussex, England 1828

Robert sat in his office, the window before him showing the crisp autumn evening outside. Moonlight glinted on the river in the distance, beyond the windswept bluff. No more smugglers made use of this particular stretch of river, not since the squire's business had fallen to nothing. It seemed that without his uncle's influence Clive wouldn't been shipped to Australia, but since he now languished in New Gate his welfare was blessedly none of Robert's concern. As to Arundel and its inherent gossips, he paid them as little attention now as he had in the past.

Taylor and Blake paid frequent calls at Shelby Manor, daring those in Arundel to diminish their happiness. Robert took a page from that particular book, and faced life with an optimism he had previously believed had died at Trevor's hands.

Matthew Ashley was proving to be a worthy investigator, though his zeal often left him open to dangers Robert now knew better to avoid. The constable was pleased that his son worked on the proper side of the law if just outside of it, however.

The case Robert worked on at present, one of pilfered goods blamed unduly on a beleaguered servant, didn't fully draw his interest. It was only a matter of time before his partner uncovered the truth from the country folk involved.

A rap came on the door, light and brisk. Turning with a smile, he faced his companion as she breezed into the room.

"I've got it!" Diana beamed. "Fran's maid wished to leave her employ and truly, who would not wish to do so? Nan wanted the girl for her own, so she engineered the discovery of the purloined brooch."

He relished the triumph glinting in Diana's beautiful eyes for a moment, then offered a shrug. "Of course."

She clicked her tongue and rolled those lovely eyes heavenward. "You knew."

Robert came to his feet. "Not precisely, love. But once the inimitable Fran described the horrid piece in detail, I had serious doubts that anyone took it for the money or pleasure it would bring."

She nodded and stepped closer to him. "You do have a gifted mind, husband."

He wrapped his arms around her. "I have a gifted wife."

She laughed and kissed him. He began to deepen the kiss, stilling as the office door banged against the wall.

"Papa!"

Robert released Diana, taking her hand in his. He faced the tiny newcomer, smiling at the nightshirt dragging the floor.

"John Robert." He stepped toward the little boy named for Robert's father, the grandfather he would never know. "Did you not seek your bed well before now, young man?"

Diana clicked her tongue and bent to face their three-year-old son. "Did you slip away from your nurse again, darling?"

John Robert shrugged and peered up at his parents, his deep blue eyes sparkling with what Robert knew was pure intent. Hadn't he glimpsed that intent in Diana's gaze time and again?

"Mama said you'd tell me a story."

Diana straightened. "That, I did."

Robert gave up the battle before it began. He swept his son into his arms, eliciting a whoop of joy from the child, and caught Diana's eye.

"Join us, love?"

"Of course."

They made their way toward the staircase, nodding to Sterns who ruffled John Robert's golden hair.

"Good night, little master," Sterns said.

"G'night, Sterns."

Once in the nursery, the boy climbed out of Robert's arms and settled himself in his bed. They told him a story recited from memory, one of smugglers and sleuths and secret chambers laden with booty. It was a favorite of the child's, a story which told of a beacon of light which led the hero straight to the truth, and soon the little boy drifted off to sleep.

Robert and Diana left the nursery hand in hand.

"He never tires of that story," she whispered.

"Bloodthirsty little mite," he chuckled.

Much later, as Diana smiled sleepily on top Robert's chest in their big bed, he gazed at the guttering candle on the bedstand. It was such a tiny light. Yet it cast a golden sheen over the lovely woman in his arms.

So long he was in darkness. In a prison of his own making long after gaining his freedom. Diana had brought him out of that blackness, her light a beacon which drew him, heart and soul. She drew him still, and he would never surrender to the darkness again.

About the Author

JoMarie DeGioia is a bestselling author of Historical and Contemporary Romance. She's known Mickey Mouse from the "inside," has been a copyeditor for her tiny town's newspaper, and a bookseller. She is the author of over 40 Romances, and writes Young Adult Fantasy/Adventure stories and Paranormal Romance too. She gets lost in DIY projects around the house and works out plot ideas during long runs. She divides her time between Central Florida and New England.

Discover other books by JoMarie DeGioia

The Bridgewater Brides series, including

The Heir's Treasure

The Viscount's Vixen

The Earl's Beauty

The Gentlemen Undercover series, including

A Hero and a Gentleman

A Hero and a Rogue

The Shopgirls of Bond Street series, including

That Determined Mister Latham

The Dashing Nobles series, including

More Than Passion

Pride and Fire

Just Perfect

More Than Charming

The Cypress Corners series, including

Cypress Corners Boxed Set

Finding Harmony

Taming Jake

Loving Cassie

Winning Ben

Showing Jessie

Seeing Shannon (Barefoot Bay World novella)

Dreaming Eli

Giving Chase (Barefoot Bay World novella)

Kissing Bree

Wishing Joy

Bugging Nate

The Gifted YA Fantasy/Adventure Trilogy, including

Gifted

Braunachs of the Dell series, including

Luke's Gold

Patrick's Promise

Connect with me online

Get the latest news!

Be a VIP Reader!

Twitter: https://twitter.com/JoMarieDeGioia

Facebook:

https://www.facebook.com/JoMarie.DeGioia.Author

Website: www.jomariedegioia.com

www.ingramcontent.com/pod-product-compliance
Lightning Source LLC
Chambersburg PA
CBHW051315250626
47155CB00007B/2324